Fatal Designs

Friends In Crisis Series (Book 5)

Lucy Appadoo

Copyright© 2023

Lucy Appadoo

Dedication

This book is dedicated to those who have struggled with multiple losses. It is also about the need to be true and honest with yourself.

Dedication

Contents

PROLOGUE

Sex and cigarettes hung heavily in the dark room. On the bedside table, the syringe he had put there over an hour ago lay against a burnt spoon. A scalpel nestled in a thick red smear of blood on the dusty dressing table. In the corner, the TV droned out stories of unsolved true crimes.

The woman on the bed moaned, bloodshot eyes unseeing as her body twitched, regaining some control over her limbs. The drawn blinds kept the room just dark enough to accentuate her hollowed out features and made every time she opened her mouth look like a scream. When her head lolled to the side, he curled a lip in disgust.

The man pulled down his pants and pushed them and several pieces of dirty underwear out of his way with his foot. Running a finger along the angry red marks on his bare chest, he relished the sting her claws left. She had put up a fight. Even drugged, the bitch cried when he forced her down to cut her, but the more she screamed, the more excited he became. Kicking and screaming, as he preferred, he dragged her with him into dark, delicious fantasies which were a far-cry from her prim and proper life.

Picking up the syringe, he stuck it into the vial and withdrew the plunger slowly. Approaching her, she slowly roused from her weak state, and when her terror-filled eyes met his, he smiled. Then he was on her. Jabbing her arm with the needle and injecting her again with Ketamine. Underneath him, her heart beat rapidly. Yanking the needle out and casting it aside, he pressed a firm hand across her mouth and nose. She writhed like a snake, but he was strong. Through his thighs he felt her heart slow, and he lifted a few fingers to give her air again. Finally, her dilated eyes relaxed and her limbs stilled.

Slapping her gaunt cheeks and making her blink, he said, "We are going to enjoy more of each other."

It had been a rush, fulfilling his every dream with her and pushing her past her limits. He had pushed her into the dark side, eons away from the world she knew. That stopped now. She was not going back to her life.

The woman started wheezing and convulsing. No, not now. It was too damn soon.

Chapter One

HOPE IN SIGHT

Sitting at her desk, Joy Warrier undid the top button of her bright-orange linen shirt with its rolled-up sleeves and fanned herself. Her bangles clinked as she flicked through fabric samples and jotted down notes for the home she was designing. On one corner of her desk an office phone blinked and the in-tray stacked with current design jobs threatened to topple.

On her crowded cobalt steel-framed desk was a computer and drawing tablet, currently pushed to the side to make room for her samples, piles of sketch pads, cups of pencils and highlighters, and a lone bonsai tree. The tree butted up against a small building model teetering between the edge of her desk and the neighbouring stack of cardboard file and sample boxes. The long white shelf behind her held manilla folders filled with projects past and present, and more potted bonsai trees.

Photographs of the city landscape and staff portraits lined the cavity brick wall on one side of the office, and the other side consisted of large windows with views of Melbourne's city skyline.

The grey padded chairs in front of her were empty and she stared at them as she recalled a discussion with her client earlier that day. Resting a hand underneath her chin, she glanced across the room at the other steel-framed cobalt desk in the room. It was Kathleen's desk, now vacant. Filing cabinets and stacks of folders stood beside it too, but all of them remained untouched. Where was Kathleen? Joy missed her colleague and friend. Kathleen could be anywhere out there. Maybe she had run away and started a new life with a whirlwind romance, or maybe she just needed a break.

Through the door to their shared space was an L-shaped hallway, leading to the other offices, tea room, and reception desk.

Her coffee had become cold and Joy thought about walking down the corridor to the tearoom, but then decided it was too late in the day for more coffee. She heard the click of shoes on the hard floor from the corridor as her friend and manager, Lian entered through the doorway. She approached Joy's desk. "How are you doing with those couch samples? We needed them yesterday."

Lian owned *Tasteful and Trending Designs* with two other designers, a stylist, and investment partner. Her long, brown hair flowed down to her shoulders and her dimples deepened with her tentative smile. Her white blouse and fitted black skirt accentuated her petite frame.

Joy had worked with Lian for two years and thrived on the hectic pace of their regular client work. She pointed to a pink and a peach sample. "We should go with one of these pastel colours. What do you think?"

Lian nodded. "Great. Go with the peach sample. It's the client's preferred colour. Ring the supplier. Hopefully, it won't take too long to deliver."

Joy picked up her phone from the table. "On it." Hunger pangs soon set in. "Let's have lunch, girl."

"Yes, I could eat."

Marching to the tearoom with Lian behind her, Joy greeted the two other interior designers, who offered brief acknowledgements, and swung open the fridge. Her friend pulled out a small dish from the microwave while Joy took out her salad roll.

In the overhead cupboard, her hand hovered over the glass. A familiar mug, abandoned by its owner, made her chest ache. Joy pulled the glass out and shut the cupboard. She filled it up with water and walked to the table to sit across from Lian, who was forking up her chicken stir-fry. Unwrapping her lunch, Joy said, "That smells good."

Lian stared at the cupboard and pinched the skin at her throat. "I keep looking at that mug and missing her every day."

A chill ran up Joy's spine. "I can't believe Kathleen's been missing for two weeks. Where is she?" At their last lunch together, Kathleen had been unusually withdrawn and down. Joy had asked if anything was bothering her but she said no. Nothing else. But what if she'd been in trouble and Joy hadn't pushed hard enough to get to the actual truth? If Kathleen had needed a break from her problems, she could at least let them know.

Lian bit a nail, with most of the others having been chewed off in the last two weeks. "I wish I knew. Your detective friends Marco and Angelo haven't found her. Where the hell is she, Joy?" Lian hadn't slept or eaten much since Kathleen had been missing.

"I don't know. They mentioned having priority cases, so who knows if she ran away or ..."

Lian leaned forward. "Or what?"

Joy hesitated. "I don't know." She didn't want to say it might be something sinister. Lian said nothing. "I worry about her sister, Ariana. She's always looked up to Kathleen. I need to check on her."

Lian slipped her hands into her pockets, averting her eyes. "She'll turn up one of these days. I know it. Probably took a much-needed vacation or met the man of her dreams. She is most likely going to surprise us."

Joy wanted it to be the truth but had mixed thoughts. "Of course. That's it," she lied. "She loves this job, Lian. I'm sure there's a perfectly good explanation for this." Joy had been through many losses in her life, including the death of an old friend a year ago and her sister fourteen years ago. Her hands clenched. No, she wouldn't go there. Kathleen was fine. She was on a sabbatical and just needed a break.

Threading a hand through her shoulder-length, wavy blonde hair, Joy wondered about Ariana. Joy had a brother, Jesse, and couldn't imagine what she'd do if he disappeared and she didn't know what had happened to him. It must be torture for Ariana. All they could do until they heard otherwise was wait, but she held on to hope. Until they knew more, Joy had to get on with her life.

It was nearly the end of the day, so she closed down her computer and gathered her things. Tonight she had the night to herself. After a bad date the night before, she was sworn off men for life, and wondering if the right man even existed for her.

Chapter Two

CLOSE BROTHERS

Edward Astbury gripped the pencil tight as he scrunched up his nose, totally focused on his brother. "Please hold still, Ray." He rested his back against the steel chair in Ray's dining room, colouring in the rounded cheeks and adding bushy eyebrows. He sketched the finishing touches to Ray's shoulder-length blonde waves and placed the portrait face up on the table. "It's done."

Ray let out a sigh. "Finally. Let me see."

Edward passed it over the table and sat back with squared shoulders, waiting for his brother's opinion. It hadn't been the first time he'd drawn for Ray, who never kept still. He had drawn Ray dozens of times, attempting to improve on each one. Drawing portraits and landscapes was his creative outlet, and he had sold his work to friends and family over in England. "What are your thoughts?"

"I love it, man," said Ray. "This one's better than the last one you did. You have a real talent. I should pay you this time. How much do I owe you?"

Edward put up his hand and shook his head. "Complimentary, Ray. I only charge those who are overseas, given I have to pay for postage."

"Thanks, man. You are too kind."

"I know." Edward deadpanned then flashed a cheeky grin.

"So tell me about this woman, Lian, we're working with? What's she like?" Ray was a self-employed carpenter and Edward an architect; they were working together on Edward's next project.

Edward pressed his lips together. "I only met her once but she seems pleasant enough. She has a few designers working for the company, but I believe only one of them is coming on board."

Ray nodded. "I'll appreciate the change. My last job was a ball-breaker, so I'm sure this new home we're working on will be a breeze." He rubbed his hands. "I like us working together, bro. It's been too long since that last project."

"It is better late than never, I suppose. That seven-year break between us was harrowing."

Ray looked down at his fingers, picking at his cuticles. "How many times do I have to damn well apologise, Ed? Don't you think it's time you got over it?"

Edward ignored the stinging comment. He pushed down his pain. Edward was only nine years old when Ray left him alone with their parents. He had missed his brother.

Edward got up and swung open his fridge, picking up two bottles of orange juice. He handed one to Ray, who fumbled with it and spilled some on the floor, stopping to wipe it down with a paper towel. He poured the other one into a glass for himself.

They carried their drinks through the open-plan dining room into the living room with its beige two-seater sofa. A thin, black-patterned rug covered timber floors. The house featured high ceilings and bay windows overlooking the Williamstown Beach. A 65-inch TV sat against the opposite wall, and a bookshelf in the corner displayed books on design and the modern structure of commercial and domestic buildings.

A close-up framed portrait hung on the wall, showcasing a woman's heavily made-up eyes and long eyelashes. It was a drawing of Ray's ex-girlfriend, Mary, who had broken up with him a few years prior due to a misunderstanding. It had hurt him like hell as he had loved her with all his heart. Mary had left him a note and walked out of his life. He had attempted to rekindle their relationship, but she refused.

Edward reached for the remote and switched to the news. "It is unbelievably tragic. These murders. Two of them so close to each other and both in the local community. I wonder if it's the same perpetrator."

Ray scratched his neck as he leaned forward on the couch. "They are bad." He started coughing. "I need a drink." He tossed down his juice and wiped his mouth with the back of his hand.

"Are you all right?" asked Edward."

"I'm fine. Just a tickly throat. Nothing to worry about." He leaned back against the couch and placed his right leg over his left. "How about one of those British shows? Give you a taste of home, Ed."

Edward sometimes missed his hometown of London, but he'd been in Australia for the past twelve years—since he was sixteen, when his father had been offered a lucrative position as a stockbroker. He missed his old friends and the culture but his home now was Williamstown, Victoria.

"I would rather watch the news. I am curious about these two missing women whose bodies were found locally. The latest is this poor woman who died from drugs but was missing for two weeks. There has to be more to that story."

Ray averted his eyes. "Too dreary for me, man. What does it have to do with you? Crimes happen all the time."

"Why do you always do that?"

Ray grimaced. "Do what?"

"Avoid the reality of life. The statistics show—"

Ray put up a hand. "Oh, leave the stats, man. You and your damn facts. Can't we just take a breather and watch a British show? Enough of the downer of the news."

Edward loved his brother, and they'd been close given their family situation, but he was curious lately about why Ray had become ultra-sensitive to the news. The more Edward thought about it, the more he realised that Ray had been angrier and more distracted lately, but every time Edward asked about it, Ray brushed it off.

"Sure, Ray," Edward said and changed the channel. Something about Ray's reaction to the news nagged at him, but he decided it was best to let it go instead of risking a fight.

Edward glanced at the time. He had a date to keep and excused himself from Ray's, hurrying home.

Once he arrived at his townhouse, he placed his keys into their usual kitchen drawer. Swinging open his fridge door he stared at its contents: left-over pasta, assorted lunch containers for the working week, fresh fruit and vegetables, assorted cheeses, and a carton of eggs. Selecting a small container, Edward filled it with fruit and cheese.

The clock ticked the time and Edward ensured that he left precisely in eight minutes to be there in time. Collecting the container and a small bottle of wine with two glasses, he opened his back door and stepped inside the garage. A motorcycle and helmet stood beside his car. It had been a gift from his late fiancée, Evanthia. The memory tugged at his heart and brought to mind her beautiful smile, kind eyes, and open heart.

Edward tucked the fruit, glasses and wine into the seat's case and climbed on. He pulled on his helmet, leaving the garage with the roaring engine of the motorbike. His whole world eased away as he rode towards an overarching gate and breathed in the mild, fresh air. He got off the bike, gathered his belongings, and walked the grounds, surrounded by lush trees and flower beds with their rustling leaves and petals in the cool breeze. The freshly-mowed grass smelled sweet and sharp. The loose stones and rocks created a path as he walked further to his destination. *She always waits for me.* He sat down by Evanthia's gravestone, pulled out a cloth from his jeans pocket and cleaned off the dust. His heart ached as he picked up his bottle and poured the wine into a plastic glass. He drank up. "I know you wanted me to love again, Evanthia, but no-one will ever be you. No-one will ever belong to me like you did. I miss you so much,. I know you only want me to be happy and find love again, but I have to admit...I'm too scared to love again. I don't know if I'll ever get over you, my darling."

Edward bowed his head and spent an hour by her gravestone, He dug into his container of fruit and ate a piece of rock melon in honour of his beloved. Would he ever be able to move on?

Chapter Three

BAD TO WORSE

Joy sat inside Lian's office the next day, tapping her wedged heel on the plush carpet. She played with the stitching around a hole in her faded jeans, getting away with occasional casual attire when she didn't have client meetings.

Lian's desk featured stacks of files on one side, assorted invoices piled high, a computer monitor with a laptop, and a desk phone. She pulled files over to one side so Joy could see her. "I know you're busy but I couldn't turn this one down. It is an opportunity for us to expand if this project does well."

Joy's spine straightened and her heart fluttered. "What is it?"

Her boss leaned in, holding a pen in the air. "It is a single-story home belonging to a wealthy family. The husband and wife are gifting it to their daughter. Please say you are open to this?" She gave a cheeky grin. "Otherwise, I will have to fire you on the spot."

Joy's shoulders lifted. "Sounds like another challenge. When do we go on-site?"

"Tomorrow. The client will meet us at the house. They have a solicitor, Thomas. He will be managing the practical details. I doubt we'll see the client much." Her desk phone rang. She picked it up. "Hey, Val. What's up?" Her eyes turned a shade darker. "Send them in." She hung up and rose, cross-armed, watching the doorway.

"What's wrong?" Before Lian replied, footsteps sounded behind Joy. She turned as Angelo and Marco entered the office. Joy's back tensed up and she stilled her foot, tilting her head. "Hey, guys. Do you have news?"

Marco scratched his stubble and his brown eyes dimmed. "Hello ladies." He declined the chair offered by Joy who sat stock-still.

"What is going on?" said Lian.

Angelo had dimples and jet-black hair. He pulled over a chair from a corner of the office. "We're sorry to interrupt but this couldn't wait."

Lian shifted in her seat behind her desk. "What couldn't wait, detectives?"

Marco's posture straightened. "We are sorry to give you this news, but Kathleen was found dead yesterday."

Joy's vision blurred and she couldn't catch her breath. Squeezing her hands, she dug her nails into her sweaty palms as flashes of Kathleen's beautiful smile and boisterous laugh arose in her mind. The room around her spun and her heart raced. No, this couldn't be happening again. Marco leaned forward and grabbed her hand gently. "Joy, are you all right?"

She had to keep it together. "How?" she croaked.

Angelo glanced at her reassuringly. "It appears to be from drugs. An overdose."

Lian sat with a rigid posture, eye twitching and cheeks pale. "That's crazy. Kathleen was never into drugs. How can that be possible?"

Marco shrugged. "We will investigate further and keep you up to date."

The bile in Joy's throat stopped her from speaking. Kathleen could not be dead.

Angelo said, "We are sorry. I know you all loved her here."

Joy nodded. "This keeps happening, Angelo. First Mia then Erica ... and the others lately stalked and kidnapped and ...why?" She rubbed the heel of her palm against her chest.

Marco approached her and wrapped his arms around her as her life changed forever, again. "I'm sorry, Joy." He released her. "Do you want me to call Bella?"

Shaking her head, she said, "No. I'll call her and the others in a bit."

"Maybe you should take the day off?" Angelo suggested.

"No. No." Joy rubbed her arm. "I'd like to focus on my work. It helps ... helps me."

"I have to let everyone in the office know. We'll shut down early," Lian said as he led the two men out.

The world went quiet. Kathleen was gone. Clearing her throat, sheer will drove Joy to her feet and back to her office. She flipped open a folder and went to work.

Sitting on a padded bench inside a cafe across from her friends, Joy stared out at the entryway as patrons walked in and out. The servers rushed from one customer to another, carrying trays of orders in a circular fashion. It was a full house with chattering voices giving her a headache, and smells of greasy food and coffee making her nauseous. Normally, she relished the hectic pace of the café, but not today.

Joy sipped her water, savouring the cold down her throat. "I can't believe Kathleen is dead."

Gabriella squeezed her shoulder. "I am sorry you had to go through that, Joy." Sunlight shone on her face, making Gabriella squint. Threading her fingers through her chestnut brown bob-style cut, she shooed away a fly that landed on one of her blonde highlights.

Joy hated making Gabriella nervous. Her friend always fidgeted with her hair when she was upset or nervous. "I can't believe she died from a drug overdose," Joy said, voice cracking.

"It might have been a one-off. All it takes is one bad injection." Bella sat on Joy's other side. Her emerald green almond-shaped eyes radiated sympathy.

Joy nodded. "You could be right, but there's still this part of me believing that I should have done more. I should have noticed something was wrong. Why would she even try it once?"

Gabriella shook her head. "Oh, Joy. Stop that, will you? You can't help someone if you have to read their minds. Nothing more you could do."

"Exactly right, girl. You can't take responsibility for this," said Liz from across the table. She towered above them all, even sitting.

"If I have learned anything these past few years, it is never to assume anything," said Jamie from Liz's right." She had a regal look about her.

Her eyes darkened. "I hope you are taking care of yourself, Joy. I know you are likely to be triggered after —"

Joy flailed her hands. "I will be fine, Jamie. All good. Please. Don't be such a mother hen."

Jamie laughed. "I am sorry, but a leopard does not change its spots."

Joy drank down the remainder of her drink. "I should see how her sister, Ariana, is doing. I met her a few times when she visited Kathleen at the office. They were total opposites. Each time she visited, Ariana barely spoke to anyone, but Kathleen described her as a party girl."

Jamie straightened her shoulders. "People can change."

Bella brought up her glass. "Let's make a toast." She waited as each woman lifted their drinks. "To Kathleen."

They clinked their glasses and took a sip, letting silence fall between them.

Bella leaned forward. "You do need time to process the grief, Joy, and if you are feeling overwhelmed, please call on me any time."

Joy nodded. "Thanks, Bella. But I am sure if I ring you at midnight, Marco would have something to say about it."

Bella chuckled. "He is the most understanding man I know, and he would be there for you and the others in a heartbeat. We are all here for you."

"You'd think I'd be used to it by now. The grief. The pain." Joy didn't want to be reminded of her past, and the loss of Kathleen just brought everything back up. "But I will get through it." She shifted in her seat, fighting against tears. The empty, dark pit in her stomach was hard to ignore, but she had to. It was best to move on and not dwell.

Chapter Four

CLASH AND CONSULT

Joy hurried towards a recently built, grey brick-rendered home, a black satchel bumping into her thigh. The weight of her bag—filled with books, markers, and supplies—slowed her progress.

The warm wind swept against her skin as she made her way down a concrete path surrounded by mounds of dirt. Stopping at a heavy opaque glass door, she pulled it open and entered the bare living space. Lian stood next to a tall, handsome man with a short regal beard and hazel eyes. His light brown crew cut framed his oval face well. Joy rubbed her hands against her pants and struggled to catch her breath. "Hi, I finally made it."

Lian smiled. "Good morning."

"Sorry. Traffic was a nightmare."

Lian looked at her sternly. "This is Edward Astbury. He's the architect on-site. Edward, this is Joy, our esteemed interior designer. Ray is over there. He's part of the construction team and Edward's brother." Ray took a moment to offer a wave before getting back to work.

The man put out his hand. "A pleasure to meet you, Joy."

She shook it firmly. His touch sent a tingle up her wrist. "Same here." She made her way around the living space and reached for the blueprint sitting on the table. "Impressive design. This was all you?"

Edward nodded. "Yes, it is to the client's exact specifications. They want trendy decor, the most modern furniture and accessories, and I believe that is where you come in. The flooring is done, as you can see, but now I need to order the lighting fixtures and kitchen cabinets."

"Do you have samples of the fixtures or cabinets? I'd like to make sure the furnishings and accessories match this space and other rooms."

"Of course."

Lian handed Joy a design contract. "I made a copy of this so you can be ready for when the clients arrive. They'll be here in a half-hour. I'm heading for a cigarette break. I'll be back."

Joy bent down to her satchel, retrieving her notepad and pen. "Let's take a tour of the rooms and discuss options."

Edward's eyes seared into her own, studying her. "Certainly."

Joy appreciated his British accent; she had always thought the British sounded distinguished. "I can envision the bedroom space here, with a modern armoire, a lift-off bed for storage, and plush carpeting."

He stood close to Joy and gave her his phone. "Scroll through these for the lighting fixture ideas."

Joy scrutinised the photos but found them drab. "I don't like these. Too archaic. Sorry. But I have my own thoughts."

Edward stiffened and his brow raised. "These are the latest designs."

Joy swallowed. "I know they are the latest designs, but they don't suit the home and won't match with my ideas."

He sighed. "Right. It sounds as though we need to come to a compromise. Why don't we speak to the clients and tour the remainder of the house I designed?"

"Sounds fine to me." Joy made her way to the next room.

As they stood inside one of the bedrooms, Edward peered through the window. "I have ideas for the curtains, too." He showed a range of dressings on his phone and she scrolled through each one.

"Why are you crossing into my territory? These are old-fashioned styles and I don't think the clients would like these. Let me explore that. You can deal with the cabinets and kitchen fixtures."

He crossed his arms across his chest and pursed his lips. "I did not mean to offend you, but I had a bit of extra time and wanted this to match the structure of the home, which I designed. These are modern, in my opinion."

This guy wanted to take over her work. "Let's see what the clients say. But this is my speciality, and I can do my job if you give me at least five seconds."

"Like I said, I know what I am doing, and I am certain the clients have a more elite taste than what you have in mind."

She stared at him open-mouthed. How dare he criticise and judge her work before she'd had a chance to give the clients or him ideas? She'd worked her butt off to be successful in her job. "Why don't we see what the clients say when they get here? Judging each other is not going to help us succeed now, is it?"

Edward stared her down. "Fine."

Joy pulled out a notepad from her satchel and jotted down ideas, turning away from him. It was going to be a long project.

Fifteen minutes later, Lian returned. "I need to go to another site. One of the other designers missed the brief and I have to mediate. You can handle this right?"

Joy glanced at Edward, his back to her as he worked with the other man, Ray. From their banter, Joy believed the two acted as brothers. "Yes, I can handle it."

Edward flicked open his measuring tape and passed it to Ray who stretched it to the end of the other kitchen wall. "Okay, we need to order the cupboards. Let's place an order for the white gloss timber after we speak to the clients."

White gloss? Joy inwardly groaned. Well, they were modern and would go with a variety of options. Her brain started working over changing her décor to match.

Ray let go of the tape. "Are they coming today?"

The front door opened and footsteps sounded close by. "It appears they have arrived early," said Edward.

The clients, June and Richard Stubble, nodded in greeting. "Hello, gentlemen." Joy avoided Edward's eyes when he flicked his gaze to her.

Edward grinned and his whole demeanour changed. Gone was the stern and pushy man, replaced by a charismatic professional. Joy's cheek twitched as she held back a sneer at his masquerade. "It is a pleasure to meet you, Mr and Mrs Stubble." He shook their hands.

Ray inched forward and did the same. "Good to meet you both."

What was she? Invisible? Joy stepped forward. "Mr and Mrs Stubble. So good to meet you. I'm Joy your interior designer from *Tasteful and Trending Designs*." She held out her hand. Richard waited a bit too long to reach back and shake it. Joy offered her hand to June Stubble. The woman looked at her wide-eyed then her face melted into a warm smile as she extended her hand and shook Joy's with a hesitant grasp.

June was everything Richard was not as she silently hung by his side. He was a skinny man with cold, sharp grey eyes, short grey hair and a stern expression on his thin face. Something about him made her uneasy. "Well, let's get started. I don't have all day, Richard said."

Joy intervened. "I can make a list of all the items for the kitchen first, and we can plan out the other rooms. It'll give you an idea of budget."

"Sounds great, darling. I already agreed with Edward over the phone on the sort of cupboards I'd like, but you can give me a list of other items that will match the design." June's hair was tied up in a chignon framing her square-shaped face. Her jewellery looked expensive and expertly matched her equally fine outfit. She had an eye for style.

So Edward hadn't picked the cupboards just to try and take over the project. Joy's brows knit. She'd have to start sharing some of her new ideas before she adjusted her designs. "Of course."

"It has to be the exact style for our daughter. We only want the best for her, Ms Warrier. You do understand, don't you?" Richard's eyes pierced into her as he stepped towards her.

Joy took a step back as Richard neared her. She felt an instant dislike for the man. "I strive to create my best work. We will triple-check my list and I will show you all possibilities. We'll meet again and work through all the rooms to make sure everything aligns. I'll create a physical design model and a computer-generated one to make sure it meets your needs." She took a breath. "I'll be advising as they come to mind when we walk through each space again. It might be wallpaper here, sheer curtains there, something we could do to improve each room so it suits your daughter's style."

"Oh, I'm sure Sue will love it, Richard. When have we steered her wrong?" June said.

Richard scoffed. "Hmm. I never have, but you are quite a different story, my dear." He held her tightly by the arm. "Come along, June. Why do you always take forever to move? I should have come on my own and you could have had one of your expensive luncheons that I pay for."

Joy cringed and noticed Edward had an equally uncomfortable expression. Ray kept his head down and resumed taking measurements.

Richard grunted and turned to Edward. "I like the work so far, Mr Astbury." He cleared his throat. "Thomas, our solicitor, should be here any moment and will be our liaison on this project. We are far too busy these days."

"Of course, and thank you, sir. I have the catalogue here for the countertops." Edward gave it to him. "I can get samples of benchtops that match the white gloss cabinets. You'll have an array to select from."

Richard squinted. "Yes, yes. Please do so. We do not want any delays on this house." He turned to June. "I assume you're in agreement with the benchtop samples?"

June waved a hand. "Oh, Richard darling. I would like to get a sense of the samples and go from there. You know I'm very tactile."

Richard sighed. "Yes, tactile when it suits you, but we are on a schedule so do not dilly-dally on this, June."

"We will get you on schedule." Edward's lips were tight and his now free hands were balled into fists. *Interesting*, thought Joy. Did Edward find Richard's treatment of his wife as terrible as she did?

"Follow me," Joy said. She led the couple into the bedrooms and went over her designs and colour palettes. Richard grudgingly accepted some of her suggestions, and once or twice, insulted her choices. The noise of the drill started getting to her. Between Edward and Richard, her nerves were frayed.

Joy led them back into the kitchen. A familiar face stood in the doorway with the other two men. He was tall and in a stunning suit that did everything for him. The collar of his white shirt enhanced the precise cut of his beard, and the blue tie brought out the man's vibrant eyes.

"Oh my God! Is that you, Thomas?"

Edward moved away from Thomas, giving him more room.

Thomas grinned. "Joy? Oh my goodness." He approached and took her hands in his. Edward crossed his arms in front of his chest and looked downright sulky, but Joy chose to ignore him and focus on Thomas.

"It's a small world," said Joy.

"It certainly is. You have aged with grace," said Thomas.

Edward interrupted them. "I take it you two know each other?"

Joy turned to him and let go of Thomas's hands. "Yes, Thomas was my neighbour and dear friend when I was about twelve. After we moved house, we lost touch."

Thomas nodded. "I have missed you, Joy. It is so great to see you, and a famous designer, no less. I saw you in the paper last year. Quite the accomplishment."

"Same to you. A solicitor," said Joy, beaming with pride.

Edward took a step forward and opened his mouth.

Richard intervened. "Why don't we get back to work? I am certain that you two can banter another time. We are on a schedule."

Thomas gave Joy a reassuring smile. "Of course, Richard. Joy, let's exchange numbers before I leave."

Joy nodded. "Great idea."

Joy walked up the brick-paved path to her parents' house as the summer wind brushed her cheeks and the sky above turned darker. She passed two tall green ferns, a water fountain, and freshly-clipped grass in the front yard. Their beige rendered house had a pitched roof with colonial timber windows, bushy trees and plants lining the front yard. A Cupid statue stood beside the fountain. She loved the house she lived in with her parents, but they had their fair share of conflict, and planned to move out one of these days as soon as she could save up enough in this market.

She unlocked the door and sauntered to the open-plan kitchen which merged with the dining area, featuring a pine wall unit, wall to wall paintings of flowers, and a round dining table with solid timber chairs. The dining room led to the living room, where her parents, Margaret and Jim, sat curled up on the couch.

"Hi, honey," said her mother. She had vibrant, green eyes and her black hair was tied in a bun. She was in her late forties. "How was work?"

"Challenging, thanks to my new co-worker Edward, who does not play well with others."

Her father grunted. His dirty-blonde hair was like her brother Jesse's, but his personality was different. Instead of being friendly and warm like Jesse, he was stoic and emotionally reserved. "Why so critical?"

She frowned, ignoring the ache in her chest. "Because he's trying to take over my job and has no problem crossing boundaries."

"You can't be so obstinate your whole life," said her father. "Maybe you should bend a little. It's only décor after all."

Joy sat on the armchair beside the couch and turned to the TV playing a comedy show. "It's what I love, Dad. You know I like to keep busy." The last thing she wanted to do was debate her life with her parents.

"But darling," her mother said. "You've got to look after yourself. Why burn yourself out unnecessarily by getting into conflicts at work? You're already doing yoga, the gym, volleyball, going out with your friends and partying, not to mention having an extremely busy job. Slow down a little."

Her self-care was the topic of discussion every week and she was tired of it. It was too late to care about her at twenty-five when they should have cared about her when she needed them. "I gave up yoga and I am fine, Mum. You guys don't need to worry. I am an adult and know what's good for me." She rose from the seat.

"Where are you off to?" her father asked.

"My room. I have a few things to do." She bent over and kissed them. "Goodnight."

Her father put up his hand. "Wait, young lady." He faced her mother with a weary look. "Why are you always in your room, Joy? If you're not in your room, you are out. Your mother would like to see more of you. Do you understand?"

Joy sat back down. "I need my space. It is not personal. Please understand. Pretty soon, I'll be looking for my own place just like Jesse."

Her father scoffed. "Jesse is more responsible than you are. You do things without thinking and that can get you into trouble."

Joy contained her fury. If only her father could say one nice thing about her instead of pointing out her faults. Why couldn't he love her like a normal father? She fought back tears, got back up, and walked off. "I'm going to my room." She ignored his grunt.

When she reached the bedroom, she threw herself on the bed and lay down with her arms behind her head. She had to get out of here. Her mother was overprotective, and her father always criticised her, not appreciating her for who she was. She knew they blamed her for her sister's death all those years ago. If she had told her parents how her sister liked to leave the house at night through her window, she might still be alive today. Their blame translated into everything they said and did, and she had to get out of here and look for somewhere else to live.

She got up from the bed and switched on the TV on top of a solid timber cabinet but stopped when a notification beeped from her phone.

Retrieving her phone from her pocket, she saw text messages from Thomas. "It was good to see you again. Call me when you get a chance."

Tapping on his number, she waited for him to answer.

"Hello. Thomas speaking."

"Hi Thomas. It's Joy. How are you doing?"

"Great, now you've called. I have had a trying day. Richard is a hard taskmaster, I must say, but he pays me and I have to say yes to everything."

"I am sorry to hear that." She hesitated, then voiced her thoughts. "He is strange. It's the way he talks to his wife and puts her down. Is he always like that, and why doesn't she stand up for herself?"

"I know. She's submissive and he controls her, but we have to be the professionals and do whatever they want with the house."

"True, I guess."

"I am so impressed by your design ability, Joy. You have a true talent."

Her heart lifted. "Thanks, Thomas. It's what I love to do." She took a breath. "Was there a reason you wanted me to call?"

"Yes, I would like to get together with my old friend. How about a breakfast Saturday? My treat."

She smiled to herself. "I would love that. It's been such a long time and we have a lot to talk about."

"Great. I'll text you the details then." She ended the call and instantly thought about Edward. Why did he flash in her mind? Her going out with a friend had nothing to do with him.

Chapter Five

BROTHERLY CONFLICT

Edward leaned over Joy's worktable on Thursday and rolled out his blueprint while scrutinising her 3D design model situated on her desk.

She stood beside him with her soapy, floral scent filling his senses. "This is my design model for the house so far. What do you think?"

It had the living room and kitchen with its furnishings, window interiors, and lighting. He was impressed. "Interesting."

"Lian mentioned you wanted to remove one of the cabinets in the kitchen. Why would you?"

He contained his annoyance at her questioning his expertise. "I spoke to Richard about this, and he agreed it would create more space for the pantry they had selected."

Joy placed her arms over her waist. "Right. So did Richard want a pantry the size of the globe?" She screwed up her nose in thought.

He scoffed. "Listen, I am working with the client here. Besides, aren't the kitchen cabinets my area? Why are you now crossing the boundaries?"

"Fine. If it suits the client, but I still don't understand why they want such a huge pantry. Are they planning to host a party every night?"

He shrugged. "If they are, it is their business. We are here to achieve outcomes and schedules, so please do not give me a hard time, and trust my work as you would like me to trust yours."

"I *would* like you to trust my work. This is my work. You would've made changes to your blueprint. Did you at least charge Richard for the amendment?"

This woman would be the death of him. "Are you questioning my professional expertise here? I know what I am doing, and yes, he has agreed to an extra cost to the amendments."

She stared at the ground with her hands on her hips. "Fine. If it works, it works. I assume you're mostly done with the kitchen cupboards?"

Could they ever learn to work together? She was questioning his judgement and expertise and stepping into his territory. Why did she have to be so feisty, demanding, and irritating? She should focus on the facts rather than moving willy-nilly into his affairs. Right now, he was helping their client, and she had no right to question his customer service when he'd had more experience than her in this industry. If Richard wanted changes, he would appease the client. "Ray has completed them." His brother had left them alone together to go take a call.

"We'll need to check out the space in the living room again," said Joy.

He nodded, moving closer towards her as he scrutinised her model again. "Richard and June want to refurbish their old couch to make it look new, but I explained how it might not fit the specification here." Their shoulders brushed and a sense of calm took the edge off his irritation. Edward was keenly aware of her proximity, his mind turning to how easy she would feel in his arms. He was too tired to be thinking straight.

Joy nodded. She took a step back, blushing as she put cold distance between them. "Possibly, but what if we shave off a bit of this wall and make it fit that way?"

"That sounds good. We can talk to the clients and see what they want to do. They'll either want a narrower wall or a new couch."

Joy moved further away from the desk towards the counter with a water jug and glasses on it. Was she just as nervous by their proximity as he was?

"Would you like a drink?" she asked.

"Sure. Thanks." He watched her fill up two glasses of water with shaky hands. His eyes turned to displays of her designs pinned on the wall above her desk. She was talented, he had to admit. She was smart and creative, and she managed to create a space that fit in with his blueprint even as it changed. They needed to learn to get along and compromise on the project.

She handed him a tall glass of water. She held hers and took a sip. Her eyes peered at the ground beside her as she tapped one of her feet.

Footsteps came from the entryway. "Hey, guys," Ray said, "Just wondering how long you're going to be? I need help with a few bathroom fixtures at the house, and Johnny, the plumber called in sick today. I'll have to do some of his work to keep us on schedule."

Edward hesitated, a part of him wanting to keep working with Joy, finding their rhythm. But he knew they couldn't delay work on the house, which could cost them money. "Give me a few minutes."

Ray nodded. "Sure." Ray closed the distance to Joy. She flicked through papers inside a manila folder. "Listen, Joy. I was ... ah ... wondering if you'd like to catch a bite to eat tonight. My treat."

Edward's heart hammered and his shoulders deflated. Ray hadn't mentioned having an interest in Joy. Quickly regaining his composure, Edward focused on making his final notes. What did he care anyway? It wasn't as if they had a relationship. They weren't even friends. At best, they were slowly learning to tolerate each other.

Joy abandoned the file folder, drew her hands through her glossy blonde hair and drank down her water. She moved away and poured herself another glass, glancing Edward's way. Did she want his approval? "I am sorry, Ray, but I have plans tonight."

Ray's eyes darkened. "That's cool. We can do it another night. What about tomorrow or the next night? I have a few nights free this week." His eyes looked hopeful, and a part of Edward would feel bad if she said no.

Joy gave him a reassuring smile. She looked at Ray with pity in her eyes. "Maybe. Can I let you know for sure in the next few days?"

Ray's eyes lit up. "Not a problem."

Edward's chest ached, but he put it down to tiredness and overwork. What did he care who Joy socialised with, least of all his brother? She was free.

Closing his notebook, he took long strides around the desk and over to Ray. "How about the work you needed help with? We can leave now." He turned to Joy. "I will see you at the house tomorrow."

"Sure, Edward. Bye Ray. I'll be in touch."

Forty minutes later, Edward and Ray hefted a basin to fit into the bathroom and lay it on the ground. He watched as his brother filled the bottom of the basin with sealant.

"All done," said Ray. "Help me put the basin in place then I'll add the faucets."

Edward nodded. "Of course." He shifted his feet as he bent down to the basin and lifted it up, leaning it against the wall and pushing it in place.

"We should be paid extra for doing a plumber's job. But at least we are on a schedule," said Ray.

Edward took a breath and clenched his hands. "Johnny will need to connect the water tomorrow. Hopefully he'll be in then." Ray shrugged. "Listen, Ray. I ... I wanted to talk to you about Joy."

He wiped his hands against his dirty pants with knit brows. "What about Joy?"

He hesitated, not wanting to hurt his brother when he had been hurt before. Looking past him, he delved in. "I don't know about you asking Joy out. We work together and it could ruin our working relationship. I believe it's best if you don't get involved."

Ray reached down to pick up a faucet from the nearby cardboard box, then pulled out washers and a wrench. "I like Joy, and whether we go out is none of your damn business."

Edward sighed. "But you cannot mix business with pleasure, Ray. It will destroy what we are building here, and I don't want there to be any conflict. If things don't work out, it will surely impact our work. Please leave her be."

Ray gritted his teeth and threw the wrench back into the box, the clanking noise deafening. "I can do what I damn well like, bro. I don't need you to live my life for me. Last I checked, this is a free country, and if Joy wants to see me, why not? We are both two consenting adults, Eddie, so just back off."

Edward shook his head, hating to be hard on his brother, but he knew what Ray was like with women; he got too attached. It wasn't because he thought of Joy as attractive. It was more about Ray or Joy getting hurt and it impacting their work. He couldn't have it happening. "Please, Ray. Think about this, at least. It is definitely not a good idea."

Ray inched his way closer to Edward. "Why don't you leave, Eddie? I can do the rest myself. Besides, I can't look at you right now. Just leave."

Edward frowned. He hated hurting his brother, but he was right. The ensuing conflict if they were in a relationship would affect them all. He had to keep the peace. "Fine Ray. But please think about it."

Ray grunted. "Get the hell out before I throw you out."

Edward left before Ray got angrier. Was it wrong of him to tell his brother what to do? He'd never listened before, but he had to at least try.

Later that evening, Edward rested back against his chocolate brown sofa at home. He had worked hard to buy his brick veneer two-bedroom townhouse which had plenty of space. His living room featured a wallpaper design of abstract shapes and beige curtained windows with a view of the street..

He let his mind drift where it wanted. Joy worked creatively and had passion. But he wasn't sure if he liked her friendship with Thomas. The man was smooth and charismatic and appeared to care about Joy. But did she care about him as more than a friend?

Edward shook his head. It wasn't his business. She was free to do as she liked, and if she liked Thomas that way, then who was he to stand in the way? Then there was Ray. Would Ray's attempts at dating Joy ruin their project? It could put another wall between their tenuous working relationship.

He rose from the couch, picked up the remote from his gold-rimmed glass coffee table and glanced at the TV hanging on his wall. He changed channels, but his mind was not on any show. It was on Joy. This thing with Ray, it would interfere with their professionalism, and he didn't want it to be awkward between them.

His phone rang. Picking it up from the coffee table, he checked the display. "Hi Ray. It's late. Is everything all right?"

"I cut my ... hand ... on ... glass," he slurred. Oh, great. He was drunk. Again. "Need help, man."

Edward sighed. "I will be right there. Stay put." He rose, turned off the TV, picked up his keys and sped the entire fifteen-minute drive to Ray's in Laverton. He had purposely bought a home closer to his brother as a way to keep an eye on him. It paid off, as drinking and whirlwind relationships usually caused trouble for Ray. Edward was there for his brother and would do anything to help him, especially when no-one else in their family cared.

He arrived at the house and let himself inside with his key. The stench of cigarettes, alcohol, and burned coffee permeated the air as he flinched at the mess around the living room. Loose newspaper pages lay strewn over the carpet, dirty t-shirts littered the stained sofa and at least twelve empty beer bottles lined the table and part of the floor. He had cleaned the place only days ago. Now look at it.

Stepping into the kitchen, an overflow of dishes lay scattered in the sink and on the counter. When he turned, he found Ray behind the island with his eyes closed and blood dripping from his hand. "Jesus, Ray. What did you do?"

Ray slowly opened his eyes. "Sorry, man. Tried to ... get a glass." A wine bottle stood open on the island. A broken glass lay shattered beside Ray.

Edward picked up a dirty tea towel and wrapped it around his brother's hand then rushed to the bathroom for disinfectant and a bandage. Returning to the kitchen, he sat across from Ray and dressed his wound with the liquid and wrapped his hand with the bandage, careful to tie a tight knot. "Have you eaten anything?"

Ray shook his head. "No, wasn't hungry." Of course, he wasn't when he'd filled himself up with beer and wine.

"Let's get you over to the couch." He lifted his brother up and led him to his seat after throwing the newspaper on the floor to make space. "Now, wait here and I will clean up and make you dinner." Edward opened the fridge but all he found was mouldy cheese, a bottle of sauce, a bottle of orange juice, greasy sausages and blackened vegetables.

He approached Ray. "Stay here. I'm going to the shop to buy groceries. You have nothing in your fridge." His brother nodded, then closed his eyes.

Edward stood over the stove, stirring a cheese and mushroom omelette, one of Ray's favourite foods. He turned off the gas, plated it up and brought it over to Ray, who had since mostly sobered up with coffee and water. He set the plate on the kitchen table and took a seat opposite him. "You need help, Ray. You cannot keep doing this to yourself with the alcohol. It is literally going to kill you if you do not stop. How long has it been since you checked your liver?"

Ray finished swallowing a piece of his food and shrugged. "I'm fine, man. I don't need help. I can stop any time. You don't need to worry."

He scoffed. "It is always the same story with you. I am your brother and I love you, but you need to acknowledge you have a problem. It is the first step."

Ray devoured the rest of his food and then washed it down with water. He wiped his mouth with the back of his hand. "I don't need you on my case every single damn time. Just put a lid on it or leave. Your choice."

Edward knew it would not help to keep badgering him, but he was tired of seeing his brother hurting himself this way. If he died because of the alcohol, Edward would never forgive himself for not trying harder to make him stop.

He'd already had the discussion once about using his flask at work on another job and how he'd been making mistakes, and Ray assured him it would not happen again. A part of Edward wanted to believe him but the other part wondered if he would ever change.

After washing the load of dishes, he started picking up piles of clothing from the couch and dropped them into the laundry basket. Then he filled up the washing machine and turned it on. He moved to the living room while Ray lazed back against the couch, scrolling through his phone. He didn't want to nag him, but hopefully one day, Ray would realise this affected Edward too.

Edward sat on the couch with Ray and stared at the TV, a British comedy show he forgot the name of. Laughing at a few scenes with Ray until the end of the show, he forgot the world for a second. Then he was faced the chaotic mess on the coffee table. More clutter. Getting up, he picked up the newspaper pages and sorted them into a neat pile. The top page had a headline: POLICE SEARCH FOR LEADS TO MURDER AT BRAYBROOK PARK.

He turned to Ray. "This murder. It is terrifying to know there's a man in the area killing these women. A possible serial killer." Ray remained silent, continuing to scroll through his phone. "I am talking to you, Ray."

"What did you say?" Ray looked up at him with disinterest.

"These murders. I hope the police find out who is doing this before anyone else gets hurt."

"Yeah," Ray said then went back to his phone.

Nothing seemed to phase Ray. Well, nothing except women and beer.

Chapter Six

VOLLEYBALL RESPITE

Joy perused samples of paint colours, flicking through an array of shades which might be to the Stubbles' daughter's taste.

Lian stood beside her, pointing at one of the colours. "I think this colour might suit, based on her taste. What do you think?"

Joy nodded. "I can offer them this one and the mint green that's similar. It offers a fresher and relaxed ambience."

"Hmm. Possibly."

Joy reached for her notebook and jotted down notes, eventually looking up to see Ariana ambling towards them. "Ariana?"

She knit her brows and clutched on to a suede bag. "Hi. Your receptionist let me in to collect Kathleen's belongings."

Joy had got a phone call from Marco, explaining how they ruled Kathleen's death an accident and would no longer be investigating. She still struggled to come to terms with the conclusion. Why hadn't she seen Kathleen was in trouble before she went missing? It was hard to believe—Kathleen and drugs. "Of course." She approached Ariana who was twirling her long, blonde hair absentmindedly. Her bloodshot hazel eyes gazed at nothing. She was petite, with a diamond-shaped face that made her look angelic.

Lian approached. "I can help you." Ariana had been to the office a few times and knew where her sister's desk was located.

Joy stared over at Kathleen's desk, highlighters, design supplies, and satchel all clumped together in the cluttered area.

"I am sorry I didn't clear this up for you, but it was hard to touch her things. We weren't quite ready."

Ariana appeared to fight back tears. "It's fine. I ... I have to do this."

Joy inched her way forward. "I'll go get a box for you to put her things in." She headed to a small storage room, opened the door and rummaged through various-sized boxes clumped on top of each other. Grabbing a medium sized box, she carried it back to her office. She lay it on the ground beside Kathleen's desk.

Ariana picked up a tissue from her sister's desk and wiped her nose, sniffling. "I am sorry. This is harder than I thought." She stood stock-still opposite the desk, observing.

"Listen, why don't Joy and I do this? We can bring you her things."

Ariana shook her head. "No, it's fine. It is my responsibility but thank you." She bent down low to pick up the box, settled it on a side of the desk and gently placed a large notebook and highlighters inside it. Tears ran down her face and she wiped them away with the back of her hand.

Joy walked back to her desk, watching the poor woman. "I'll be right here if you need help." She wanted to give Ariana a warm hug but the way she clammed up whenever someone got close to her stopped her.

"Thank you, Joy."

Ariana slumped, and her chin dipped to her chest, her hand resting on her satchel. Taking a deep breath, she reached for Kathleen's set of three interior design books on a high shelf and hefted them into the box. The sleeves of her shirt shifted with her movement to reveal track marks over the inside of her arm. Bruises lined the inside of her palms.

Twenty minutes later, Ariana plastered a fake smile on her gaunt and pale face. Those dark eyes of hers seemed to be more than pools of grief. Was more going on with Ariana? "Thank you, Joy and Lian. I have everything." She swallowed hard and took a shuddering breath, her eyes darting past them.

Joy inched her way towards Ariana. "You take care of yourself."

Ariana looked past her. "Thanks. I will." She walked away quickly.

Joy turned to Lian. "Did you see the marks on her arm?"

Lian nodded. "I did. I wonder if she's in trouble too. We should make sure Ariana's okay. We should take her out for coffee."

"Do you think if we both go, she might feel like we're ganging up on her?"

Lian shrugged. ""Perhaps you're right. You should go. She's always connected more with you than me."

Joy nodded. "Okay. I'll give her a bit of time. I'll have to be tactful and careful with my words." If Ariana was in trouble, she had to help. Kathleen would have wanted her sister safe. It was about helping Ariana in Kathleen's memory.

Lian nodded. "Don't forget, it's Friday so we have volleyball tonight. Oh, I've invited Edward too and he's coming. Ray and Thomas couldn't make it."

"Right." Joy prepared the samples they had decided on before Ariana's visit and sent them by courier to Thomas's office. She pondered. Edward and volleyball. She couldn't picture him letting loose enough for team sports.

The spacious indoor gymnasium featured glossy, brown floors with high ceilings. Low lighting created a soft glow with two basketball rings on either side of the space. A volleyball net stretched across the middle of the gym.

Edward stood alongside Lian and the five other players on his team. Joy opposed them on the other team with a few of the other designers and work colleagues, and her friend Camilla. It was a social team, with no actual participation in competitions, and a way to release work stress. Edward gave Joy a curt nod and she nodded in response. Sportsmanlike of him. Maybe she had misjudged him. She wore tight red shorts and a yellow singlet top, grateful she kept her gym bag in her car and didn't have to go home to change in rush hour traffic. She bent over her legs for warm-up exercises and touched her feet, stretching out the tension in her back and legs. She tried not to notice Edward staring. What was his problem?

He turned away and sipped water from his bottle. No way would Edward win against her. Joy would see to that.

Lian touched him on the shoulder. "Hey, Edward, are you ready to start or are you still daydreaming?"

His face reddened. "No, I'm ready." Other players stared, and he stood close to the net and directly opposite Joy, ready to play. Joy served the ball towards Edward. He bumped the ball but it bounced inside the net.

Ha! He'd lost them a point. Just as she suspected. He was not a regular player. Joy served again and the ball bounced around until Edward pushed himself in front of Lian, accidentally, and hit the ball over the net.

Lian glanced at him. "I had that."

"Sorry, but at least I got it over this time."

Not so sportsmanlike after all. "Don't get too cocky," said Joy across from him.

He stepped closer to her and she smirked at him. She focused back on the game and hit the ball over the net towards Lian who bumped it up. Camilla spiked it over the net, her chestnut brown hair bouncing with the effort, and it landed on their opponents' side. Joy gave Edward a satisfied smile and he frowned at her. Okay, so she was gloating a little bit. Joy was competitive. What could she say?

The referee shouted, "Half-time. Let's switch sides."

Edward walked over to the other side of the court, avoiding Joy.

Joy served the ball and hit it hard over the net, reaching his side. He threw it over, and it knocked into a player's chest and bounced. *Yes, one point for them.*

As the ball moved from side to side in a rally, Joy hit it towards Lian. Lian sent it up over to Camilla. Camilla hit it back over and Edward lunged, slamming it back to Joy. She missed it, the force of the ball leaving a sting where it grazed her arm. She frowned in his direction, sighing heavily with a shake of the head. Another round, and he passed the ball but made it fall into the net.

"Better luck next time," Joy said with feigned sincerity. Serves him right.

He snarled. "You are unbelievable."

She lifted a brow.

By the end of the game, Joy's team won twenty-five to fifteen.

She wiped her forehead with a towel and sat on the floor. Edward made his way over to them with Lian. The others made their excuses to leave and it was just the four of them left: Camilla, Lian, Edward, and her.

"I am not much of a sportsperson," Edward admitted.

Joy scoffed as she rose from the floor. "I can see that."

"I played the best I could and it's not as though we are competing for a trophy. It is purely social, isn't it?"

"Yes, I guess it is, but I love to win." She lifted her shoulders and put her hand on the other woman's arm. "This is my friend, Camilla. She's only recently joined the game and is another star player. This is Edward, the architect I'm working with on the new house."

He put out his hand. "Nice to meet you, Camilla."

She shook his hand. "Hi Edward. Great to meet you. I am not much of a player either but I am getting better."

"You did well. Better than I did, in fact," said Edward.

"No debating that," said Joy.

Lian glared at Joy and rubbed her hands together. "How about drinks? My shout."

Joy nodded. "Sure. Sounds good."

"Okay," said Camilla. "But I can only stay for an hour or so. I have to pick up Mariana."

"I will take a raincheck." Joy and Lian wouldn't want him around after his bad game.

Lian pursed her lips. "Nonsense. You can have at least one drink. No arguments. Let's go."

Joy averted her eyes; she didn't want him tagging along. Edward agreed. "Okay then."

A rowdy bunch of patrons sat in their groups inside the city cafe with its square timber tables and blue chairs, a TV set high above the bar, and a mural with colourful abstract art painted on the walls. The smells of beer and spices clouded the pub. Bottles lined the counter shelf, and waiters bustled from one area to another.

Joy's heart beat fast at the way Edward intermittently glanced her way. The man was stiffer than a pole.

Her eyes shifted towards the muscular outline of his chest in his skin-tight t-shirt, the way his square jawline and well-rounded toned legs reminded her of an actor who took great care of his physique with a well-oiled exercise regime because of the value of their public persona. He might work out at the gym, but it was obvious he wasn't a sportsman.

She wondered if she was a tad too hard on him, but she couldn't help it. He wanted to control her at work, and she'd had enough of others trying to control her to last a lifetime.

"Penny for your thoughts, Joy," Lian said. "What's with you?"

Joy smiled reassuringly. "Sorry. Just thinking about the game and how we won."

Edward leaned forward, sipping his beer. "I keep hearing the same message. We cannot all be talented athletes."

"Okay, fine. I am sorry to be bragging but I can't help this competitive streak," said Joy.

Camilla frowned. "Oh, Joy. I wish I could be half as great as you are but I'm not an athlete either."

Joy shook her head. "No, that's where you're wrong. You've improved your game since you started a few months ago. But as Edward said, it's a social game and we don't need to get competitive, but ..."

"You can't help yourself," finished Edward. "Why can't you view the game as a way to unwind after a stressful day."

"Hmm," said Joy. "For me, work is not a stress, most of the time. I get my rush through my work."

Lian intervened. "What do you do to unwind, Edward?"

He hesitated as if he didn't like the spotlight on him. "I go to galleries to look at abstract art, read literary classics and thrillers, and sketch portraits and landscapes."

Joy's gaze seared through him. "Interesting." She couldn't imagine Edward portraying his emotions in a drawing. She imagined him liking the classics and abstract art, but she didn't want to judge the guy without knowing him. Had she misjudged him?

A notification sounded in Joy's handbag. She rummaged into it and pulled out her phone, thinking it might be one of her friends. It was Thomas. She ignored the call, intending to return to it later. She didn't want to be rude.

"You look surprised," said Camilla. "Is everything okay?"

She nodded, ignoring Edward who, from the corner of her eye, appeared to be watching her. "All good. It's Thomas. Probably confirming our breakfast for tomorrow. I'll get back to him later. How's Mariana doing at school?"

Edward's hand stilled around his drink, and he quickly looked away from her, lips in a tight line. Joy would bet he was judging her for socialising with Thomas and misinterpreting her as playing Ray. He could think what he liked. Thomas and Joy were just friends and there was no way she and Ray would become a thing. Edward should stay in his lane, not that he knew how to do that.

Camilla's eyes shone every time she spoke about her daughter. "She is excelling and has made a lot of friends at school. Every week, she's invited to a party or a playdate and if we're free, we go. I still have a few things to work out because of my past, but Matthew and Liz have been a godsend and help with Mariana when I have errands."

"If there is anything I can help you with, let me know. But it's great to see you for volleyball every week. I'd miss you otherwise," said Joy.

As they engaged in further discussions about work and volleyball, Joy couldn't help but notice Edward's continued glances in her direction, lingering just a bit too long. She ignored the flutter in her stomach.

Chapter Seven

A NEW WOMAN

He waited, watching the woman in her early twenties parade around in that skin-tight leopard-print dress, cleavage bursting over the top.

His mouth salivated and his adrenaline kicked in. Blonde hair flowed neatly around the soft outline of her jaw. Bright-blue eyes flicked in his direction then flitted away. He licked his lips, waiting to pounce but he had to take it slow. He didn't want to scare her. Yet.

Approaching her table at the restaurant, he straightened his shoulders. "Hi. I'm Gerald. Care for a drink?"

The woman beamed. "I already have one but thank you."

Flowers and cinnamon; that familiar scent kicked up his desire, making his skin itch and his loins ache. "Happy to grab another one. It looks like you've almost finished." He maintained eye contact, softened his expression, and kept space between them.

The woman leaned closer.

"Then I would love another drink. Gin and tonic." She brushed her tongue over her upper lip and he knew he had her.

He was about to leave to buy her the drink when he turned back around. "Would you care for anything else? A snack?"

The woman beamed. "Just the drink is fine. Thank you."

He had to show he cared for her basic needs. "Not a problem. I'll get you that drink and we can get to know each other."

Approaching the counter, he leaned forward. "I'll have a gin and tonic and a beer."

"Of course, sir." The server smiled pathetically as if he was doing him a favour.

While waiting for his drink, his eyes darted at the patrons surrounding the other tables and how they all pretended to be having fun, bantering with each other. It was all a game when truthfully they hated their humdrum lives. Where was the real excitement of life when each day was like Groundhog Day?

He knew how to break up the day-to-day by tearing down a woman piece by piece. Full of life and fake smiles, he eventually brought out their true colours. Finding a new woman to charm until he pushed her to the brink. It was art.

He returned with her gin and tonic and placed it on the table, taking the seat opposite her. "What's your name?"

She gave him her winning smile. "Diane Jeens, but you can call me Di."

"Di. What a perfect name."

Chapter Eight

IT'S A DATE

Overlooking Victoria Harbour from the cafe at the Docklands Saturday morning, Joy cut into her toast topped with a slice of bacon, poached egg, lettuce, and grilled piece of tomato. She enjoyed the crunch and the tangy and salty flavours of her big breakfast. Thomas had chosen a great place.

Thomas bit into his warm croissant filled with cheese, ham, and tomato. He had a cappuccino at the side of his plate that smelled heavenly. He frowned as if he didn't like his food.

The sun shone brightly as the light wind outside brushed her flushed cheeks. The sails of boats in the near distance flapped against the wind, with several boats out riding along the waterfront. Coffee and aromatic herbs whetted her appetite. She wondered whether this view would instil a more relaxed demeanour in Edward.

Shaking away her thought, Joy smiled to herself. She and Thomas fell into easy conversation and comfortable silences. It was as if the years had never passed.

Joy picked up her orange juice and sipped, peering over her glass at him as he wiped crumbs off his beard and froth off his moustache with a napkin. "You scoffed that one down easily. I am so full. I don't think I can finish this toast."

Thomas shook his head. "Of course you can. Afterwards, we're having pancakes with blueberries and ice cream for dessert. They're the best here. I will not accept no for an answer."

"How fat do you want me to get? Jesus. I don't know if I can eat another bite."

"Take your time. We have all day."

"I don't have all day, Thomas. I have a few errands and a prior engagement with friends. Why don't you finish my last piece of toast? Then I will have room for dessert."

He shrugged. "All right. Challenge accepted." He picked up her toast and devoured it in three bites.

Joy laughed. "Wow. You must've still been hungry."

He beamed. "I work out a lot. For my career, I need to stay fit and have energy to keep up with my client caseload. It takes a lot of work to keep up with the changing laws, and exercise makes my mind sharp, which energises me physically. Constant training, workshops, you name it. The law changes more often than I go out for breakfast."

She chuckled. "It's good for mental health too," said Joy. "You seem energised by your work. Did you always want to be a solicitor?"

He wiped his mouth. "Not always. Initially, I had an interest in carpentry, but I figured that by the time I turn thirty, I'd most likely need surgery on one part of my body. I prefer the mental challenge of the law. As I said, it keeps my brain sharp."

A rowdy bunch of people left and the place immediately grew quieter. "I never pegged you for the law growing up. You always had an interest in making things with your hands. Remember the bookshelf you made me?"

He chuckled. "Sure do. But by the time you put your books on there, it broke apart. Luckily, I didn't become a carpenter. It was not my forte."

"Hmm. You might have got there in the end."

A buxom female waiter walked over to them. "Can I get you anything else?" She stared hard at Thomas, obviously taking a liking to him.

Thomas ordered. "We'd like your blueberry pancakes for two, with lots of cream and blueberries. Thank you."

"Certainly sir. It shouldn't be too long." She lingered and kept gazing at Thomas.

Joy cleared her throat. "Oh, can I have a glass of water, please?" The waitress nodded and walked away.

Not that Joy was jealous, but Thomas was a handsome man who was worthy of a second look, and so far, several women passing by had gazed a minute longer than was expected. But Thomas didn't seem to notice how women flocked to him. She imagined Edward would also have women gazing at him intensely too. He was a pain in her side but easy on the eyes.

Joy clasped her hands. "From memory, you'd be twenty-seven?"

He nodded. "I am getting old, but from my memory, you're twenty-five?" She nodded. "Such a success at a young age. You were born to be an interior designer, Joy. I truly respect your work. It's exceptional."

Joy waved him away. "Do not exaggerate, please. But it makes all the difference when you are passionate about something, as you are about the law."

He leaned in. "It does. Without passion, life becomes meaningless." He stared into her eyes a bit longer than expected. She quickly looked away at other customers laughing and chatting at the next table. Was the way he looked at her as only a friend or was it more? Would she and Edward ever be friends? *Stop that!* You're here with Thomas, not Edward.

The silence between them was filled with something unspoken and broken when the waitress returned with their pancakes. "Enjoy." This time she didn't linger with Thomas and rushed off.

Joy picked at a blueberry and tasted the sweet juices. "Mmm, nice." She cut into her pancake and mixed it in with the cream and ice cream, then bit into it. "You're right. This is delicious."

"Yes, the best I've tasted," Thomas said as his eyes lit up at the food. He put down his fork and sipped his iced coffee.

"I might need to go on a diet after this," she said. Joy was having a nice time.

He inched closer to her and grabbed her hand, caressing between her knuckles and scrutinising her hand as if it held secrets. He brought it to his lips. "You're beautiful the way you are. No diets." He looked up at her, his hand trailing the side of her eyebrow then moving down to her lips. The tender way he touched her gave her shivers.

"What are you doing, Thomas?" she said softly.

"I care about you, Joy. Even when we were kids I wanted you, but the timing was wrong. I'd like for us to go out. See where it goes. Enjoy each other. We're both adults now."

Joy swallowed, not sure of what to say. She wondered why Thomas was still single, given he had both charm and good looks. Was Edward single? What an absurd thought. Clearly Thomas's caress had muddled her brain. "I don't know Thomas. We're friends, and I don't want to spoil that."

"Is there someone else?"

Joy hesitated. What did she have to lose by getting closer to Thomas? "No, there's no-one else."

He leaned in and smashed his lips against hers. His breath tasted like a blend of mint, blueberry and espresso, and she hungered for more as he guided his expert tongue inside her mouth, tantalising her. He pulled away then kissed the side of her neck. Joy took a few moments to recover before they returned to their meal. It was a pleasant kiss.

Late afternoon, walking along the stone fence opposite the Williamstown Beach with her friend, Gabriella, Joy breathed in the salty air as the seagulls perched on the fence. The day had been packed. She returned Ray's calls, declining his invitation, and ran a few errands before coming here to meet her friends. Stepping down from the hardness of the concrete to the yielding feel of the sand beneath her thongs, her mind kept wandering back to Thomas's kiss this morning. What would it be like to taste him, hold him, and have him caress her down the centre of her chest down to her navel and even lower? She was feeling hot all over and gasped for breath. Her mind conjured Edward's face interrupting her daydream and she blinked. Edward was not the man for her. Why was she thinking about him when she had Thomas?

Joy set herself down on the picnic blanket as she watched the rolling waves, hordes of people throwing a ball, and others lazing on towels or swimming in the sea.

"How's the new project going?" asked Gabriella.

Joy gave a thumbs-up. "Amazing house. Lian and the clients like my design ideas so far. Not sure about the architect, though."

"Ooh, who's the architect? Is he handsome?" said Gabriella.

Joy blushed. "He's okay, but not really my type. A stuffy Englishman who seems to have his own ideas for the house. I guess he's come around to some of my thoughts, but he does have less trendy designs in mind. We've had to compromise."

"Why are you blushing?" Gabriella poured herself more wine.

"I'm not. Can we change the subject? How are things with Jesse, Gabriella? Is my brother treating you well?"

Gabriella's eyes lit up as she touched the base of her throat. "He's amazing. Tonight, he's taking me to a new Korean place where you cook your own food. I'm looking forward to it. He spoils me rotten."

"That's what I like to hear, girl. My brother should treat you like a princess after what you've been through."

Their other friend, Jamie, trudged through the sand towards them. "Hello young ladies. Sorry I am late."

"Where are the others? I thought Bella and Liz were coming."

Jamie shook her head. "They got caught up at work, and I have a free few hours before driving back to the hospital." She sat opposite them on the blanket and Gabriella unscrewed a wine bottle and poured it into a plastic glass.

"Here, Jamie. It looks like you need this."

Jamie gave Gabriella a reassuring smile as she took the proffered wine from her. "Thank you. I need this after the hectic day I have had." Facing Joy, she pursed her lips briefly. "You are not looking well, Joy. Is everything all right?"

Joy chuckled, having grabbed a wine glass too. "You're always the mother hen, aren't you? But I am fine. Just a little tired after playing catch up with my sleep."

Jamie's eyes darkened. "I would like you to take vitamins. Are you worried about the new project you have started or the architect you are working with?"

Joy wanted the focus away from herself, craving respite. "No, all good. Tell us about you and Angelo. What is happening with the engagement party?"

Jamie's eyes roamed. "I know it is short notice, but Angelo and I plan to have our engagement party in the next several months. I will text you the date, followed by invitations."

Joy rubbed her hands, then hugged her friend. "You did mention an engagement this year, but I didn't think it'd be this soon. How exciting."

Jamie beamed. "Why wait when we want to move forward in our relationship? We are not getting any younger."

Gabriella's eyes lit up. "We are both looking forward to the party, aren't we, Joy?"

"Of course," Joy said.

Jamie touched Joy on the shoulder. "I know something is on your mind. Please tell me what's wrong."

"Edward's brother, Ray. He's a carpenter on the job and asked me out. I tried to let him down gently but he just didn't get it. He called me a few times until I set him straight this morning."

"How did he take it?" asked Gabriella.

"Not great," said Joy. The warm wind feathered her cheek but she was chilled to the bone. Her whole body ached as she thought about Ray's sombre voice over the phone. She sipped her wine, gripping the glass tightly. "I feel guilty hurting the guy."

"It's understandable why you would feel guilty, but you need to do what is right for you," said Jamie. "I am sure you would have been tactful in your approach."

She could always confide in Jamie and get her wise counsel. "I was nice about it, but he asked if Edward spoke to me about the situation. Why would he?"

Gabriella downed her wine. "Do you think Edward's jealous his brother asked you out? Do you care about the guy? What would he even say to Ray?"

Jamie put up a hand. "My goodness, Gabriella. Please take a breath. Is there any particular order you would like her to respond to those questions?"

She shrugged in Jamie's direction and turned to Joy. "Sorry, but it does sound like Edward might be a factor in this equation if Ray's talking about him."

Joy stared at her hands. "I don't know, Gabi. But I hope we can move on from this and not let it affect our working lives. I don't want it to be awkward between us. Besides, Thomas kissed me when we went out."

"Interesting," said Jamie. "Do you care about him?"

She nodded. "I do."

Gabriella looked at her strangely. "Why am I not convinced?"

"He knows how to kiss," said Joy, avoiding the question.

Gabriella tapped her on the shoulder. "Ah, Joy. There's this guy staring at you. He's coming this way. Do you know him?"

She sat up straight and looked where Gabriella pointed. What was he doing here? "Hi, Ray. This is a surprise."

Ray took off his sunglasses and knelt in the sand beside Joy. Gabriella and Jamie exchanged a glance and shifted to create space for him. "Thanks." He cleared his throat. "I usually take a drive here because it's close by. I didn't expect to see you here."

"Is Edward with you?" Joy asked, only out of curiosity.

His eyes darkened. "No, he's not."

She pushed down the disappointment. "These are my friends." She introduced them one by one, fighting a sense of tightness in her chest.

"Great to meet you, ladies." He gazed intensely at Joy. "Listen, can we take a walk? I wanted to show you photos of my work at the house and talk about something else." He had a light in his eyes. "I left my phone in my car across the road. I can quickly show you."

Joy didn't want to talk about work but couldn't be rude either. "Sure." She dusted the sand off and made her way towards the playground and past the road towards the barbecue areas with Ray. He unlocked his car in the parking space and retrieved his phone from the glove box.

They walked in silence until Ray found a bench and sat down. She joined him but kept distance between them. The best way to deal with this would be to make it clear right away, she decided. "I am sorry about turning you down earlier today, but like I said on the phone, I'm only in the headspace for work. I am not looking for anything else, Ray."

He averted his eyes. "No problem. I was only wondering if you might have changed your mind since then. We can grab a bite to eat now if you don't mind leaving your friends?"

She shook her head. "I'd rather not." Joy squeezed her hands. "I like you, Ray, but as I said, I'm not looking for anything at the moment."

He grew tense and silent, jaw ticking." I understand."
One of his nails pressed into his palm. "Let me show
you these photos." He scrolled through his phone, and
images of the completed bathroom came up, as well as the
installed kitchen cabinets.

"It looks good."

Ray moved his body closer, and Joy slowly eased herself
away. "You know, you remind me of someone."

She gasped. "Who?" She looked into his eyes, drawn
into the pained look in his expression. What was going
on with this guy? Joy wiped her hands on her pants
and checked for her friends. She couldn't see them from
here. She was being silly. Surely, he was harmless. He was
Edward's brother and a co-worker.

When she turned back, Ray inched his mouth towards
her and kissed her before she could stop him. His hand
squeezed her shoulder hard. Joy abruptly pulled away and
put up her hand. "No, stop this." She jumped to her
feet. "Why did you do that? I told you I didn't want a
relationship."

Ray smiled briefly as if he'd won a prize. "I couldn't help
it. You're so beautiful, Joy." He stood up. "If you get to
know me, we could have something special. Please give me
a chance?"

Joy couldn't believe the nerve of this man. Why couldn't he take no for an answer? "I'm going now. Please don't ever do that again."

"No, please, Joy. Get to know me." He stood closer, his hands clenched.

Joy stepped back, swallowing. The hair at the back of her neck stood on end. His eyes bore into her as if he desperately needed her. "I have to go." She rushed off without looking back, her knees threatening to give out. She didn't relax until she saw her friends again. When she turned around, Ray was gone.

Chapter Nine

A REAL CATCH

"Please. You don't have to do this. I promise I won't say anything. Let me go."

Her hands were bound behind her back in red cuffs and she bowed her head, contorted on the mattress and pressed against the wall as far away from him as possible. Purple bloomed on her cheeks and angry slashes on her legs puckered. Strewn around her were locks of dishevelled and dirty bleach-blonde hair that he had cut away while she sobbed. Dried semen stained the blankets. The terror in her eyes had made him release with a powerful crescendo. The more he tortured, the higher the rush.

A bottle of whisky rested on the bedside table. As he picked it up, he squeezed her cheeks. "Now open up wide." The woman shook her head, pressing her lips tight together. "Open up, bitch, or I'll cut your damn tongue out." She relented and he poured the alcohol into her mouth, making her gag and choke. Alcohol dripped down her chest. Releasing her, he tilted his head back and guzzled from the bottle himself, throat warming.

The man grabbed a glowing cigarette on the bedside table and flicked it to the ground, grinding it into the cement with his shoe as he surveyed his countertop.

He kicked off his shoes, having left them on in his haste, and made his choice. He picked up one of the implements and climbed back on the bed with her.

Facing the bitch, he thrust his chest out. "Call me Master and I might let you go."

The woman's lips quivered. "Master." Her hazel eyes showed a hint of hope, but he was about to snuff that out.

Chuckling, he murmured in her ear, "You're going to have the ride of your life, Di."

The light in her eyes darkened. "Please. Don't hurt me. What do you want? I can give you money. Lots of it."

He scoffed. The need to cut that tongue of hers prominent. He could practically taste her coming terror, could hear her screams. Blood raced and warmed his core. Grasping the trembling shoulder, he sliced with the scalpel precisely. Barely a whine, a muffled cry. "That's not so bad, is it?" he cooed. With the next cut, he pushed the scalpel into her shoulder even deeper, her scream music to his ears

Her eyes dilated and teeth clenched as she squirmed and turned her face away. He slapped her. "Do not turn away from me, woman. I want you to look at me when I handle you. You might get excited too." The woman's gasps and trembling made his body feel light, as if he was floating. The terror in her eyes made him hard and he stroked himself, but when she closed her eyes, his manhood softened. "Open your fuckin eyes. Look at me or I will cut your tongue out." As she opened her bloodshot eyes, he picked up the whisky bottle and took a long sip. Putting it aside, he repositioned the scalpel, beginning to get hard again.

She screamed. It was time to get to the real work.

He slid the handcuffs off her. Red welts where the metal pressed against her skin stirred his arousal. "Touch me." The bitch lay back against the cast iron bed like a rag doll, cowering. "I fuckin' said touch me or I'll make your death painfully slow."

"Please, don't do this." Diane had the brightest green eyes he'd ever seen, pools of terror he fell into. She was living on borrowed time, and he couldn't wait to destroy her.

He pulled her arm hard and made her wince in pain. Inching closer, he closed his eyes as she glided her hand up and down his manhood. Moaning, he wrapped his hands around her throat, choking her. Her grip tightened then relaxed as her gasps grew quiet. The way her eyes drooped and she grew limp made his heart palpitate. He let go and he leaned in, kissing her and forcing air into her lungs. She sputtered and tears poured down her face as she stared up at him. Hands finding her throat again, he repeated his attention to her throat three times and his arousal escalated. When she loosened her hands around him and let them fall to the bed, he didn't care. The darkness in her eyes and wriggle of her body was enough to keep him going. One less bitch in the world once he snuffed her out.

He needed to see the fear and hopelessness in her eyes, the light dimming, and her body getting smaller as he tortured her. Maybe it was time to try something a little different. Giving her a few seconds to recover, he walked to his table of supplies. Picking up a jagged knife, he approached Diane again and sliced deeply into the palm of her hand, cutting into tendons and muscle with the dull blade. She screamed, his chest soaring with excitement as he closed his eyes to take in the sounds. Her terror was like a beautiful symphony, and a rush of adrenaline coursed through him as he laughed at her. Gripping the knife, he made a small, deep cut into the other palm until she blacked out. The blood oozed out of her hands and he slapped her cheeks. "Wake up, woman. Wake up. I have more surprises in store for you."

Kathleen, his last one, died prematurely. At least they had ruled her death an accident, which it was. Oh well, she was one less problem to worry about and Diane was making up for it.

She slowly roused. Pulling at the woman's short hair, he cursed. "Fuckin' wake up. Call me Master, bitch." He was getting hard again and needed release.

"Mas … ter."

He guided her still functional bloody hand back to his penis. "Make me come again. Call me Master."

Lips quivering, she squeezed tighter, wincing as her grip slipped in her own blood, scraping her nails into his flesh. She was fighting back a little, taking her anger out on his cock as if it would hurt him. The sting of pain sent him twitching to attention. He wanted to stuff her face full, but the tension in her jaw meant she might use teeth inappropriately, so he wrapped his hand around hers and clenched tighter, digging her nails deeper into his flesh. He laughed at the lost look in her eyes as a flood of semen poured out of him, splashing onto her cheek and chest and mingling with her blood under his grip.

Once his excitement was over and the woman's eyes closed, he pounded his fist hard into her eye. She cried out weakly and hit her head against the bedhead. "Wake up. We're not done yet." He slapped her cheeks until she became conscious again. He picked up his bottle of bourbon and sipped the cool liquid, energising himself even more. He poured the drink over her nipples, bending low over her body, biting hard into her breast as if it was his last meal. She winced then screamed, her body quivering. Music to his ears.

Chapter Ten

GETTING CLOSER

First thing Monday morning, Edward walked around a furniture store at the homemaker centre in Maribyrnong, gliding his hand over a charcoal sofa. Joy stood beside him. "This is the kind of sofa the client would appreciate. It would be perfect for the house." He turned to Joy, who looked radiant in a white shirt and a tight-fitted black skirt which showed her long, bronzed legs. Short, feminine, long, black boots finished the outfit. The lines her choice of clothing created over her body was downright architectural.

Joy scrutinised the sofa and sat on the end recliner. "It is soft and comfortable."

The seven-seater sofa curved into a semi-circular shape, with four out of seven seats as recliners. "The price is within our budget, too."

Joy rose from the sofa and stood cross-armed in thought. "It's the right size based on your specifications. The Rhino fabric is smooth." The rise and fall of her chest drew him into the slender olive-toned curve of her neck. "This is similar to the couch June wanted but was out of Richard's budget. This is more affordable. I can call June about this one. I love it."

Edward nodded. They were starting to agree on selections for the house. "You arrange a hold on this and I'll take a photo for the client." Narrowing her eyes, she pressed her lips together but didn't protest. He reached into his back pocket, took out his phone and snapped a photo. Joy made her way to the salesperson as he took a call. It was Ray. "Is everything handled over at the house?"

"Of course," said Ray. "I wanted to know what time you were coming back. Richard and June are here wanting changes to the design in the living room."

"About what specifically?" It would have been nice if Richard called ahead. Didn't he realise they had other projects? They couldn't always be on site.

"I don't know. They insisted on talking to you and Joy."

"Tell them we are putting a sofa they might like on hold. We're not far so we'll be there in about fifteen minutes if they can wait."

Ray sighed. "Sure. How is Joy?

"Fine. Why do you ask?" He didn't believe Ray had backed off from Joy, but he couldn't ask her about it without ruining their rapport. "Did you take my advice?"

"No, man, I didn't."

Edward's shoulders deflated. "Did you go out together?" Silence. "Ray?" His heart beat a mile a minute.

"No. She called me to give me some detail about not wanting it to affect our working relationship. Then I bumped into her at the beach when she was with her friends. She doesn't want to go out."

Edward breathed a sigh of relief. He didn't want it to be awkward between them. It was best they kept it professional. "I told you the same thing, Ray."

"Yeah, whatever. I don't give a crap anyway. I'll see you at the house." His brother was hurt. Would it send him into a spiral of drinking again? Edward wished there was some way he could ease the sting for Ray, but there was nothing he could do. He ended the call and joined Joy at the front counter.

She watched him. "All sorted. Now, how about that other kitchen manufacturer you know? We need to check out the countertops and get more samples."

"We'll need to do that later. Richard and June are waiting for us at the house."

As they crossed the car park their shoulders brushed. Apologising, he held a hand behind her, leaving a respectable distance between his hand and her back, and motioned her to continue ahead of him. Pressing the key, the car beeped and she let herself in to his vehicle before he could get to the door.

Joy stared straight ahead, hands balled into fists. Her dress shifted to reveal tanned, toned thighs, and he imagined what it would feel like to glide his hands over her soft skin. Get it together. He needed a date, maybe a good tumble, if he was thinking about Joy this way.

He started the motor and drove in silence for the next five minutes. "I am glad we are finally collaborating on the house. It is slowly coming to life."

Joy faced him. "It sure is. For now we have to deal with Richard and June." She crossed one leg over another and placed her palms on her knee. "I get a rush during a project and at the end of it. I love to see my ideas and inspirations coming to life. You must feel that way too."

"I do. The way each measurement aligns to create a purposeful home in such a limited time is rewarding when the plan works. I have made my fair share of mistakes with specifications, which were costly, and I vowed that I would always triple-check and quadruple-check the blueprint.

I even have my contractors check it. Ray has been my wingman of sorts."

Joy stiffened. "Right."

Was she embarrassed that Ray had asked her out?

Edward swallowed, focused on the way her eyes remained downcast. She looked nervous. "Is everything okay?"

"Fine."

He had to know more about her and Ray. "I heard you met with my brother at Williamstown Beach."

Joy averted her eyes. "Hmm. Small world."

Edward gripped the steering wheel as he made a turn into the street, noticing Richard's four-wheel drive parked by the kerb. "It is a small world." He parked, and before they stepped out of the car he turned to Joy. "Listen, about Ray. He explained how you didn't want to go out with him because of the working relationship." Her hands clenched beside her. "I don't want you to feel awkward in any way, Joy. He will be fine."

Joy nodded. "It's all good, Edward. I'd like to focus on my work and this current project. I don't ... I mean, I wanted to keep our working relationship professional and I hope he'll be okay."

Edward's breath hitched. "He will get over it. Before you know it, he will forget all about it. But are you sure you're all right? You seem nervous about something."

She shook her head. "All good. Water under the bridge." She put her hand on the door handle. "We shouldn't leave the clients waiting."

"Of course," Edward said. Why did he get the sense she was holding something back about Ray? Had he said something to upset her? Things had been going so well.

Inside, Joy was already handing Richard and June the samples of the countertops from the first place they visited this morning. They stood inside the kitchen around their worktable. She pointed to the sample. "This is granite." She waited as they felt the sample, then pointed to other samples. "This is marble, laminate, and engineered stone. We can get samples of others if you don't like any of these. But if you do like any of these samples, I can order what you like today."

Ray came and stood cross-armed beside Edward. Joy spared a glance at them and then turned back to the clients. Had he imagined wide-eyed fear?

Richard's nose twitched as he reached over for the granite and turned to his wife. "What do you think, June? Are there any here that you prefer?"

June shrugged. "Oh, I am happy with any one of these, darling. You would know about the durability of these."

Richard chuckled. "Yes, I must say your little brain most likely wouldn't know the best material for our needs, particularly when you have a maid that cooks for us. She'll be the one we should call, shouldn't we?"

Heat flushed through Joy's body as she deepened her tone. "You know, Richard, June still has an opinion. I'd like to know what her preference is."

Edward's eyebrows hit his forehead. Good for her. Richard was an ass.

June gave a nervous laugh. "Well, if I was to state my preference, I would say the engineered stone is my favourite."

Richard frowned. "Tell us about the engineered stone. Would you recommend it?"

Joy nodded, returning to her professional self as her shoulders inched down. "Engineered stone shares many of its attributes with natural stone. It's manufactured primarily from quartz, one of the hardest minerals available. I would recommend it." She turned to Edward. "What do you think?"

Edward moved beside Joy, grateful to be at her side to contend with Richard. "This type of material has a superior durability. It is resistant to scratches, chips, cracking, and heat. I must say that engineered stone is one of the most popular choices for kitchen counters. You can select from a range of colours. It has low-level maintenance and is easy to clean. This would be my preference too."

Richard nodded. "It has been decided then. The engineered stone it is."

June touched her husband on the shoulder, her bangles shifting across her wrist. "I am happy, Richard." She pressed her lips together. "Order these please, Joy."

"Of course," Joy said. "But before you leave, I wanted your opinion about the Rhino sofa. Edward would have sent you the photo."

Richard scoffed. "We will discuss that later."

Joy swallowed. "I have placed it on hold and only wanted to know if you would like us to order it. They can only hold it for a short period of time."

Richard shook his head. "We need to leave. We will discuss it later."

Edward wanted to throttle the man.

"When exactly will you have time?" Joy pushed.

Richard leaned in closer to Joy. "Are you deaf or stupid? When I said we will discuss it later, that's exactly what I meant. I am extremely busy so we will get to it when we get to it." He glared even harder. "Goodbye for now."

Before Edward could say or do anything, Richard pulled June by the arm and stormed out of the house, slamming the front door behind them.

Joy cringed and muttered, "Okay. I guess we will wait." She walked to the living room, giving Ray the widest berth. She reached for her laptop, sat on a chair and began clicking away, likely adjusting the design model of the kitchen to add the countertop choices. Ray got to her before Edward, squeezing her shoulder. She cringed away from the touch. Joy was oddly standoffish. Richard must have put her on edge, Edward guessed.

"Are you all right, Joy?" said Ray.

"Of course. All good."

He shifted his feet and looked over his shoulder at Edward. "Richard is a force, isn't he? He has strong opinions, so don't take it personally. I'm sure he didn't mean to be that harsh."

She chuckled. "I said I'm fine, Ray. He is who he is."

Ray stepped closer to her, but she shifted back her chair. "Listen, I don't want things to be awkward between us. Is it?"

Joy lied. "All good. I'm fine so you can go back to it."

"Okay."

Ray blew past Edward. He considered checking on Joy, but Edward decided against it to give her space. Focusing on work was the best option to move past Richard's unprofessionalism.

Edward bent down and checked the positioning and safety of the electrical switches and plugs, making a note for the electrician about the extra switches Ray had mentioned that Richard wanted earlier that morning. He went to check in the master bedroom.

The important thing was that Joy was consoled. Why did it matter if his brother got to her first? She clearly wasn't interested in his brother. He was sure it would all work out and Ray would eventually get over it.

His phone buzzed, and he slipped his hand into his back pocket. The display showed Richard's number. "Hello, Richard. Is everything all right?"

"I wanted to ask whether Ray mentioned the extra switches I'd like in the master bedroom. I will pay for the amendment to your plan."

"Yes, we are making provisions and getting it done."

"Good. See that you do."

Edward ended the call, an uneasiness settling into his stomach. There was something off about Richard but he couldn't pinpoint it. His eyes and demeanour were cold, and in spite of being friendly at times, it appeared to be inauthentic. He obviously liked to control everyone around him, and no doubt his wife was content to spend his money while he overpowered her. She must have allowed it to happen because he brought in the money.

Joy had taken control over Richard in the conversation, and it must have triggered his own need to lash out at her. At least they would be rid of him once they completed this project.

After checking all the switches in each room, Edward liaised with Ray on the measurements of the countertops, who grumbled answers from a closet as he hung an organisation system. He couldn't ignore his rumbling stomach any longer, and found Joy where he'd left her, bent over her laptop. "Sorry to interrupt, but I was wondering if you would like to step out for lunch. I need my fuel to keep working today."

Joy looked up at him, not replying instantly. "Sure." Her eyes darted around her, searching. Richard was gone. What was she looking for?

Lunch would be a good opportunity to ensure for himself that she was all right after her encounter with Richard.

The noon crowd in the cafe basked in the bright sunlight streaming through the bare bay windows, loud voices coming from the table behind theirs. Joy sat across from him on a comfortable padded chair. A stocky waitress dropped menus in front of them, her feet stomping on the hybrid flooring underneath her.

Edward scanned the menu, quickly deciding on his meal. Joy ran her finger over hers, taking her time. Five minutes later, the waitress returned. "Can I get you anything to drink while you decide?"

Joy cleared her throat and said, "I think we've decided." Edward nodded. "I'll have the chicken burger and a glass of your Lambrusco."

Edward put aside the menu. "The char-grilled octopus salad and a Blonde Beer, thank you."

After the waitress had smiled and walked away, they sat in silence for a minute. Joy's face reddened and he wondered what she was thinking. "Are you all right after the way Richard spoke to you? It was harsh."

Joy nodded. "I'm fine. All forgotten." Joy angled her body towards him and pushed her hair away from her face. "Let's talk about other things. I'm curious, Edward; what drew you to architecture?"

"I always had a fascination with buildings when I was a young boy." He paused, remembering. "My father once took me to his work when our nanny got sick. My mother was working too. He visited a client at his home. This man had three-dimensional models of department stores, homes, and a supermarket sitting on a table in his dining room. I studied those models while they were talking about money. My father was a stockbroker. The man noticed my fascination and handed me a building kit to take home. He'd bought them as gifts for his sons and had a few spare kits."

"I take it you built something with that kit?"

"I did, and it was the best time when my father wasn't a ..." He averted his eyes. "Never mind."

Thankfully, Joy didn't press into his personal matters. "Well, good thing you stuck to it as you do have the talent."

Edward couldn't believe it. A compliment. From Joy. "Thank you."

The waitress returned to set down their food and drinks. "Can I get you anything else?" They both shook their heads and she scurried over to the next table.

Edward forked his salad and chewed a piece of octopus. "Now that you've asked me about my career, I'd like to ask you the same thing." He put down his fork. "When did you know you wanted to become an interior designer?"

Joy let the silence between them stretch a bit too long and Edward feared he had overstepped. "I guess that's fair," she finally said. "I was always the type who needed to keep busy, so if I was waiting somewhere in a queue, I would always make sure I had a handy notebook with me. I liked to doodle. I'd draw random things in school, in any waiting area, and in the lounge if I was watching a boring show. Something tragic happened in our family and my parents neglected the house for years. I needed to bring the light into our house again, so I made changes in our own home and realised how much I loved doing it. I decided to study interior design and completed my degree. I've worked with Lian for the past two years. It was the best decision I ever made."

Edward smiled. "Wise decision. I know we clashed at first, but I hope we can keep working well together. Even Ray has surprised me with his work. He usually struggles to follow rules and regulations."

Joy sipped her wine. "You and Ray seem to be close."

Edward hesitated, taken aback by her observation. "Ray and I have always been close but have had our fair share of challenges. We helped each other. But he left home when he was seventeen and I was still a child. It was a challenging time."

"I am sorry to hear that. At least you get to see him often now." Edward nodded and Joy continued, "I am close to my brother, Jesse, too. It's a special relationship."

Edward knit his brows, chewing another piece of seafood. "Are you okay? You seem wistful all of a sudden."

Joy nodded and focused on her meal. "I'm good."

Edward pressed his lips together. "I get the impression that there is more to your story with Ray. Is there?"

Sitting taller, she stared him down. "As I told you earlier, I wanted to keep our working relationship professional. Nothing else to it."

"Okay. He'll get over it. But know that Ray has a tendency to draw women towards him like a magnet."

Joy sighed with relief. "You and Ray are complete opposites. No doubt you would have fought a lot in your younger days. Did you?"

She was incredibly observant. Edward chuckled, recalling a time that Ray had consoled him after his parents failed to show up at his school play. He had gone in their place instead. "He was there for me when my parents weren't, and I have a lot to thank him for. Ray was there for me at school events and birthdays with my parents' no-shows. But, yes, we fought sometimes. He is a force to be reckoned with."

She nodded. "It is hard when parents disappoint their children but having an older sibling helps. It must have been hard for you when Ray left."

Edward shifted in his seat. "It was hard but he had his reasons, and I managed. I had a nurturing nanny who was more like a mother to me than my own mother was. She helped me cope."

Joy's smile warmed his heart. "It sounds like you both have each other's back."

"We do, and I would not have it any other way."

Later that evening, Edward rested his back against the padded seat in the pub with Ray and his friend and boss, George, who guzzled his beer.

"Slow down," Edward chided.

George wiped his mouth with the back of his hand. He was a magnet to women with his piercing dark eyes, short jet-black hair with shaved sides, and a robust build to match. "Hey, we're off the clock now, mate. Let me enjoy my drink."

Ray laughed. "You two are always bantering." He checked his watch then scrolled through his phone.

What was going on with Ray? His brother furrowed his brows and kept looking over his shoulder. "Do you have an appointment?"

Ray shook his head. "Nah, just have to get home soon. A friend's coming over so I can't stay out too late. How about you? Don't you have an appointment with pretty girl? You've been in another world ever since you had lunch with her." Ray sneered.

George frowned. "What pretty girl?"

Edward glared. "Can you not call Joy that? It's patronising. She has a name. Use it. She's our colleague and you need to treat her with respect." Ray was clearly not in his right mind.

Ray put up a hand. "Sorry, but she is pretty." He drained his whisky glass.

"Am I missing something here?" said George. "Do both of you have a crush on Joy?"

Ray liked Joy, but she had turned him down. She was as free as a bird and could do whatever she liked. Edward definitely did not have a crush on Joy. "That's crazy, George. I don't have a crush on anyone."

"Hmm," said George. "I doubt that. I can sense a lighter energy in you since you started this job. You're less uptight than usual. Admit you've got feelings for her, Eddie boy. You'll feel better." He faced Ray. "Sorry she turned you down, man, but you've got plenty of fish in the sea."

Ray's face paled as he gripped the edge of the table, focusing past Edward. "Damn right, man. She's not really my type, George. I mainly asked her out as a friend."

Edward shook his head. "I barely know her."

His brother's phone buzzed. Quickly, he answered the call, his eyes becoming steely as he held the phone to his ear. The person at the other end was loud, but the pub was louder so all Edward picked out was that they were angry. With a nod, he ended the call.

"Is everything all right?" asked Edward.

Ray nodded. "Sure. I have to go. Sorry, guys." Quickly, he got up, placed a fifty-dollar bill on the table and rushed out.

Edward stared at George. "What is happening with Ray?"

"Beats me, but I do know he's been acting strangely ever since this new project started. What do you think's going on, man?"

Edward ignored the ache in his chest and shrugged. "Strange, in what way?"

"I had a complaint from one of the new architects on another one of his jobs. He's been making mistakes, forgetting his tools and getting these strange calls in the middle of his work. He's also been carrying a flask and drinking on the job again. The worker called him on it and Ray said it wouldn't happen again."

"Did you talk to Ray about it?"

George beckoned the waiter. "Another beer, thanks." He shook his head as the server left. "Nah, I thought you might want to talk to him. You have a knack for listening to people but I'm better with my hands than communication. I'll give him the benefit of the doubt for now."

"Fine. I will talk to him. Do not let him lose his job until we sort this out, George. I don't want him to lose his contractor work with you." Ray had a tendency to go through these bouts of mood changes but he never opened up about them. Edward assumed it had to do with Mary's death, even though it had been years ago. The heavy alcohol consumption didn't help matters. Grieving or not, Edward was getting tired of cleaning up Ray's messes.

Chapter Eleven

INTENSE CONNECTION

J oy stood by the window and held the measuring tape, turning to Edward in the living room. "Would you mind holding the other end? I need to order those drapes for this window."

Edward nodded. "Of course." He stood at the other end of the window and held on to the tape.

Radio music played in the background and she tapped her feet in rhythm to the music. How long had it been since she'd had fun and let loose? After this project she needed to go dancing, or on a vacation. Maybe both.

Joy jotted down the measurement and bent low to reach the samples of white lace curtains she'd placed on the floor. When she rose, Edward's eyes briefly skimmed her bare legs underneath her skirt but looked past her quickly. Was he attracted to her or was it only her imagination? She had enough going on with Ray and Thomas. She didn't need to add another man to the mix.

Joy kept on task as she thumbed through her samples. "The voile sheer or the voile wave curtains are an option. Both are modern and chic in style."

Edward leaned close. The scent of eucalyptus and his proximity made her heart flutter. He was too close and he smelled so good. "They do look modern. If you present both of them, they can make the choice. They might have other options in mind."

"They should be coming in later today. I'll ask them." She scanned through her phone for more window furnishings but couldn't find any other options. The music stopped, interrupted by a news story:

"Breaking News. This morning, Tuesday the fifteenth of March, the body of a woman discovered at Braybrook Park several days ago under suspicious circumstances has led to the police appealing to the public for any witnesses. The police are enquiring whether anyone might have seen a suspicious person around the area. The local community is banding together to try and find whoever is responsible through their neighbourhood watch programs. Please come forward if you have any information."

Joy went cold and she stared into the distance, dropping her measuring tape. "Christ," she said to herself.

"What's wrong?" asked Edward.

A knock startled her out of her shock. Edward answered the door. "Come in, Thomas." He gave him a firm handshake. "Joy's here. I will be back in a moment." He waved Thomas in her direction and disappeared into the kitchen.

"Hi, Thomas," Joy said as she straightened.

"Hi, Joy. I am so happy to see you again. Sorry, I haven't called. Richard's been keeping me busy." He put down his suitcase and wrapped his arms around her, leaning forward and kissing her. She reciprocated and held the back of his head, savouring his warm mouth and the gentle glide of his tongue. As she pulled away, she thought she heard a sound, but realised no-one was around.

Thomas let her go and picked up his briefcase. "Richard and June couldn't come today and wanted me to meet with Lian to sort out a revised version of the contract. Is Lian available? I couldn't get to her office as I had business in this area, so she agreed to meet me at the house."

"Lian mentioned you'd be coming but she's not here yet."

Thomas grinned and his eyes crinkled with mirth." Thanks. How about us going out tonight? Are you free?"

Joy nodded. "Sure. What did you have in mind?"

"Hmm. How about dinner at the Docklands? You deserve the best, the fanciest. Does that sound good?"

"Great. Text me the details."

"Will do. Now, is it okay if I wait and watch you and Edward do your magic?"

She choked a little. Magic? Edward and her? "Of ... of course. Lian shouldn't be too long, but for now, come with me. I think Edward needs help in the kitchen."

Joy located Edward. He was holding a leveller and set it against the counter as he turned to her.

"Do you need any help?" She was met with silence. He must not have heard her.

Thomas leaned forward, getting Edward's attention. "I can help you there if you wish."

Edward stared at Thomas curiously. "Do you have building experience? I could use a hand here in the kitchen. Ray is running late."

Thomas chuckled. "I'm afraid my capabilities are limited to finance and law, though I dabble in woodworking, but I am happy to help wherever I can." His eyes roamed. "The place is looking good, quite contemporary yet cosy. They'll be impressed with your progress."

Thomas was very different to the way she remembered him, so mature and professional, so far from the awkward but kind boy he had been. He had that billionaire vibe and yet he was humble enough to get his hands dirty helping Edward. He really was a catch. She'd had a nice time at breakfast on Saturday and was looking forward to their dinner tonight. So why didn't she feel more connected to him? He was a great kisser but there was just something missing. "Can I get you a coffee? We have some left in the thermos."

Thomas shook his head. "No thanks." He beamed again. "I am happy to tour the house while you work. I don't mean to take you away from it."

Edward nodded. "I can show you around the rooms and give you an idea of what we are planning. Joy can show you the design for the drapes in the living room later."

"Excellent," Thomas said.

As they moved towards the bedrooms, Joy made her way to the table inside the kitchen and opened her laptop. She clicked on her design and made changes to the living space by adding the sofa they had ordered, the window furnishings and the TV space. The couple had already chosen most of the furniture, and she had a few rugs in mind that would match the colour tone of the living room.

Closing the laptop, she made a phone call to request samples of the different rug choices before showing them to the client.

The door opened and Ray and Lian walked into the kitchen.

"Hi Joy. Is Thomas here?"

She pointed towards the bedroom. "Edward's giving him a tour." Lian rushed to the bedroom while Ray's gaze raked over Joy from head to toe. An uneasiness settled in her spine, but she ignored it and reached for the thermos, pouring the hot liquid into a cup. Ray came up behind her, his breath fanning the back of her neck. Quickly, she moved away but he stepped closer towards her again.

"I'll need to finish my work on these cabinets," said Ray. "What are you working on?"

She took a step closer to the living room. "I'm just going to, ah, finish measuring all the windows in the living room. I'll talk to you later."

Ray put up a hand. "Wait, Joy. It doesn't have to be awkward between us. I apologise for ..."

Edward walked back into the kitchen. "What are you apologising for?" She cringed at the way Ray's eyes drank her in. It was as if his eyes were attempting to see beneath her clothes. She had no ounce of attraction towards Ray. Sure, he was a good-looking guy, but she didn't feel anything. She wished he would get the hint and stop making working together so difficult.

Ray picked up a plank of wood. "Nothing. I'm going to finish these cabinets. I could use your help, man."

Edward pressed his lips together. "Why were you late?"

"I had errands to run, Eddie. Don't bust my chops, man. I'm here now, so let's get started." His expression turned from a glare to a fake smile at Joy.

Edward gazed in Joy's direction as she stood cross-armed, not liking the tension she was creating between the brothers. It was unnerving. "If you need help, let me know."

"I'll be fine. I can do the rest on my own. No sweat." She would eventually need to tell Ray how his flirtatious behaviour was making her nervous. He needed to stop. An alarm on her phone went off. She had to meet with Ariana.

As she hurried down the hall, she found the men in the master bedroom. "I have another engagement I need to get to."

Edward frowned.

Thomas stepped to her and kissed her on the forehead. "Okay, I have to run. I'll see you tonight."

Beaming up at him, she nodded. When Thomas stepped back, the look on Ray's face sent a chill down her spine. He muttered something to Edward and pushed past her. Thomas's eyes darkened. "Hey!" he called after Ray, rubbing her shoulder and holding her to his chest.

"It's okay, Thomas," Joy said.

Thomas whirled around to Edward. "Get your employee and brother in line."

Holding up his hands, Edward nodded and excused himself as he moved around them, going after Ray.

"I really have to go or I'm going to be late." Joy patted his hand. "I'm okay. Ray's probably just distracted or having a bad day. Don't be hard on Edward. It's not his fault."

"Alright." He let her go and she rushed out of the house, grabbing her bag on the way.

Thirty-five minutes later, Joy sat inside the cafe, waiting for Ariana.

Joy checked her phone. Ariana was fifteen minutes late. She couldn't blame Kathleen's sister when she was likely still grieving, but Joy had a packed day and hoped Ariana would show. She and Lian were worried. Were the marks new? Old? Was she caught up in drugs like Kathleen had been and needing help? Heart racing, Joy tapped her foot under the table as she scanned the cafe.

Another ten minutes passed by, and Joy was about to call Ariana when she finally appeared, wearing a shy smile.

"Ariana. Great to see you again."

"Hi, Joy." She twirled her blonde strands, with droopy eyes.

Joy rose and wrapped her arms around her. "Again, I am so sorry for your loss." Ariana gave her a reassuring smile. "I tried calling once or twice but missed you."

Ariana sat opposite, her hands fidgeting. "I have been busy. Sorry about that." She took a breath. "How are you?"

"Good. Now, what would you like to drink?"

The woman shrugged. "I would like a flat white."

Joy put up her hand, signalling the waiter. The middle-aged server approached and kept his hands behind his back. "What can I get you?"

"Can we get a flat white and a macchiato, please?"

"Certainly." He walked off with a nod.

Joy didn't know where to begin. "Thanks for coming, Ariana." She lifted her shoulders. "How are you doing?"

Ariana played with the collar of her shirt, staring vacantly as if in her own world. "Fine."

"And your family?"

She shrugged again. "Not well. I don't see them much."

Joy took a breath, knowing that she had to rip the bandage off. "I know we've only met a few times and don't know each other well, but is there anything you need? Anything I can do to help?"

She shook her head and smiled without it reaching her eyes. "No, thank you. I am fine. It is a process, but I do miss Kathleen." Her eyes misted.

"I know this must be hard for you." Joy toyed with the napkin on the table, running it between her fingers. "I wondered what happened to her, Ariana. Why did she go missing for two weeks? Did Kathleen ever talk about being in trouble?"

Ariana focused on her for a minute. "No, she didn't say anything."

Joy wrinkled her brow. They were interrupted by the waiter who set down their mugs. When he left, Joy pressed on. "Did you ever wonder why she went missing or where she was?"

Ariana peered into the distance, and her face flushed. "Why are you asking me this, Joy? She's gone."

Joy's throat stung, hating the pain she was putting Ariana through. But she had to know what went wrong with Kathleen. Maybe it was happening to Ariana too, and maybe Ariana would share more. She would never forgive herself if she didn't try. "I'm sorry. I know this is hard." Ariana looked down into her mug and took a sip. "Do you know if Kathleen had ever taken drugs before?"

Ariana hesitated. "I don't know. I didn't see her much before she ..."

After a moment of silence, Joy pressed on. "I assume you spoke to the police?"

"Yes. They mentioned the drugs in her system, and like you said, they believe it was an accident. That's all I know."

"Are you sure there's nothing I can do to help?"

Ariana sighed and shifted in her seat. "I'm fine, Joy. I know you worked with her. It must be ... be ... hard for Lian."

Joy nodded. "It is hard, but we are dealing with it." She wanted to ask about those marks on her skin, but she had already pushed Ariana far enough for now. "Are you sure everything is all right with you? Are your family and others treating you well?"

Ariana sipped her drink with her hands shaking. "Good. How is work?"

Joy swallowed. "Fine. Always busy." She picked up her cup, letting the warmth of the liquid moisten her dry throat. "Listen, I noticed your skin ..."

"Kathleen made her own choices." Ariana's lips pressed hard together and her eye twitched. She scratched at her wrist and peered into her drink. She drank it down then checked her phone. "It's getting late. I really need to get back to work."

Joy nodded and tried again. If she was in trouble, she had to help. "Before you go, can you tell me about those marks on your arm? I only want to help. How did you get them?"

Ariana hesitated and looked past her. "It's a chronic skin condition, psoriasis, and the skin gets itchy so I scratch. Nothing to cure it."

"The bruises?"

"I fell at work when I was tired one evening. Clumsy. I have to go now."

Joy wasn't sure she was telling the truth.

"This is on me." Joy waved her off when she tried to pay. "But, please, if you ever need anything, someone to talk to, or feel troubled in any way, give me a call. I would like you to feel you can talk to me."

"Thank you." Ariana raced out of the cafe.

As Joy drank down the remaining hot liquid, she worried about Ariana. "Well, that went nowhere." She checked the time. Paying and rushing out the door, she was soon back at the house for a meeting with a supplier.

The day raced by as Joy kept busy and managed to avoid Ray. Edward was never available to help so she made decisions without him. If he had a problem with it, he could deal with her later. Finally, at the end of the day, Joy had just enough time to get ready before meeting the car Thomas sent for her. He had spelled out everything in a text late afternoon.

Joy sat opposite him in the dimly lit restaurant, eating a tasty Chicken Caesar salad. Her companion dived into a sirloin steak with pepper sauce, savouring every bite as if it was his last.

Smells of herbs, spices, and minty sauce permeated the air.

Joy thought Thomas looked rather handsome in a white cotton shirt, a suit jacket, and black, pleated pants. She had opted for more colour and current trends. Her vibrant green blouse and airy white pants contrasted with his dark attire.

The restaurant filled up quickly with its haphazard setting of candlelit tables, and the muffled voices of patrons who came as couples or in large groups.

"I cannot believe we found our way to each other again, Joy. Who would have thought after all these years we would meet yet again."

She tilted her head. "It is a small world." She beamed. "How's your mother doing?"

He shrugged. "She's enjoying life, travelling to every part of the world. I must say I envy her, but who has the time to travel when my work keeps me plenty busy?"

Sipping her lemon, lime, and bitters, she relished the cold sweetness for her parched throat. "I would love to travel one day but my work keeps me busy too. It's one of my true passions, as the law is for you."

"Oh, yes, the law. It is hard to keep up with sometimes, which is why I often need to take up one course after another to follow the changes. But it keeps me on my toes." He wiped his mouth with a napkin. "How is your brother Jesse doing? I must visit him one day soon."

Joy grinned. "He'd like that." She gripped her glass and took a quick sip. "He's happily in love with his girlfriend, Gabriella, who is also a friend of mine, and he's a physiotherapist."

He leaned forward. "Impressive. Healing the sick. An occupation that helps out the community. Good for him."

Ta finished the rest of their meals and drinks when Joy rubbed the back of her neck, feeling an ache. "You know I love my work, but it ends up doing my body damage sometimes. I'll need to get a massage."

He stared her down, focusing on her lips. "I've been known to be an amazing, amateur masseuse," he teased.

She laughed off his suggestion.

"How about we finish off the night with dessert and coffee?"

She nodded. "Sure. Sounds great.

Joy undid her seatbelt in Thomas's car when he stopped to drop her off. "Thanks for the great night, Thomas. I had a nice time."

He nodded. "I did too. But don't go just yet."

She angled her head. "Why not?"

He leaned forward, held her chin up and proceeded to kiss her with such tenderness as if she'd break like a porcelain doll. His tongue delved in deep and she reciprocated. No heat or fire bloomed in her belly despite the expert and gentle way he kissed her.

"Oh, Joy," he said between kisses. "I love the way you taste."

Pulling away, she said, "I had better go. It is late, but thanks for the night."

"Of course, Joy. I'd like to see you again. Can I?"

"I'll call you."

Chapter Twelve

IN DENIAL

Edward gazed at his computer screen, clicking on changes to his design on AutoCAD. Three other architects sat around him, speaking on the phone, hunched over computer screens and scrutinising blueprints at their desks. He wrinkled his brow and ran a hand through his hair. A dry mouth drove him to pick up his forgotten glass of water. His head hurt as he focused back on his design while the loud voices between his manager, George, and a co-worker unnerved him.

The image of Joy kissing Thomas at the house yesterday bothered him, making his throat tight and his stomach hard. It was none of his business.

Ray's behaviour to her was inexcusable and he made sure Ray knew it. Thomas's commanding attitude set Edward's teeth on edge, but he had been right. Pushing past Joy like that could have hurt her. What was his brother thinking?

"Edward, come into my office," barked George.

He rose from his ergonomic chair after clicking out of his design model and entered the partially open door. The look on his manager's face made him swallow hard. Had he done something wrong?

Taking a seat opposite George in the small, closed office, he gazed at the cluttered desk filled with three-dimensional models, in-trays of documents stacked high, and his laptop near an old desktop computer amidst architectural books, invoices, and stationery. The window behind offered a view of city skyscrapers and vast blue horizon. "What is it, George?"

His boss stared at a pen twirling from his fingers. "It's about Ray. I gave him another contracting job the other day, and the two times he's come in to meet with Tommy, he's been drunk on the job. Another time, he was hungover. He had these heated phone calls but wouldn't share who it was. Only mentioned he's doing private jobs, but I wonder if there's more to it, though it's not my place."

Edward slouched in his chair. "I will speak to him again and make sure he doesn't drink. He enjoys his work."

George shook his head. "This is happening way too often, Eddie, and our reputation with our clients is on the line. We can't have him keep doing this to us. He's already had one warning and didn't listen to that. How many chances can I give him?"

Edward hunched over. "I understand George and I would be happy to talk to those clients, but please, he needs the work. If you take it away, he will get worse. Let me manage this situation."

George rested back against his chair, processing. "Fine. One more chance, but if he screws up again, man, he'll be out on his ear."

Edward nodded. "Noted. Thank you, George." He got up from his chair, turned, and opened the door fully. He sat at his desk, pondering how he would confront Ray again without making him defensive. Something was going on with him. He had been drinking more heavily after Joy had turned him down. Or was it more than that?

After working for another hour, he peered at his watch, closed his office door and headed out to meet with Joy to apologise for yesterday. He had to put this matter of Ray behind him.

At the restaurant at Southbank, he peered at the menu while waiting for Joy. He couldn't wait to see her. One look at her face and he should get an inkling of her emotional state, whether she opened up to him or not.

Joy wandered towards him, gripping her shoulder bag as she glanced in his direction with a fleeting smile. As she got closer, he noticed her tightly pressed lips, tired eyes, and flat demeanour. She wore a tight-fitted white blouse and a short black skirt which accentuated her toned, tanned legs. She sat opposite him. "Sorry, I'm late. I had to respond to a late call from a client."

"Perfectly fine," said Edward.

"What is this about? You said you needed to talk to me about something."

How could he explain it tactfully as a friend without intruding on her space? He had to be sensitive to this issue. "It's about yesterday. Ray shouldn't have acted that way. I wanted to see how you are."

She swallowed. "Can we order first?"

He nodded.

Joy ushered over a waiter who came quickly. He was an elderly man with a moustache and a smile. "Can I have a pineapple juice and a BLT, please?"

"Certainly, ma'am." He turned to Edward. "And you, sir?"

"I will have the calamari salad." The waiter walked off.

She glanced at her hands as she rubbed them. "Did Ray say anything?"

Edward's stomach tightened. What was going on with Ray? What might he have said that made Joy nervous? "No, just that he had a bad day and got your message loud and clear. When I pressed him on it, he ignored me, but he agreed to not push you or anyone like that again."

"Hmm."

Edward wasn't convinced she believed what she was saying. "I am sorry and take personal responsibility for his behaviour. I won't have anyone's personal life or issues ruining the project."

She avoided his eyes. "I appreciate that."

Edward leaned in. "How are you doing? Did he hurt you?"

Joy shook her head. "No. I'm fine."

"I'm glad to hear it." He swallowed. "About Ray. Is everything all right between you two?"

Joy's eyes lingered on his as if she had to make up a reply. "Of course. Why wouldn't it be?"

"No reason. But Ray can be intense at times." He turned to the waiter setting down their food. The silence was comfortable as he dug into his calamari.

"You don't need to worry, Edward. I'm a big girl and I always land on my feet."

"I have no doubt. But if you ever need to talk, I am a great listener. I do not judge. In fact, I'm a better listener than a talker."

She nodded. "Are you telling me you'd rather be the type of British man who keeps his emotions to himself? Is that how you define yourself?"

He laughed. "Such a stereotype, Ms Warrier. I could be offended by that." Her face paled. "It is a joke," he reassured. She leaned back with a sigh, and he noticed a subtle dimple on the side of her face. "We are all unique, and I have no doubt I don't speak as much as you do, but I can assure you once I get started I can talk non-stop. It depends on my mood on the day."

"What's your mood like today? Stiff upper lip or a talker?" Joy asked.

"I notice you have minimal tact, don't you?" His throat dried up. "I'm not here to talk about me. Just to apologise on behalf of Ray and make sure you're okay." Her eyes softened. "As I said, if you'd like to share anything, you can. Whatever it is."

"Thank you."

But Joy didn't elaborate. They ate the rest of their meal in silence.

After he paid, he said, "Let me know if Ray makes you uncomfortable in any way or does anything like that again.

I take the work we do seriously, Joy. I won't have anyone undermine that, not even if he's my own brother. I won't be at the house today as I'm working on another project, but you have my number and you can call or text anytime."

Joy nodded and followed him out to the carpark. Awkward seconds stretched between them and he blurted out a question, instantly regretting it. "Are you and Thomas a couple?"

She stopped walking. "I don't think that's any of your business."

Well, at least she was back to her old self, Edward thought. He coughed. "Sorry. I didn't mean to intrude. I just saw the two of you kissing yesterday—"

"That was you! Were you watching us?" Joy snapped.

Edward's face heated and he began stuttering. "I—I didn't mean—didn't want to intrude." He huffed and got a hold of himself. "I didn't want to interrupt you two when I came into the room to check if I left my pencil in there so I politely left. I would never." He strode forward to his car.

When he looked back, Joy hadn't moved. She said something he couldn't make out. "What?" he called to her.

"I said, 'I'm not really sure if we're a couple.' It's new still. It's clear you're concerned about decorum so don't worry. Thomas and my relationship will not affect the job." She stomped past him. "I have to get back to work." She slammed her car door.

Serves him right for trying to get to know her and blurting out his question. He should know to stick to things he was good at; the job.

Chapter Thirteen

ROSE TATTOO

Thursday, and Kathleen's funeral along with it had come too soon. A good crowd turned out. It was a lovely send off, but Lian and Joy decided to do something more to remember not only Kathleen but also others they had lost. Joy closed her eyes and gritted her teeth as the needle penetrated her upper left arm. Lian watched from a chair opposite. The room was dark and smoky.

The tattoo artist, with his bulky frame and arms the size of tree trunks, chuckled. "It's not as bad as it looks. You need to relax and stay still."

Lian leaned forward in her seat. "Take a few deep breaths, Joy. You can do this."

Joy nodded. "I know." She faced the artist, who hovered over her, holding the machine in his hands. "I'm ready." She could do this. Taking a deep breath, she waited, but the man sighed when Gabriella rushed inside and sat in the empty chair beside Lian.

"Sorry, I'm late," said Gabriella.

Joy waved her hand away. "It's fine, girl, but thanks for coming. I appreciate your support."

The tattoo artist angled his head. "Are you ready now, Miss? I do have other clients after you."

Joy nodded, pressing her lips together as she braced herself. "All good." With a click, the machine hummed again. She closed her eyes and winced at the initial pricking sensation of the needle, feeling like tiny, shallow stabs gliding over her skin. Breath catching, she literally couldn't breathe and clenched her teeth as the searing pain tore at her skin. *Distract yourself, girl.* Edward's face popped into her head, but she needed to think of something else.

Her back started aching as he kept drawing over her, but the discomfort would be worth it. She would be honouring Erica and Mia by writing their names inside a red rose on her arm.

"How are you doing, Joy?" asked Gabriella.

"Fine. I'm adapting to the sensation. It's not as bad as I thought it would be," she lied. The heavy scratching sensation made her short of breath as she focused on the needle.

The tattoo artist stopped for a moment. "Keep still. I am putting in one of the names inside the rose now."

"Sorry," said Joy.

"Hang in there," said Lian. "You are doing well so far." Joy smiled, grateful to have her friends here. Her chest tightened when the artist shaded in the rose. Clenching her teeth, she closed her eyes, the deep vibrations causing her to lose her breath again. When would this be over? She had thought that she had a high pain threshold, but boy was she wrong.

An hour later, the man put down the tattoo gun. "All done. It looks good if I do say so myself." He walked over to a small table and picked up a mirror. He approached Joy and reflected the tattoo in it so she could see.

Joy nodded. "I love it. Amazing detail in the rose and I like the fancy font for the names. Thank you."

"A pleasure." He instructed her on self-care.

"Your turn, Lian," said Joy.

Two hours later, Joy munched on a piece of salmon. "It was painful enough." She took in the views outside the cafe in Brooklyn, which was close to the Stubble's project, as people walked by. The pink-striped umbrella over her table swayed in the light breeze.

Lian drew a hand through her hair. "Not so much for me. I love mine. It's given me peace, that's for sure."

Gabriella munched on a lettuce leaf. "Oh, Lian. Tell me about your tattoo and what it means. It is fascinating."

"The Chinese character symbolises to commemorate or remember, and then a stylised K for Kathleen." Lian changed the subject. "What do you do for work, Gabriella?"

"That's beautiful. Sorry I didn't get one myself." Gabriella's eyes peered into the distance. "I don't know if Joy mentioned it, but I work with drug and alcohol-affected clients and have almost completed my social work degree. I plan to eventually work with youthful clients impacted by broken homes and neglectful parents. It is so widespread these days."

"I hear you, Gabriella, and couldn't agree with you more. I can see you doing that. You seem nurturing and calm."

Gabriella frowned. "Me. Calming? Jesse would disagree with you there."

Lian laughed. "Really?" Gabriella nodded. "How is Jesse doing?"

Gabriella's eyes lit up. "He is amazing, and every day I love him more and more. My true soulmate. Only the other day, he surprised me in the bedroom when ..." She blushed. "Never mind."

Joy knit her brows. "Oh, please. I don't need to hear about your antics with my brother." Secretly, she wished for a love like that; unconditional, romantic, and real. She just wasn't feeling it with Thomas and she worried about letting him down.

"How is work, Joy?" Gabriella asked.

She shrugged. "You know I love my work, but I never have a say about the clients. You need to deal with a diversity of characters, that's for sure."

"What do you mean?" asked Gabriella.

"Oh, the current client is controlling, and puts his wife down at every chance he gets. He's intimidating, to say the least."

Lian nodded. "I second that. He is like a cold fish, but we have to respect what he wants and not question it, Joy. I know you'll be professional about it, as the customer is always right." She sipped her sparkling wine.

"I know. But something about the guy rubs me the wrong way. It's something I can't understand. He is creepy and sleazy and he watches me in a strange way."

"He might be that way with everyone," said Gabriella.

Joy nodded. "You might be right." Taking a sip of her lemon, lime, and bitters, a familiar pair stopped at their table.

"This is a surprise," said Edward. He stood beside Ray, who stared past her.

Joy felt her face warm. "Hello. Edward, Ray. This is Gabriella, my friend."

Gabriella locked eyes on both men. "Good to meet you, Edward. Ray." She turned to Joy with a raised brow.

Edward's phone buzzed. He picked it up, stared at the display and turned to Joy. "It's Richard. Excuse me a minute."

Ray shifted from foot to foot. "I have to get back to the site. Just stopped in for coffee." He made a hasty exit.

The women exchanged glances and finished their meals in silence.

Edward returned ten minutes later. "I'm sorry to interrupt, but could I borrow you Joy? Just need to go over some things about Richard's changes."

Joy froze.

Lian blinked and said, "Of course you can borrow her. Let me know if there is anything I can do for the client."

Swallowing a mouthful of coffee, Joy reluctantly followed Edward out of earshot.

"I apologise for taking you away from your friends, but I needed to talk to you."

His fingers brushed her back as he steered her to a quiet spot. Her cheeks felt warm and she resisted the urge to lean back into his touch. Thomas's kiss, her grief, they were leaving her confused. "No worries. What did Richard want?"

"Richard wanted to know about the delivery date of the kitchen counters. I must have told him three times. He calls me every other day to complain or question things. He is micro-managing our work and I wish I could tell him exactly how I feel. He is a hard taskmaster. He was pushing about some of the finishing touches that I'm not sure if you've even started on based on where we all are. Something about no baubles and frilly things with no purpose."

Joy nodded. "I appreciate the heads-up." She angled her head. "It's his personality. Strong-willed and stubborn." Someone brushed past her and she flinched.

"Are you okay?"

Joy covered her arm gingerly. "I just got a tattoo, and my arm's a bit tender. Remind me not to do that again." Joy shifted and pulled up the short sleeve of her t-shirt and the clear bandage covering it. "It's not quite defined yet, but it will be."

"I admire your courage. I could never succumb to such pain." Edward shivered.

Joy chuckled. "Oh, it's not so bad. Surely, you've taken worse risks in your life?"

"Life is a risk in general, Joy." Sullen and stern Edward returned. For a second there, he seemed almost relaxed, thought Joy.

She shook her head. "True."

"I like your tattoo. Can I ask about those words?"

She nodded. "Sure. They're actually names. Erica was my friend and Mia was my sister."

He angled his head. "Was?"

"They both died, and I wanted to honour them. Lian got one for Kathleen."

"Right. Lian mentioned you were at a funeral today for a coworker. I am sorry for bringing it up." He ran a hand over his face.

"It is what it is. Their deaths aren't quite so recent as Kathleen's. Erica died just over a year ago and Mia died when I was ten years old."

Edward's hand twitched and he leaned in closer. "You've had to deal with a multitude of grief, Joy. Were you close with your colleague?"

She nodded. "We were acquaintances, but Kathleen was best friends with Lian. It hit her hard. She died of a drug overdose. We never even knew she was in that kind of trouble."

"Drug abuse is a disease and very hard to shift. People can be experts at hiding secrets."

There was something in the way he said that, like he knew what it was like. "Have you lost anyone close to you?"

Edward remembered the nanny who had treated him like her own son. "I had a nanny growing up. She died of cancer when I was twelve but my parents refused to let me attend her funeral. It pained me to know that I could not honour her and give my condolences to her family."

"That's rough, Edward, and I am sorry. Loss is the worst guarantee in life. It sucks."

His hands clenched. "I better let you return to the others." He turned and took a few steps then stopped and looked back. "If you need anything, you can call anytime. As I mentioned, I'm a great listener," he said softly and left.

Joy stood stunned. Who knew that Edward had a soft side?

That evening, Joy lazed back against the couch, attempting to read a romance novel, but instead found herself rereading the same sentence three times. Edward's face was firmly planted in her mind, interrupting her focus as she replayed their earlier conversation. She pondered the deep pools of despair in his eyes when he spoke about his nanny, akin to the eyes of a famous Melancholy painting by Edvard Munch. The way his eyes stared past her as he recounted how he hadn't been able to attend her funeral. It sounded like he'd been closer to his nanny than his own parents. She could relate.

It was that distance between her and her parents after her sister died. As if they had stopped living, forgetting they had two other living children to care for. Her father drowned himself in long hours at work and her mother had become an empty shell, locked in her bedroom. Jesse had been more of a parent to her.

Joy abandoned the book and scrolled through her phone to check social media and the news until a headline drew her attention: *Murdered Woman at Cherry Lake*. The police were still investigating, appealing to witnesses. They had no leads. Cherry Lake? She had played there as a child. Joy shivered. Having these murders so close to home struck a nerve.

The doorbell stirred her to action and when she swung open the front door, she smiled at her friends, Octavia and Claudia.

"Hey, lovelies. What brings you two by?" She ushered them inside after they leaned forward and kissed her on the cheek. Their faces were sombre, not like their usual selves.

Claudia sat at one end of the couch and crossed her legs, her hands fidgeting. She was petite, with grey eyes, and strawberry blonde hair tied in a high bun. "We apologise for not catching up sooner but work for both of us has been crazy. We meant to visit you earlier and wanted to see how you are doing. We know you've been struggling with your colleague's death. I spoke to Bella this morning at work and she said the funeral was today."

Joy knit her brows, her hands clenching. "I'm fine. I still wonder how she could have taken drugs. Lian and I had no clue. It's still a mystery."

Octavia's long hair, brown with auburn highlights, cascaded neatly down her shoulders. A mole on her right upper lip accentuated her natural beauty. She was a forensic psychologist and worked with the police. "It had been ruled an accident, Joy. Don't go ruminating about Kathleen when you need to take care of yourself. Focus on processing it."

Joy rubbed her palms, ignoring the searing ache in her back from sitting at a funny angle too long. "Hmm. I still wonder about that, Octavia. Kathleen might've been mixed up with the wrong people. I wish I knew what went wrong. She seemed distant and preoccupied at work, but when Lian and I asked her about it, she said she'd been having family issues. Nothing more than that."

Claudia nodded. "Listen, whatever the poor girl was going through, she might have been coping with her issues through drugs. Plain and simple."

"I don't know, Claudia. Maybe you're right."

Octavia's warm, green eyes fixed on her. "She is right. Your first and foremost priority is yourself." She leaned forward and touched her hand. "Is there anything you need? Something we can do for you?"

This talk about death made Joy queasy. She rose. "How about a drink?"

Claudia's eyes lit up. "I won't say no to a dry red if you have it."

"I'll have a glass of water," said Octavia.

She returned with two glasses, then sat back with her legs underneath her, discussing safe topics such as work and family until Joy could no longer wait to ask. "Octavia, I saw the news about the young woman found at Cherry Lake. Also, those two others in the local area before that. Are you guys investigating these?" It was likely Kathleen's death caused her to see death everywhere, and it made her feel unsafe. If her friends were working on them, Joy could sleep more soundly.

Octavia hesitated and stared at the ground. "We might be, but I can't give you details, Joy. You know that."

Joy bit her bottom lip. "Do the police think it's a serial killer?"

Octavia sighed, turning to Claudia, who put out her hands as if uncertain. "Possibly."

Claudia looked at Octavia. "Oh, for heaven's sake. Tell her the truth, woman. She can handle it."

Octavia leaned forward. "I don't want to say anything as nothing is certain at this point and it is an active investigation, but the police and I are looking into the backgrounds of a few people. Some, you may be acquainted with but I can't say more at this stage. Please keep it to yourself."

Joy swallowed. Someone she knew could be involved with the murders somehow? Her mind worked over what she knew of the murders.

Octavia reached for her hand and patted it. "We're here for you, Joy. Whatever it is you need, do not hesitate to ask."

Claudia stared at her strangely. "Something's on your mind, isn't it? Spill."

Joy was seeing connections where there wasn't. She voiced her observations so Claudia and Octavia could put her in her place. "It's creepy how the last woman killed was found near a place I would visit with my family growing up."

Octavia touched her on the shoulder. "That was a good memory with your family. Don't let it be tarnished by this case or jump to conclusions. You're safe. We will find the perpetrator."

Despite her friend's support, Joy's gut twisted. She was being ridiculous. The death might have been close to home, but it didn't need to mean anything.

Chapter Fourteen

CHARMED

H e silently scoffed, subtly shaking his head as he stared at the abstract painting. The woman beside him gazed at the same painting. Her eyes sparkled in the bright lights of the room showcasing a range of local art he loved. Her legs seemed to go on forever underneath her short skimpy black dress, her breasts hanging out of the low cut top of her dress. He was getting a hard-on, imagining what it would feel like to pull those blonde strands right out of her scalp.

He smirked at at the thought of her slightly boisterous nature She would be a challenge. He loved challenges.

She threaded her hands through her short, blonde hair. The smell of her strong perfume enticed him, and he turned towards her. "Don't you love the angular lines and mix-up of colours?"

Flicking a hair strand out of her eye and thrusting out her chest, he realised she would be easy to manipulate. Her eyes lit up. "I do. It reminds me of a summer rain."

"Yes, totally agree." He had done his research on her. "There's almost a shadow in there but ..."

She shifted closer. "But what?"

He took a breath, throwing in one of his popular lines. "It reminds me of the time I took my nephew out for a walk. He loved the rain, but his parents would fume at the times he'd dirty his clothes. What child doesn't love to get dirty in the rain?"

"I agree. They're so adventurous and love every small thing that adults take for granted."

"Yeah, I miss that. I miss him." He bowed his head, evoking sympathy. He hated kids with a passion but he would never hurt them. He wasn't a monster like that.

She touched the base of her throat. "Don't you see him anymore?"

He exhaled, feigning sadness. "He died and I miss him every day." He didn't dare look up at her yet, needing to be in the emotion.

The woman expelled an audible breath but didn't say anything for a few seconds. "I'm so sorry. It's hard losing someone you love."

He finally looked up at her, ignoring people passing by. The woman focused on the same painting. "It sounds like you're speaking from experience."

She shrugged. "I would rather not say."

He nodded. "I understand." Nice and slow. "What's your name?"

Light shone in her eyes. "My name's Gina. And you?"

"Gerald. Great to meet you. I don't often meet anyone who shares my love of artwork." A waiter came around and held out a tray of champagne. "No thanks, but the lady might like one."

She grinned. "Oh, you're so sweet." The woman reached for a glass. "Thank you." Taking a sip, she glanced over at him with interest.

He waited until they were alone again and people had scattered. "How about dinner? I would love to get to know you." He licked his lips. "It is hard talking privately here."

She looked over her shoulder. "Oh, I don't know. I'm here with a girlfriend."

"Bring her along too." He knew he had her with that statement, as she would think he had nothing to hide. But he could work with two women if he had to. It would be more of a challenge, but he could get twice the amount of dessert.

She peered at her watch, hesitating. "Let me go find her and then I'll come find you."

No, he couldn't let her leave. Damn! I need this one. He would lose her if he let her leave now. "How about I help you find her?"

Her eyes pierced into his as she debated whether to take him up on his offer. One last ball to play with. He undid his top button and played with the chain around his neck with a cross pendant on it. He knew she was religious and this would draw her in further, gaining her trust. "Two heads are better than one."

She grinned. "Sure. Let's go."

The man followed her, a rush of adrenaline soaring through his body. "Great."

The woman's phone buzzed in her hand. She answered the call. "Okay, no worries." He tilted his head, waiting for more. "It's okay. We can go get a drink. My friend got called into work and had to leave. I guess I need a ride."

He sighed with relief, as his job would be easier with only one woman. Divine intervention was on his side.

Oh, he couldn't wait to break her down piece by piece.

He grinned at his latest conquest, Gina, with her hands tied behind her back, her head drooping to the side, unconscious. Welts and bruises lined her chest and arms, and a broken lip ensured she didn't answer him back the next time.

When he'd met her at the art gallery he had known he'd hit a pot of gold. The bitch played right into his hands and her capture had gone according to plan. He had to give her credit for her huge cleavage, gleaming blue eyes, long, blonde hair and slim physique. She was attractive but she deserved what all women deserved; to be put down.

Scanning his tray by the bed, he picked up a scalpel and twirled it through his fingers. Where was it? The hammer, needle, surgical scissors, forceps, blades, and a variety of saws filled the tray, but his knife was missing. He dropped the scalpel back on to the tray. About to search the room, he remembered having it in the kitchen last.

Swaggering out of the bedroom, he walked down the narrow passageway and headed to the kitchen. The bloody knife lay in the sink, and he licked his lips at the hard-on he was getting. It was time to have a bit more fun with her before he snuffed her out.

Smiling to himself, he washed the knife and wiped it thoroughly with a towel.

He grinned to himself. He'd be adding to his collection soon. He had kept all their hair in a sealed bag inside a box in his wardrobe. Each time he sealed another bag was another time he had won against the weaker race.

Swaggering back to the bedroom, he swung the knife high up in the air and stabbed it deeply into Gina's arm. Music to his ears when she woke up with a jolt and a scream. The dilation in her eyes and shaking of her head sent his blood pumping right to his core.

"No, please. I promise I'll behave. Don't kill me."

His heart soared. "We are going to have us some fun, Gina." He gripped the knife and twirled it in the air. "Hmm. Which part of your body should I stab next? The other arm or your thigh? Decisions, decisions."

Gina lay on his stained mattress. He had chained her to the bed posts and the welts on her body were slowly fading. He reached for the whisky bottle, stomped towards the barely alive woman, and poured alcohol down her throat. Gurgling, she choked. He slapped her cheek hard. The smell of dried blood, urine, and sweat heightened his adrenaline.

"So, things weren't good last time, Gina. I didn't get what I wanted from you."

Gina's eyes were pools of terror, her face gaunt, but it didn't quite reach his core. Her face was all wrong. Her breasts were too large. This would be her last day of survival. "Please. Don't do this. Please."

He chuckled and threw his head back. "It's already done, sweetheart. I am the master and king of your dim world. Why don't you call me Master and I might let you live another day."

"Master. Master," she said.

Did she believe that even if he was telling her the truth she could get out of her tight situation? The woman had deep cuts around her breasts, chest and legs. He had bruised and battered her face and had broken the bone of her little finger when he couldn't come inside of her.

Maybe it was his technique. Choices, choices. Should he use the hammer for breaking bones, the scalpel for deeper cuts and to let her bleed out slowly while strangling her to death, or the knife to chop off her fingers one by one?

He opted for the hammer to break more bones before he grabbed that rope to strangle her to death. His senses heightened and he became breathless as he toyed with the hammer in his hands and got to work. Bones crushing under his blows, Gina screamed as he struck again and again.

He was inside of her, thrusting into her and she quivered around him. This time he got close to the climax as the life left her eyes and her screams grew silent. So close. But it wasn't enough. It just wasn't what he wanted. It wasn't who he wanted. Blind rage had him smashing wildly, the crunch of bones louder in the silence. Blood pooled and he finally stopped. Panting, he discarded the hammer.

He walked over to his dressing table and retrieved a photo of another woman. He had taken the photo of her at the beach and he couldn't stop looking at it. He pulled down his pants. She was everything. His hand pumped over his semi-erection, fingers flexing as he studied her features: the not-so-innocent pout of her mouth, the delicate curve of her neck, the plunge of her cleavage. What would it feel like to be nestled between those perfect mounds? What would her screams sound like? His cock jerked to attention in his hand and he pumped faster. How deep would the hue of purple in her lips get as the rope tightened around her throat? Lavender? Violet? Or would they turn red and plump and ready to take him in as he filled her with himself, choking off her breath until they turned blue-black? He groaned and spurted as he closed his eyes, imagining her lips encased around his penis as he gripped the scalpel and made a cut into her chest. The edge of his arousal sharpened, his release barely touching the growing urges deep inside him. Clenching his teeth, he had to do more to her. He had to have her.

Chapter Fifteen

NO SPARK

Over an extended lunch, Joy wandered through the Fitzroy Gardens in East Melbourne with Thomas along the tree-lined footpath, watching passersby and the array of colours surrounding them. Tall elm trees with flowers between them lined their way. Low shrubs and trees over extensive lawns created a painting-like layered landscape.

They stopped by the conservatory opposite a large round fountain with benches. Earthy bark from the dense woodland and freshly-cut grass grounded her as she took a seat on the bench beside Thomas. "Thanks for dinner the other night. I enjoyed the food."

"My pleasure," said Thomas. "I enjoy your company. Both when we were children, and in an adult way now."

She looked past him at a child splashing water from the fountain. If only she could be as carefree as that child. "There were many great times back then."

He nodded. "Do you remember the time the neighbour across the road came rushing out the door and accused me of kissing her daughter? An extreme lie."

Joy nodded, knowing he had been a handsome Lothario back then, and even more so now. He could have had his pick of women. "Did you truly not kiss her?"

Thomas shifted beside her on the bench. "Of course not. She wasn't my type. Besides, it wasn't as if I didn't have my pick of girls. She wasn't on the list."

Joy chuckled. "It sounds as if you had many girls after you, which you kind of did."

"Perhaps, but I set the mother straight. It came out she was trying to get her mother's attention. But things were good between them after that. Great, in fact."

Groups of people walked past them hand in hand and Joy found herself wishing she was here with Edward. He would appreciate the architecture of the place. It was all so well thought out and symmetrical. Lately, Joy had begun noticing exterior design—the symmetry of places, arches, texture of the exteriors—and wondering what Edward would think about it. What was modern in his world versus hers? Sometimes it seemed like they were in different worlds, but lately, more and more, they had found an easy pace between them, compromising. Edward had stepped back and given her choices more support, too. Maybe she had misjudged the man.

"Penny for your thoughts," said Thomas.

She breathed out. "I am sorry. I have a few things on my mind." The child ran around the fountain while a woman chased after him. "Nothing I wish to burden you with, Thomas."

He touched her shoulder and leaned forward, their thighs brushing. "I am a great listener and can give great advice. It has been known to have happened before."

She laughed. "Vain much?" Edward had said something about being a great listener yesterday too. She forced her attention to Thomas. "I appreciate you taking me out for lunch and taking my mind off things. You are special, Thomas."

The trees rattled in the breeze and clouds shaded the park. Would it rain? The throng of people trickled out into the conservatory or abandoned the gardens altogether, and in that moment, it had become as desolate as if Thomas and she were the only two people in the world.

"Only the best for you, Joy." He caressed her cheek with the back of his hand.

Joy considered him. She cared about Thomas, but it wasn't enough. There was no spark between them.

Thomas leaned forward and smashed his lips across hers. She sank into his gentle, skilful kiss as she delved deeper into his mouth, his hand stroking the back of her head. His tongue expertly gliding in and out as he moaned in her mouth. He became hungrier as he dived in deeper. His hand massaged her breast.

Joy pulled away from the kiss and plucked his hand away from her breast. "I don't think this is the right thing for us."

He focused intently on her. "Oh, Joy. I care about you. I always have. Don't go back to work." He feathered her cheeks. "I can book us a room at one of the hotels on St Kilda Road. We'll have champagne, roses, and everything you surely deserve. Are you willing to take a chance on us?"

She swallowed. "No, I'm sorry."

He drew back as if slapped.

"I truly am sorry, Thomas. I think we're better off as friends. Can we go back to being friends?" She clenched her fists in her lap and avoided looking at him.

"If that's what you think is best." His voice was flat. "I'll take you back."

Struggling to keep up with Thomas's pace, she hurried back to his car. He started the motor and drove in silence, zipping in and out of lanes and avoiding slow truck drivers. She gripped the edge of her seat in the passenger side and took a deep breath. Why was she having second thoughts? No, she and Thomas didn't have chemistry, not on her end anyway. What if she was mistaken and Thomas was her soulmate and the one person she could count on, and she was throwing it all away based on a vague feeling?

Clicking into park, Joy realised they had reached the house. "I'll see you around?"

"Yeah." His cold expression stretched into a gentle smile. "I am happy to have you as a friend, Joy. If you ever change your mind, though, let me know."

She nodded and opened the door and stepped out, waiting until Thomas's car was out of sight to go inside.

A cacophony of construction assailed her.

"Oh, hey. You're back," Edward said. "The paint is done drying just in time because the beds showed up early. They're assembling them now. Everything is coming together."

Joy followed Edward down the hall.

Joy bent forward and caught her breath. Reaching for her sports bag, she unzipped it and rummaged inside for a towel. With one big swipe, she dried the sweat off her forehead.

Footsteps receded as most of the team members headed outside of the gym, waving goodbye to her, Lian, Camilla, and Edward.

As she wiped the back of her neck, Edward rubbed his lean and tanned biceps. He sipped his water while squaring his shoulders, standing tall. His eyes briefly fell on her cleavage. She was curious about those lips and what they would taste like. How his strong, muscular hands would feel against the small of her back, not just hovering to respectfully guide her around?

"Earth to Joy," said Lian.

Joy broke out of her reverie. He shifted his gaze and proceeded to dry himself. "Sorry, what?"

"I said I can't come for drinks tonight. I've got this family thing," said Lian as she swung her sports bag over her shoulder.

Camilla approached. "Mariana's got her first friend birthday party tonight and I need to take her. I can't come out either. Sorry."

Joy nodded. "That's fine, ladies. I'll stay home tonight. I could do with the rest anyway."

Lian looked over at Edward. "You can go out, can't you?"

Edward replied quickly. "I don't mind going out."

Joy yawned, not having slept the night before in anticipation of breaking it off with Thomas. "I'm going to crash. It's all good." Though, she could use a drink and Edward wouldn't be the worst social option. "On second thought, I could use a drink."

"Great," said Lian. "You and Joy can have drinks on us. We'll come next time."

Camilla eyed Lian and pressed her lips together. Joy had revealed her breakup to her two friends just before the game. "After what you've been through lately, Joy, I'd say it's good to let your hair down. You should go and have fun."

Joy grinned at Edward, realising he was quieter than usual. "We can catch up in an hour after I've showered and changed."

Edward slowly nodded. "Okay then." He looked at Lian and Camilla. "I will see you, ladies, at the next game." As they said their goodbyes, Edward rushed out, looking briefly over his shoulder in her direction.

The wafting aromas of pasta sauce, herbs and assorted spices in the Italian restaurant triggered hunger pangs while waiters bustled about. The back wall displayed a photograph of a loaf of dough resting on a board with a background of sprinkles of flour in the air while masculine hands worked the pastry. It was black and white, with the person's face hidden behind the cloud of flour.

Black vinyl chairs were arranged around rectangular timber tables with chequered tablecloths on them. A brick-tiled counter stood opposite their table. Low-tempo music and dim lights gave the space a relaxing ambience.

Edward sipped his beer. "How's your cocktail?"

Joy wrapped her hands around the tall glass. Maybe she shouldn't have worn the red dress. Was it too much? "Great." She knit her brows. "Are you all right? You seem different."

"I wanted to talk to you about Ray. I know when he asked you out, it made things awkward between you. Has he done or said anything to upset you since Tuesday?"

Joy squeezed her hands. "Not really, no." She took a quick breath. "It has been awkward, and I hope Ray doesn't hate me for it, but I wasn't feeling it, you know. I've just been staying out of his way."

The tall, muscled male waiter interrupted their moment. He smiled, with a notebook in hand. "What can I get you?"

Joy looked up at him. "I'll have the eggplant parmigiana."

Edward stared at his menu before turning to the waiter. "Can I please have the salt and pepper squid?"

"Of course," said the waiter. He walked off with a curt nod.

Joy clasped her hands. "I know you and Ray are close. I get the feeling Ray is going through something. Is he all right?"

Edward swallowed. "He got himself in a tad of trouble lately, but he is fine now."

Joy gazed at him pondering her next question. "Sorry to hear that."

"Thanks." Edward shook his head. "He had a bad breakup a few years ago and tends to struggle with relationships and ... never mind."

The waiter interrupted their moment to lay down their steaming dishes. Once he left, Edward dug into his squid. Joy picked at her food until it cooled enough.

She rubbed at a nail. "Did he ever get any counselling for that? Relationship breakups can be hard to let go of sometimes."

"They can be, but no, he never had counselling. He always tells me he is fine and has come to terms with the breakup, but I still wonder."

She nodded then cut into her parmigiana and took a bite. "I felt like that about my own brother, Jesse, after he lost his fiancée. I always thought he couldn't let go of her because of his grief, but it was more about ..."

"More about what?"

She placed a hand across her throat and rubbed at her skin. "She was killed and he knew it. We thought she'd killed herself, but the bastard who murdered her made it look that way." She stared into her glass. "I am sorry. Here we were talking about Ray, and I bring up my own brother and his grief."

"It's fine, Joy. I would like to ... I was hoping we could get to know each other a bit better? Outside of work. We have a lot in common and I hope we can be friends."

Heat bloomed over her face. He wanted to get to know her? "Hmm. What do we have in common?"

Edward cleared his throat. "Let's see." His eyes looked past her as he thought. "We are both creative. You with your interior design and me with my work as an architect. I also like to draw. We have a fascination with the design of a building or piece of structure. We both have brothers."

She chuckled lightly. "I remember you said that you draw. Do you sell any of your drawings?"

He shook his head. "No, I draw for fun. It's an outlet for stress and helps me unwind."

"That's interesting. I would love to see your drawings one day."

"Any time."

Joy rubbed her hands together and leaned forward. "I guess we do have a bit in common. I'm not really ready to go home. What about a game of bowling? I love playing. Do we have that in common? I bet I could beat you."

He grinned. "I will ask for the bill."

Joy picked up her bowling ball, held it tight and swung it down the lane, keenly aware of his eyes boring into her back. They had been bowling for the last hour and were on their last game.

Joy's eyes lit up when she knocked down all the pins. "And that's a strike." The bowling centre comprised of nine other lanes. Laughter and chattering blended with the clunky sounds of the balls hitting lanes and running through the tracks. Loud music energised her as she prepared to bowl and win. A queue of people stood opposite the bar and cafe behind them. Dim lighting gave the space a romantic ambience, but she had to keep her head in the game and not falter from her winning streak.

Edward got up and retrieved his ball from the bench. He swung out his arm and threw the ball hard down the lane, knocking down four pins. While he waited for his next ball, Joy couldn't help but stare at the way his tight, green jeans fit him. Retrieving the ball he bent down to the lane. He struck the remaining pins down. "I knew I could knock down all the pins eventually." He beamed.

Joy glanced at him, his eyes met hers, drinking her in. She looked away and wondered what was on his mind. "My turn." She picked up the bowling ball, palmed it with both hands, moved towards the lane and swung it down hard. She got another strike, then turned in his direction. "This is our last game, Edward. Make it count."

He nodded. "I still have a chance." Edward's phone buzzed in his back pocket, but he ignored it.

"Do you need to get that?" asked Joy.

"I will check it later. I need to win this game."

"Right. Good luck with that." She sat back against the seat and put her head back until the sounds of pins fell. Only two. "Try again." But when he played his second shot, only one more pin fell.

He stood cross-armed and shook his head. "That was bad. Truly bad. I need more practice, but you are more of a sportsperson than I am. You won." He lay out his hands. "Bowling's not my favourite activity."

Joy knit her brows, wishing he'd told her that earlier. "I am sorry. Why didn't you tell me you didn't like bowling?"

He shrugged. "I wanted to try my hand with a beautiful woman."

She cleared her throat and her face warmed, not knowing how to respond. "Right."

"I'm feeling sore and it's stuffy in here. How about a walk?" asked Edward.

"Okay." They made their way outside the building and passed a range of stores until they reached the streets of the city with its warm breeze. Trucks and trams passed by, and they walked in the direction of the underground parking space. They crossed the road and found a bench to sit on. "It's a nice night." Their shoulders bumped.

Edward averted his eyes. "It is. Can you believe we have almost finished the house?"

"Hmm. Let's hope it's up to Richard's standards."

"He might have micro-managed us a tad, but I believe he is content with the work so far. You've done an amazing job."

Joy nodded. "Thanks." She grinned. "You did great too."

"So how is Thomas?" he asked.

"Thomas? Oh. I'm not sure. We're not together anymore."

"You're not?" he asked. His question was a little too quick and she studied him as he stood there on the walk.

"No."

"Oh. I'm sorry to hear that." He continued their leisurely pace and she followed, puzzling at his reaction.

"Things just weren't clicking for me. We're better as friends anyway."

Edward nodded. "Hmm. Too bad. He seemed like a decent guy."

"He is."

A long silence stretched between them.

"How have you been since the funeral?"

Joy wasn't expecting the question. "Oh, um, managing. It just brought everything back up."

"Do you want to talk about it? You never reached out so I hope that means you're managing?"

She had thought about reaching out once last night but thought better of it. They barely knew each other. Her friends were supporting her through it. Yet she found herself wanting to share with Edward.

So she started to tell him everything. Letting Mia leave, her parents resenting her. Her brother Jesse getting her through and never accepting that his fiancé, Erica's death was a suicide like the police had declared. Erica's murder and catching the killer recently. She told him about missing Kathleen's presence in their shared office. About how nothing made sense about her death. About how living at home was pushing her to her limits.

"Why don't you get your own place?" he asked.

"In this economy?" She scoffed.

He held up his hands. "You're right. It sounds like you're dealing with a lot. I get the feeling that you're never enough for your parents. I'm sorry." Dropping his hands, he said, "I hope you have support and that the load on your shoulders will lighten soon."

"Thanks. I've also only been working at Lian's for two years so I still have a bit to go before I can save enough to get my own place. I'm thinking of a modest place in one of the artsy districts. Close to shops and artisans."

"Sounds like a nice plan."

A man with a black coat and dark glasses stood in front of a restaurant, watching them. She shifted her foot as the man flicked a cigarette on the ground, barely missing being burned by the cigarette and knocking into Edward, her hand brushing his.

Catching her hand, he steered her away and cast daggered looks back at the cigarette thrower. "Are you all right?"

She nodded. "Yes. Thank you." She looked down at their hands. Edward followed her prompt but he didn't let her go.

Moisture welled in her eyes and Joy briefly closed them. Heartbeat slowing at his touch, she let the tension in her shoulders melt away. It felt so good to be held by Edward. She had to get a grip. Why was she so emotional tonight? This wasn't how she wanted him to see her.

He gave her a reassuring smile, squeezing her hand. "You are so strong, Joy. You carry such a heavy burden with grace and beauty."

She didn't expect those words, and as they locked eyes, she became aware of how dry her lips were. Would he recoil at the scratchiness? Light-headedness made her surroundings surreal. Kissing him. She was thinking about kissing him. He made her feel safe and loved and appeared to understand her deepest thoughts and emotions. He knew exactly what it was like to have a missing piece of childhood, how they weren't good enough to be themselves. How their parents were too busy with their own lives and issues to worry about their children. It wasn't only deep-seated passion or attraction she felt towards Edward. It was more than that. Was this what she was missing with Thomas? Was this the piece she had been looking for?

"How about a drink at the bar across the street?"

She nodded, not wanting the night to end. "Perhaps only one drink."

Edward's phone buzzed again. He checked the display and winced. "Oh, great."

Joy stared after him. "What's wrong?"

Edward got up. "It's Ray. He sent me a text saying he got robbed and needs me to pick him up in Altona. I'm sorry. Let me ring him first." She watched as he spoke to his brother on the phone while shaking his head and sighing. "I am sorry, Joy, but I have to leave. I would like to do this again."

"All good. He needs you." As they walked back to the cars, Edward placed his hand on the small of her back. It felt as good as she imagined. She wished they could have more time together, but Ray was in trouble and needed his brother.

Joy watched Edward walk towards his car for a second before she made her way in the opposite direction. The street was dark and the night air brisk. Footsteps behind her sounded close, and as she turned around the same man she had seen earlier walked past her. Chills permeated down her spine. She ignored the man and continued on her way. He had changed course and walked across the road in the opposite direction. Given what was going on in her community, it was understandable to be paranoid.

Chapter Sixteen

HOMELESS MAN

Edward locked his car and stepped towards the bright lights from the sign above the door. Opening it, he entered the quiet bar. A small group of patrons tossed down drinks, ate hot snacks, and bantered and laughed with each other. Long-padded benches and chairs rimmed the small bar.

He sat at the counter and nodded to the male bartender with kind eyes and shoulder-length wavy hair.

"What can I get you?" asked the server.

"I'm looking for a man named Ray. Was he here?"

The man nodded and waved his hand away. "In there. Throwing up. I'd say he's had a bit too much to drink. Who's asking?"

"I'm his brother, Edward." He smiled. "Thanks." He got up and walked towards the bathroom, shaking his head.

"Wait," the bartender said. Edward turned back around. "I thought you should know he lost his wallet. Some homeless man by the side of the road took it. But if he's got money, he'll be scoring drugs at the end of the street and shouldn't be far away. I'm sure you'll find the guy."

Ray, drunk again. Why wasn't he surprised? "Thank you. I appreciate your help. I will check in on Ray."

"Good luck."

He walked down a narrow corridor heavy with smells of beer, wine, and spirits. Passing the kitchen, he pushed open the door of the unisex bathroom. Moans and a toilet flush told him which cubicle his brother was in. "Ray. Open up." He remembered his date with Joy but didn't want to hurt Ray with the truth about where he'd been. He'd keep it to himself.

"Eddie, mate. Thanks. Give me a second." His eyes roamed the bathroom with its dirty mirrors, sticky vinyl flooring and stench of vomit. No doubt many men had been nauseous in this toilet, but luckily, Ray might have sobered up a little in the time it took to get there.

The door opened. Ray's hair was dishevelled, his eyes bloodshot, and at least two days' worth of stubble covered his jaw. His shirt was half tucked in with stains on the collar, and his jeans looked worn. He wobbled and held on to the side wall for support, grunting and placing a quivering hand over his forehead. Turning on the tap, he soaped his hands and washed his face.

"You look terrible," said Edward.

"I feel like shit."

Edward sighed. "You cannot keep doing this to yourself, Ray. You need help. This could have been much worse. What if the man who stole your wallet killed you? You wouldn't be able to defend yourself when you're intoxicated. I cannot keep bailing you out."

Ray nodded. "Sorry, Eddie. I promise I'll do better." He ripped out paper from the dispenser and wiped his hands.

"I have heard that before. Now, let's leave this place and find your wallet. Did you have much money in it?"

He shook his head and made his way to the exit with Edward trailing behind. Ray only swayed and wobbled a little so he left him alone. "Nah, but I don't want to lose all my cards. That'd be a bummer if I have to contact the bank and everyone else if I don't get them back."

He wanted to say it served him right but this wasn't the time. Edward was inclined not to help the next time around but he'd said the same thing to himself before, so here he was. He owed a lot to Ray for being there for him growing up and he couldn't abandon him now. "Let's find this homeless man. He can't be too far."

As they walked outside the bar, passersby stared at them, no doubt wondering why Ray looked like a wreck. At the end of the street it became deserted.

Further ahead car horns and tires on asphalt roared and screeched. Closed shops lit up the dark night with display lighting and glowing signs as they made their way to the back of the building. Turning around, they crossed the street and went back towards the bar. Shadows appeared a few metres away from Edward's car, and as they got closer, a man wearing a jacket, gloves, and a beanie flicked through something. "Is that the man?" Edward whispered.

"Sure is."

"Let's not spook him and get closer." Walking ahead of Ray, he approached the man who jolted when he spotted Edward. In his hands, he held a familiar wallet. The man bolted and Edward chased after him.

"Hey! Stop."

Dodging people and almost tripping over a bike-rider and an old lady, he forged ahead. The man was horribly fast. Puffing and fighting against the pain in his legs, he increased his pace until he got closer, his fingers grabbing the edge of the man's jacket. They both fell, and the man groaned as his back slammed into the pavement. The wallet slipped through his fingers and dropped beside them. Edward, having landed on his knees, got up and picked up the wallet, ignoring the pain. "I only wanted the wallet." He helped the man up.

Ray caught up to them, swaying more than before. He tripped and stumbled into Edward who righted his brother then turned back to the man.

The homeless man stared over at Ray. "Sorry."

Ray nodded. "You should be."

Edward's heart ached at this man's state. His hair looked as if it hadn't been washed in weeks, his clothes were dirty, and the stench on him was unbearable. He pulled out his wallet and handed the man three hundred dollars. "Go and get yourself a meal and a night in a cheap motel. Get yourself help with your thieving too. You can't go around stealing wallets. I could refer you to a friend of mine, George, who might be able to get you labouring work."

The man nodded. "Thank you."

Edward and Ray returned to the vehicle while the homeless man strayed behind them.

"Let's hope he puts the money to good use."

Edward nodded. "Hopefully. If he's hungry, he'll get himself a meal." When they got into the car, he checked his rearview mirror. The homeless man walked away and headed towards a cafe. At least he was buying himself food.

Back at Ray's, he dropped his brother off his shoulder into the bed and took off his shoes. Wrinkling his nose,

Edward pushed his brother securely on to the mattress. Ray was already snoring loudly. The place was a mess again. Empty bottles littered the surfaces. Takeout meals and a loaf of mouldy bread were scattered in odd places. With a sigh, Edward decided to stay the night. He'd clean and get Ray a good breakfast in the morning.

Swiping crumbs and bottles off the couch, Edward found a lone blanket in the closet thrown onto a shelf, not even folded. It would have to do. Making himself as comfortable as he could on the couch, he stared at the ceiling. Would it be a good idea to meet with Joy again? He saw her in a new light. He had been so wrong about her. She was smart and disciplined, and not flaky at all. She had been through so much and was strong.

Was he betraying Ray by feeling the way he did about her? Unable to help himself, he texted Joy. Most likely, she would be asleep at this late hour, but she would see the text in the morning. *"How about dinner at my house tonight?"*

Edward walked back from the kitchen with a glass of water when his phone pinged. It couldn't be Joy. It was three o'clock in the morning.

"I would love to have dinner with you again. How is Ray?"

He was touched she thought of Ray. *"He is resting at home. All fine."*

"Great to hear. Thanks for the great time earlier. Text me your address and the time."

He sent her the information. *"You are welcome. I had an amazing time too. Goodnight, Joy."*

"Goodnight."

Edward slowly opened his eyes on Ray's couch the next morning, rubbing the back of his neck. He had stayed the night so he wouldn't drink again. His drinking usually escalated on the weekends. It was only Saturday. How was it only Saturday?

He got up and walked to the kitchen, pouring water into the electric kettle. A cup of coffee would wake him up before he spoke to Ray about getting help for his drinking. Enough was enough.

While waiting for the kettle to boil, the doorbell rang. He approached the front door and swung it open, his chest clenching when he saw two police officers standing there. "Hello, officers. What can I do for you?"

The policeman said, "Yes, hello. I am Officer Michaels, and this is Officer Abruzzo. We need to speak to Mr Ray Astbury."

"What is this about, officers?"

"We would rather speak to Mr Astbury. Is he home?"

Edward nodded. "Yes. Come inside and I will wake him up." He opened the door wider and they stepped inside. Officer Michaels was stout and of average height, his eyes darting in all directions around the house. Officer Abruzzo tucked his shirt over his protruding belly.

He rushed into Ray's bedroom and called out. The display on the digital clock read seven o'clock. "Wake up."

Ray roused from sleep as he turned to Edward. "What the fuck, man? It's early."

He huffed. Edward despised his brother's regular use of such foul language. "The police are here. Get up now." He wondered what had happened for the police to arrive here this early. For all he knew, Ray might have had a bar fight or assaulted someone while drunk. Any number of incidents could have occurred without him knowing.

Ray jerked as he pulled the blankets off himself and quickly reached for a jumper on the floor. He swung it over his head then reached for his pants lying over a chair. "What the hell are they doing here this early, Eddie? This is madness."

He stood cross-armed. "I don't know, Ray. You tell me."

Ray shook his head. "I've done nothing wrong." Edward was curious, wondering if this might have been simple questioning about an incident not initiated by his brother.

They entered the living room and Officer Michaels approached Ray. "Mr Astbury, you are under arrest for assault. We would like you to come with us to the station."

He frowned. "What?"

Officer Abruzzo intervened. "Please come with us."

Edward's blood ran cold.

Ray put up his hands. "What assault? Who did I hurt?"

Officer Michaels said, "The assault of a young woman at the local Motor Inn yesterday afternoon. You can come with us quietly to the station or we can cuff you. Your choice."

He flailed with his hands. "Fine, fine. I'll come quietly."

"Officers. This has to be a mistake," said Edward.

"No mistake. Please come with us, Mr Astbury," said Officer Michaels.

Edward touched his brother gently on the shoulder. "I will meet you at the station, Ray. We will sort this out, do not worry."

Ray nodded with dark pools of despair in his eyes. "No worries, bro."

Edward couldn't believe Ray was in trouble with the police. After four hours, he finally got to speak to Ray in an interview room. "Ray, what is going on?"

"A woman I had sex with, Eddie. She reported me. A prostitute. She said I got rough with her but it didn't happen like that." Ray sighed. "They looked into my history too. The police think I was obsessed with my ex-girlfriend, Mary. When they called her, she mentioned I got rough with her too."

Edward scoffed. A prostitute? Was that what he was resorting to? "Did you hurt this woman?" Did he actually hurt his ex-girlfriend, Mary too, and why didn't Edward know much about their relationship? Granted, they had not seen each other for a few years, but surely Ray wasn't violent?

"It's all a huge misunderstanding, bro."

He shifted his posture on the hard couch. "What actually happened, Ray? Explain it to me from the beginning."

Ray put up a hand. "Oh, that prostitute at the hotel wanted it rough, and as for Mary, she did exaggerate. I might have been a bit clingy, but I never hurt her, at least not intentionally. I loved her. Besides, I didn't know the woman was a prostitute until the end of the night. Met her in a bar."

Edward jolted in his seat. "What are you talking about, Ray? What do you mean, not intentionally? What happened with Mary?"

His voice rose. "Okay, so my ex-girlfriend said she found someone who treated her better, and that she didn't love me anymore. When I tried to convince her to give us a chance, she became rude and arrogant. I felt betrayed and hurt, and anyway, I might have shoved her a little to take control of the situation, and she hurled abuse at me. I shoved her some more and left. She was fine."

Edward swallowed, shaking his head. He didn't know his brother at all. "Did she report you to the police before?

"The police from another precinct had photos of Mary with bruising around her arms and neck. The report mentioned I might have called her a few times a day for the following week. They even falsely claimed I had stalked her at least twice. But I did no such thing. Like I said, a misunderstanding. I missed the woman and tried to get her back."

Edward couldn't believe what he was hearing. Chills ran up and down his spine. His legs felt heavy beneath him. How could he miss what his brother was doing to women? "Jesus, Ray. What did you do to Mary and to the prostitute?"

Ray remained silent for a few seconds. "I didn't mean to hurt Mary. I was a little drunk. As for the prostitute, she only had a few bruises. Nothing major. This is crazy, Eddie. I want a damn lawyer."

He struggled to breathe evenly. "I will get you a lawyer."

Edward had a thickness in his throat and his stomach somersaulted. How could Ray be violent with women? It sickened him to the core. Ray had no-one else in his life. He had lost friends along the way, and as of today, he only had George and himself.

Surely Ray needed help. But was he the right person to help when he was ashamed of his brother for what he'd done?

Chapter Seventeen

WITNESS

Joy sat on a bench at Braybrook Park, gazing at children taking turns sliding through a tube slide, swaying on swings, and tackling a steel-based tunnel. Their mothers chased them around the playground and over the wood shavings that spilled onto the delicate blades of vibrant, green grass. Trees of all shapes and sizes provided shade around the playground area. The warm breeze did nothing to ease her mind as she recalled her conversation with Octavia on Thursday. The funeral, and last night with Edward had made her forget, but now her worry was thundering loud. Someone she knew was linked to the murdered women. Who could it be?

Surely, it wasn't Edward? Not with such a kind touch and thoughtfulness. No way. She had really misjudged him. Last night made her feel closer to him. She couldn't wait for them to meet again. Ray maybe? He was a creep, and based on Edward's text last night, she suspected he was drinking too. Could he really be capable of murdering someone? She could easily believe Richard was on that list. She shuddered. He was cold and cruel to Joy and his wife, but could he really be related to the killings?

She scrolled through her phone checking the news while the warm wind feathered her cheek. No new updates. She was just letting her worry run away with her. Putting the phone into her back pocket, a prickle of unease rained down her spine, her eyes scanning her surroundings, unsure what they were looking for. She shook it off, thinking she was over-using her imagination again. Her morning reprieve had lost its appeal.

As she slid into the driver's seat, she noticed that her glovebox was open. The romance book she kept on the passenger seat was missing. Her eyes darted around the park again. Someone had been inside her car. They had invaded her privacy. But she saw no-one. Something wasn't quite right with her today, and she might need to go to the gym to release built-up tension.

It was possible she had left the glovebox open and forgot. Was she even sure she had her romance book inside the car? She might have left it at home. She put the matter behind her and started the motor, then wound down her window. A scream echoed across the park.

Near the playground, mothers and children stopped what they were doing on the slide and swings as a young woman flailed with her hands and pointed to something. Joy exited the car. People were running towards something on the ground behind a tree. She couldn't make out what it was. Mothers swept up children and fled.

She walked closer to the playground, feet unsteady. People scattered. One of the children ran towards the tree, but his mother yanked him back and shook her head. What did the mother not want her son to see?

Joy swallowed, her legs stepping forward before her brain could catch up. The sky was turning grey and the wind had become cold as it scraped her cheek. She fought back dizziness as she ignored the pit in her stomach. A few stragglers lingered, whispering to each other and one spoke on the phone. "Yes. No. No-one has touched it ..."

Joy flinched at the sight before her. A woman with blood-matted blonde hair lay at an awkward angle without any clothes on. Her arms had been cut off and lay at her side." She turned away and vomited into the bushes.

The voice of a young woman came from behind her. "Are you all right?"

Joy turned and peered at a lady whose face was pale. She threaded her hands through her auburn hair. "Yes, I'm fine. Has someone called the police?"

The woman nodded. "I have and they should be here any minute. Apparently, they're close by."

Joy shivered and felt cold all over. "The poor woman. Did you see anything?"

The lady shook her head. "No, nothing. She might have been here before we arrived."

Joy closed her eyes, but the image kept haunting her. "We need something to cover the body. I have a blanket in my car." She ran towards her car and hefted a blanket from her boot, taking a moment to gather herself before returning.

By the time she got back, police cars and emergency services personnel had arrived and the woman she'd met had directed them to the body. Joy stood back and watched as one of the officers covered the woman's body with a white sheet. People huddled around the tree, witnessing the scene.

Two policemen yelled out. "Please get back. We have a crime scene here. Nobody leaves as we need to question you all." One of them secured a yellow tape around the area.

She headed back to her car and put away the blanket, then returned to the scene, watching the officers talk to the women who had stayed back. Joy bowed her head and checked her phone for messages, knowing she was late for her lunch with her friends. They would understand.

A gentle touch on her shoulder warmed her. "Joy." She turned around and saw Marco, accompanied by Angelo and a forensics team. "Are you all right?"

"The poor woman. What ... happened ... to her?"

"We don't know yet until forensics examine the body. Angelo and the medical examiner will assess the crime now."

Angelo bent down low, lifted up the sheet and scanned over the body before the examiner took over. He approached them. "Hi Joy. You don't look too good. I am surprised to see you here."

"I was stopping here just to take in the park and relax, like I do often. I was about to drive away when someone screamed."

Marco led her towards a nearby bench while Angelo walked back to the scene. "Listen. Did you see anyone suspicious lurking around?"

She shook her head. "No, nothing."

"You should go home. We have our hands full here," said Marco.

She peered over her shoulder as if she'd find the perpetrator. "Do you think it's the serial killer in the area?"

Marco tilted his head.

"Are you sure you're okay?"

"I'm fine. But who could do something so sickening? Her arms were cut off, Marco."

Marco lay his hands on her shoulders. "Perhaps you should go home? What you saw wasn't pleasant. If we have more questions, we'll let you know."

Joy fought back dizziness and took deep breaths. "I'm meeting the others for lunch. Then I'll go home. Not that I could eat now."

He gave her a reassuring smile and joined Angelo in interviewing the people surrounding the scene.

She couldn't believe that another poor woman was dead, and that she had seen it. What was going on in the community, and would they find this killer before he murdered again?

The aroma of coffee and cinnamon in the city bar gave Joy little comfort. The coming and going of patrons gave her a headache as she pondered the notion that this murderer had fallen lower than Satan. Cutting up bodies and dumping them in parks where children could find them? Who could be this depraved?

Normally, she loved the excitement and hectic pace of this bar, but even the soothing jazz tunes of the pianist did nothing to calm her palpitating heart. The hard-backed chair made her spine ache, and her legs shook underneath her table. Get a grip, girl.

Her friends, Gabriella and Camilla were wrapped up in their own conversation while she pretended to listen to them.

Playing with the gold chain around her neck, Joy stared into her sparkling strawberry wine drink. Reaching for it, she took a quick sip and allowed the bubbles to settle her stomach and warm her dry throat. She hadn't told the girls about what she'd witnessed yet.

Gabriella stopped talking and watched her with curiosity. She curled a brow. "Something's wrong, Joy."

Camilla touched her on the shoulder. "I agree with Gabriella. What happened? You don't seem like yourself."

Joy pushed away the images of the woman at the park, steeling herself. Her hands clasping her glass were visibly shaking. "I ... I ... saw a dead body." Gabriella and Camilla gazed at her with dark expressions. They waited for more. "Marco and Angelo were there investigating." She bowed her head and gazed into her drink. She couldn't breathe and her body ached all over. Was the room spinning? Gabriella's soft hand squeezed her own, and Camilla wrapped around her as she felt a stronger gush of tears coming. She couldn't stop them if she wanted to.

Her other friends, Bella and Octavia, rushed to their table as soon as they walked into the cafe, their eyes showing their worry as they took a seat.

Bella reached for her hand, her eyes misting. "Oh, Joy. I am so sorry." She hugged her tight. "Marco and Octavia explained what happened this morning at the park. Are you all right?"

Joy pulled away. "I am fine. You guys don't need to worry. I am more concerned about that woman's family."

Octavia fixed her gaze on her. "I cannot believe you were there. You shouldn't have seen that."

"It was a coincidence, Octavia. I was there taking in the laughter and warm Saturday morning and heard a scream. A woman saw the corpse and called the police." She explained more of what happened.

Bella shook her head. "Marco and Angelo will find whoever did this. How are you truly? What can we do for you?"

Joy smiled wanly. "Nothing, Bella. I will get over it. The image is still raw but like everything else, I move on."

Octavia undid the top button of her shirt, under the tailored suit she was wearing. She knit her brows. "Don't downplay this. The leads we have so far on this case will bring this creep to justice. I do not want you to worry about these murders."

"How can I not?" Joy said. "So far, we've had a few local murders and two of them have been at places where I've been. First Cherry Lake and now Braybrook Park. It is scary to think that something weird is going on here. Is it just a coincidence, Octavia?" She remained silent. "Can you tell me anything about the leads you have?"

Octavia's eyes darkened. "You know I can't, and to answer your question earlier, I am sure it is a coincidence." Why did that sound like a lie?

Bella gave her a reassuring smile. "Let's have a drink for now. I want you to take care of yourself, Joy, and not worry about anything. This case is in good hands. I trust my husband."

"I know. I do too. It is just that I am starting to wonder if there's more to this story. Why is this person killing in the local area, particularly at places where I've visited?"

"Not killed at, but dumped in those places," said Octavia.

"You're right," said Joy. She turned to Camilla, who was visibly shaking. "Are you all right?"

Camilla leaned forward and took a sip of her wine while the waiter took drink orders from Bella and Octavia. "I am fine. I need to stop listening to the news as it can be triggering, you know?"

"I'm sorry. We don't need to talk about this anymore." Joy rested back in her seat and wondered why the killer had so far dumped two women in the local areas she'd frequented.

Maybe she should cancel on Edward. After another drink and a nibble of appetizer with the others, she was feeling a bit better, and decided against cancelling. She excused herself an hour later, head clear and excitement blooming in her chest. She needed to get ready.

Chapter Eighteen

CONFLICTED

Edward answered the door. Joy felt self-conscious. Her hair was tied low in a ponytail, free strands falling down the sides of her rosy cheeks. Her red lips were full and pink. She wore a below the knee stretch dress.

"Thanks for coming," he said.

She looked around the foyer as she stepped inside his two-bedroom townhouse.

He led her inside the kitchen where he'd set a candlelight dinner with China and shiny cutlery. A bowl of Caesar salad rested in the centre of the table. Tomato and meat scented the room and she guessed they were having a bolognaise or maybe even lasagna. Whatever it was it smelled delicious and impressed her. "Take a seat."

She sat at the round glass top cast iron table and he joined her. "This looks interesting, and the smells. Delicious."

He grinned. "My nanny taught me how to cook." He rose and opened the oven, wafting more basil, tomato, and cheese into the air. Setting the tray on the stove, he looked to her. "Dinner is served."

Joy stayed at the table while Edward plated up the lasagne and set it in front of her. "Would you like a sparkling wine?" She nodded. Retrieving the bottle from the fridge, he reached for two wine glasses from an overhead cupboard, poured it, and set them on the table.

After he sat down, they dug in. She forked a small slice of the meal into her mouth. He had cooked the best lasagne she had ever tasted. When she met his gaze, he held it.

Joy broke their lingering look. "This is tasty and well-seasoned."

"Thanks." He savoured the cheesy texture. "Do you like cooking?"

Joy nodded. "Sometimes, but I would rather spend time on hobbies than cook a gourmet meal. I resort to a simple pasta dish or take-away if my mum's not home, as she does most of the cooking."

He got up. "I will put music on. Do you have any requests?"

Joy frowned and put down her fork. She picked up her wine glass and hesitated. "How about something upbeat like the Weeknd or Khalid? I like pop music and ballads. Or whatever you have available."

"I don't mind those singers, but I also like alternative styles or music with deep lyrics, like those discussing world issues. I like to think deeply when I listen to music. Songs reciting facts or the state of the world. I am logical with sounds."

Joy nodded. "I am not a big fan of alternative music, but I do like the odd groups like The 1975."

"Hmm," said Edward. "I like their music. They're versatile with their range of alternative songs, but they do have those upbeat or pop styles of music too. I'll play a mix from my playlist." He walked away and connected his phone to his stereo, elated by how much they were different but also the same.

When he returned she closed her eyes, relaxing into the song by the Weeknd with its vibrant rhythm. The image of the body flashed in her mind and she opened her eyes, pressing her back against the solid chair. I am safe, she thought. It's over.

"It takes you to another place, doesn't it?"

Joy opened her eyes and blushed. She hadn't been paying much attention. "What?"

"Music. It saved me after Ray left and after ..."

She angled her head, holding her fork in the air. "After what?"

He cast his eyes downward. "My fiancée died of terminal brain cancer a few years back. They couldn't operate. It took me a while to move forward. We lived together and it was hard after she died. I expected to see her walk through the door. I went out and believed she was around the corner. I even stopped a few people in the street, thinking it was her." He clenched his fists around his fork and knife.

Joy placed her cutlery down, leaned forward and touched him on the hand. "I am sorry. What was her name?"

He sighed and looked at her with softer eyes. Putting down his knife he placed a hand over hers and butterflies danced in her stomach. "Evanthia." He bit into his lasagne. "I don't wish to be a downer but I wanted you to know."

She smiled reassuringly. "I appreciate you telling me, Edward." Taking another bite of her lasagne, Joy swallowed then touched the base of her throat. Poor Edward. What a horrible thing to face.

"It took me a while to manage my grief but Ray helped me through it. Not long before Evanthia died he had gone through a separation, but he put his own loss aside and helped me cope."

She leaned in. "I'm glad you had support." She beamed. "I appreciate you opening up to me too. I know it couldn't have been easy."

"You are easy to talk to, Joy." Their gaze lingered for a while before they resumed their meal. Time passed in a comfortable silence. "Do you like any particular movie genre or TV show?"

Joy rested her hand against her chin, her plate and Edward's clear now. "I like romance, family sagas, psychological thrillers. That sort of thing."

Edward rose, carried the plates to the sink and took out a tray of tiramisu from the fridge. He reached up high to retrieve dessert plates. "Quite a diversity there. I don't mind all those too." He cut a slice of the sweet and put it on Joy's plate, and then a piece on his. "Enjoy."

She beamed. "This looks good. Thanks."

Edward resumed their conversation. "I like British comedies too, of course, and action-adventure."

"I find them a bit dry myself but to each their own."

Edward laughed. "Bite your tongue. You need to appreciate the culture of British comedies. It might be dry, but that is what is amazing about it."

"Hmm. If you say so."

After finishing their desserts, Edward carried his plate to the sink. Joy took hers and placed it on top of his. Washing and drying the dishes together was comforting and easy.

He wiped his hands on the tea towel. "How about a movie? We can watch a light-hearted comedy or a suspense movie. Your choice."

"A comedy would be great."

"Okay, but not a British one. I can respect your opinion this time." As they seated themselves on the couch, Edward scrolled through a list of movies. "How about this one?"

Joy nodded. "Sure. The blurb sounds good."

He sat back on the couch and started the movie, reaching for and caressing her hand. She didn't take it away.

Joy shifted her body closer towards him, but her eyes remained glued to the TV. Struggling to watch with Edward so close, she held on until the movie ended. These new feeling flooded her and she realised she was attracted to Edward. She wanted him. It felt right to be with him.

"What did you think of the movie?" he asked

"I enjoyed it. But ..." she said softly, "it was hard to pay attention with you so near." Joy pressed her lips together and looked up at him.

"Really?" he murmured. Nodding, she parted her lips and he leaned close.

Edward feathered her bottom lip and cheek. She closed her eyes and they inched forward. Then he pulled away.

"This can't happen."

Joy angled her head. "Why not?"

He got up from the couch and stood cross-armed. Joy rose too and inched her way closer to Edward, but he stepped back and shook his head. "What's going on, Edward?" He remained silent. "I thought you cared."

"This won't work."

"Care to explain?" She scowled. "I mean, here you are, inviting me out for dinner and a show, then getting kind of intimate. What do you expect me to think?"

He paced the floor with his hands on his hips. "We work together and it would be awkward for one thing."

"For one. What other reasons are there?"

He glanced in her direction and sat back down on the couch, turning the TV off. He rubbed underneath his eye. "What if Thomas finds out?"

Joy averted her eyes. "What? He is not my boyfriend. You know that."

"It could wreck our work with the Stubbles if Thomas finds out and doesn't like the idea."

"You invited me here, Edward. I think we can both be professional and keep our relationship discreet until after the project is done. Like you said yesterday, it is almost done. Maybe a few weeks at best."

He didn't reply. Was he trying to think of more reasons? It dawned on her that this might not be about Thomas or work at all. "This is more about Ray, isn't it? You don't want to hurt your brother, is that it? What do you truly want, Edward? Tell me. I know there's an attraction here, but I want you to tell me you're attracted to me and want this too. If not, then be straight with me. What is it you want?"

He hung his head down, elbows at his sides. "I don't know what I want. I think this is a mistake."

"But you were the one who made the first move."

He breathed deeply, his eyes downcast. "I made a mistake and wasn't thinking rationally."

"Well, God forbid you need to be rational about your emotions, if you have any."

"What does that mean? I am not a robot and I do have feelings."

She sighed. "I'm sorry. I didn't mean ... You can be really frustrating, you know?"

Edward's face paled and his shoulders appeared to tighten. He avoided looking at her and stared at his hands instead. "This won't work anyway. I'm not the man for you. I ... I ... It won't work. We work together and I'm not looking for a relationship. It's too hard after ..."

"After who? Evanthia? Are you still grieving for her?"

"There are too many complications with us. Ray, Thomas, our work, and yes, Evanthia. It's too hard and I can't manage this now, if ever."

Her heartbeat slowed and her legs trembled. "God forbid. I should be worth it." She felt a fleeting dizzy sensation. "I was willing to try, Edward. You don't even want to try."

Joy got up and wiped at her face. A painful tightness in her throat made her want to scream, but she lifted her shoulders up high. "Fine. Next time, don't even consider kissing me because I'll be unavailable. Goodbye." She headed to the front door and rushed out with tears in her eyes. Bowing down, she sniffed and walked on unsteady legs to her car. She didn't care about Edward. He could go take a flying leap in the river for all she cared. Today was turning into a nightmare.

Chapter Nineteen

TORN

Edward bowed his head over his design model for a new project. With a gentle finger, he placed a miniature door on the model building. He glued another on piece which made the walls of the warehouse, cautiously pressing in his thumb and index finger to hold it up. The model was coming along, and he planned to show his design to the client in a few days. He had worked late into the night on Monday. At ten o'clock, his eyes were strained from lingering over all the small pieces. He had made the front part of the warehouse with its side walls, but now came the tricky part; the individual storage spaces of the interior.

Rubbing his shoulders, he focused on Joy and their most recent dinner together, and how they'd argued. He hadn't meant to hurt her and had desperately wanted to kiss her, but the timing was off. He didn't even know what had come over him when he was about to kiss her. It had been two days since their argument, when he had realised that he wasn't ready for anything. Too many complications.

He walked over to the staffroom, picked up a cup from the overhead cupboard, and placed it underneath the coffee machine spout. Pressing a button, the strong aroma of espresso permeated the air, the steam flowing out of the cup as he picked it up and took a sip. The coffee would keep him awake for the next two hours. He had to finish the model before he put the final touches on his blueprint and liaised with stakeholders, builders, contractors, the engineer, and manager.

His back pocket vibrated. He rummaged into it, pulled out his phone, and stared at the display. Ray. Not again. "What is going on?"

"Hello to you too," said Ray. "Can't a brother ring occasionally? What are you ... do ... ing?"

Edward shook his head at the slur of his words. "Jesus Ray, they just let you out. I know it was rough but you're drunk. Shouldn't you be staying out of trouble?"

"No bro. They got nothing on me. Just a few drinks. Not even that much. Just wanted to say I love you, man. Also, that I ... may be a little ... little late at the house tomorrow."

"Again? It doesn't matter. The clients won't be there until the afternoon. I will most likely arrive late, too. Joy is working on one of the bedrooms tomorrow. As long as you are there before lunchtime, it is fine." Silence. "Are you there, Ray?"

"Thanks, man. I knew you'd understand. You always do."

Edward swallowed, an uneasy feeling in his stomach. "Why did you drink?"

He breathed heavily over the phone, his voice low. "I don't know, Eddie. It's just that I'm alone, man. Always alone. Lost all my friends, our parents couldn't give a shit about ... us, and my ... my girl ... friends never last. I'm a loser, man." He breathed heavily.

"Are you home?"

"Yeah. But I'm fine. Wanted to say hi ... that ... s ... all. I'm fine. Always fine."

Edward's heart sank, not liking the wistful, sad tone in his brother's voice. His breathing sounded erratic, too. "I am coming over."

"Nah, I'll be fine. Going to bed."

Edward wasn't about to get anything out of him tonight. He'd speak to him tomorrow and make sure that he got help for his drinking. Ray had to find better coping strategies for stress.

"Okay, listen. Go to bed and sleep it off. You are going to have one bad headache tomorrow."

Ray hung up without saying goodbye. Hopefully, he would stop drinking. He wondered if he should check on him or if Ray truly was going to bed. He normally went to bed after drinking, so he wasn't likely to be doing anything stupid. But Ray didn't sound fine.

Then again, it was too late to see his brother now and he had his work to complete. He would most likely sleep it off, so he would check on him first thing in the morning. Ray couldn't keep dominating his life like this.

Before starting the motor, Joy checked her phone with the address he had texted her and entered it into her GPS. Speeding towards his house in Laverton, Joy took a calming breath, hoping Ray was okay. She needed peace of mind that he wasn't going to hurt himself. He'd called her saying that he wanted to meet for dinner, make amends. Something in his voice sounded as if he had given up, and the late hour worried her. She couldn't just leave him. What if he harmed himself?

The lights were still on when she arrived at Ray's house. Her heart raced. Damn! What if he got the wrong idea from her visit? Could she explain that she was worried that he'd hurt himself, or was she only imagining the worst?

Walking past the overgrowing brush in the front garden and tall hedges, she made her way along a brick-paved pathway and rang the doorbell. When he opened the door, his bloodshot eyes spoke volumes. He was in a bad way, but thank God he was in one piece. She hesitated, wondering if she should go inside. "I wanted to check on you. You didn't sound great over the phone. Are you okay?"

His stained jumper and creased jeans appeared as if he'd worn them for days, and his dishevelled hair got worse as he threaded his hands through it multiple times. "I'm o ... kay. Come in." His words were slow, like he was struggling to speak.

Joy hesitated. He was okay so she could leave. "No. I'll get going. I wanted to make sure you were all right. You should go to bed."

His eyes darkened. "Come inside."

She shook her head. "No, it's late."

As she turned around, he whispered something. "No-one loves me. I might as well kill myself," he slurred. "And ... I can't keep a damn woman either."

Joy changed course and faced him, unable to read his neutral expression. Her heart beat wildly and her legs felt unsteady. What if he was serious? What if he did something to himself and she had done nothing to prevent it? Did she want his life as well as Kathleen's on her conscience? She never had an opportunity to help Kathleen but she could help Ray now. She wouldn't have another death on her hands.

Joy sullenly stepped inside Ray's house. Take-away food scraps lay on the coffee table, clothes were strewn on the well-padded brown sofa, and what appeared to beer stained the shagpile carpet.

The stench of beer mixed in with spirits and cigarettes permeated the air and she had to block her nose. How could he live in this pigsty?

Her heart pounded when she looked into the kitchen. A round table had been set with two plates, cutlery, glasses, and a candle centrepiece. Was this the amends he was proposing? A romantic dinner?

On the walls above the TV were three photos of a beautiful woman in various poses. Was this his ex-girlfriend? The one Edward had mentioned he had trouble getting over? The woman bore a strong resemblance to Joy. Chills ran down her spine as she realised he must have obsessed over her because of his ex-girlfriend. She had to get out of here.

Ray approached. "How about a drink?"

She lifted her shoulders. "I think you've had enough to drink. Why don't you go to bed? I wanted to make sure you were okay. That's why I'm here." She paused. "Did you mean it when you said you would kill yourself?"

He chuckled. "Of course not. I'm too gutless to do such a thing."

Her spine prickled with fear. "So you lied? Why?"

Ray shrugged then grimaced. His eyes scanned her from head to toe. "You are beautiful, Joy."

She could smell the beer on his breath as he drew closer. Joy took a step back, feeling stupid for falling for his trick. "You're drunk. I'll be going now. Go to bed and sleep it off." She walked to the door, almost bumping into a floral vase on the coffee table nearby. It looked homemade.

A strong arm pulled her back and she gasped at his strength. His grip hurt her. Twisting and struggling to gain purchase on the damp floor, Joy tried to pull away. "Let me go, Ray."

He spun her around to face him and his free hand trailed down to her breast, circling it, but she elbowed him in his stomach. His grip loosened and he moaned. "You bitch! Come here."

Joy ran for the door, but he yanked her ponytail. Her scalp stung and she clawed at his hands. He turned her around, pulled her face roughly towards him and plunged his tongue deep inside her mouth. Gagging, she pushed him away, but his strength outmatched hers. Lifting her knee, she kicked him hard in the groin and he crumpled. She made it back to the door, but he recovered quickly and reached for her again, tearing the back of her shirt as he threw her down and pinned her to the floor.

"Oh, come on, Mary. I know you still want me. Remember the videos we made. The amazing foreplay and sex we always had."

Mary? Joy twisted her around as he lay on top of her, his weight squashing the air out of her lungs. His lips trailed around her neck as she felt him harden. No. Not like this. Not this!

As his hands fumbled with the button of her jeans, she palmed his face and pushed. His head jerked back and his weight eased off her chest. She sucked in air desperately, but she knew he wouldn't stop unless she took drastic action.

Aiming for his eyes, she gouged her fingers into his sockets and he screamed. "Bitch!" The few seconds when he reared back and onto his knees, rubbing his eyes, bought her the precious seconds she needed. Joy crawled towards the coffee table. Wrapping a hand around the vase, Joy swung out her right arm and hit him hard across his shoulder and cheek. He fell back, his head thumping against the edge of the couch. Blood pooled in a small stain on the carpet, the iron tang making her sick. She had to get out of here before he recovered. Fighting unsteady legs, Joy clambered to her feet, made her way to the door, ran to her car and dove inside, slamming the door and locking it. Bowing over the steering wheel, she sobbed and trembled vio lently.

Edward decided to visit Ray for pure peace of mind, having arrived and parking at the kerb. He spotted a car he recognised parked across the street from Ray's. As he stepped out of his own car his phone buzzed. When he saw the name on the display he reached for the phone and lifted it to his ear. "Joy, what's wrong?" He heard deep breaths. "Joy, are you okay?"

"No, I'm not." Her voice cracked and her sobbing and gasping breaths were a knife to his chest. "Are you ... ? Are you behind me? Did you just pull up?"

"Yes. Yes. I'm here. What's wrong?"

The line went dead.

"Joy?"

When her car door opened, he rushed out and to her. Her eyes were puffy and bruised and her cheeks red. The shirt she wore was tattered and loosely hung on her shoulders. She turned away for a second to look back at Ray's house and he saw the back of her shirt had been torn, and angry red claw marks scraped down her exposed skin. Rage brewed inside his chest. Wide-eyed, she trembled as she looked back at him. Whoever had hurt Joy, they would pay. Reaching for her, he wrapped his arms around her, caressing the back of her head. "I'm here. Are you all right? What happened? Who did this to you?"

They pulled apart, and her bottom lip trembled as she said the words that shattered his world. "It's Ray. I think he's ... I think I killed him. He hit his head on the couch. I didn't mean to, but he was ..."

Edward grabbed her by the hand. Ray had been drunk. Could he have tried to hurt her? Was Ray really that type of man? His own brother? "Wait in the car. Let me check. Give me a few minutes." He watched until she was safely in her car, his heart breaking in two. All he wanted to do was comfort her, but first, he had to check on his brother. Gritting his teeth, he stormed towards the house.

Opening the door, Edward stopped short at the scene before him. Ray's bloody face smeared the carpet red. His legs lay at an awkward angle at the edge of the couch. Shards of the vase Ray had gotten from his ex-girlfriend spread out around the floor. Closing the distance between them, Edward went to his brother's side. Kneeling, he placed his hands around his wrist and felt a pulse. "Thank God." Edward sighed. He checked underneath his head for any sign of blood, but there wasn't any.

When Ray roused from slumber, he jolted at seeing Edward hovering over him. "What the fuck, man? What ...? What are you doing here?"

"What the hell did you do to Joy?"

Ray put his hand over his head. "What? Who?" Edward's nose curled at Ray's yeasty breath.

"I am calling the ambulance. He retrieved his phone and made the 000 call." Joy mentioned he'd hit his head so the hospital would need to check for injuries. When the dispatcher ended the call, he tried again. "Did you hurt Joy?" But before he could get a response, Ray's eyes rolled back and he fell unconscious again.

Hurrying to the bathroom, Edward retrieved a small towel from the cupboard, dampened it with warm water, and wiped Ray's blood from his shoulder and cheek. "Wake up. The ambulance will be here shortly."

He moaned.

Hefting his weight with an arm behind his back, Edward propped him on to the couch.

Edward was ashamed and disgusted at what his brother had done. How could Ray keep drinking and live with hurting others and himself? He didn't think he could control his anger with his brother any longer. Edward needed to get out of there.

Closing the front door, Edward jogged across the street to Joy's car. Entering the passenger door, he took her hand and caressed it. "Are you all right?"

She hesitated and stared ahead. "I will be. How is Ray?"

"He was talking and will recover. I have called the ambulance and will need to wait until they get here. What happened?" He had to get Joy's account of the incident. Ray's version, too, when he was sober. What was Joy doing here?

She shook her head. "Listen. We'll talk about this later. Right now, you should focus on Ray." Even when she'd been hurt, she was still thinking of others. He couldn't believe she cared about Ray after this. But it was the kind of person Joy was, caring for others more than she cared for herself. He saw that now. He loved this woman with a passion. She pressed her lips together and touched him on the arm. "I made the mistake of coming here. I shouldn't have. I'm sorry."

Edward's heart ached. Pulling himself towards her, again he wrapped his arms around her. "I am not going anywhere, Joy. But I need to know what happened. I need to know everything. Please?"

Joy stared straight ahead as if preparing herself for the truth. "He rang to invite me over for dinner but I refused. He didn't listen because he texted me his address in case I changed my mind. He sounded out of sorts on the phone, depressed. I thought about it and wondered if he would hurt himself. I was worried, so I called you and when you didn't answer I came over. He opened the door and I could see he was drunk and didn't plan to kill himself. But when I decided to leave, he threatened to hurt himself outright. I thought that if I didn't make sure he was alright and he got hurt, I would never forgive myself. I already don't forgive myself over what happened with Kathleen. If I could have helped ... When I went inside his house, he ... he ... he tried to rape me. He called me Mary. I tried to fight him off but he was too strong. The vase was there and I hit him. I am so sorry for hurting him, Edward, but he would have raped me."

Bile rose in his throat. He wanted to kill his brother with his bare hands. How could he do such a thing? It was terrifying to know that Ray was capable of such a crime. How could she go through such abuse from his own brother? He was ashamed of him and realised that this was the last straw. Edward had to report him to the police as that was the only way Ray would take responsibility for his actions.

Scanning her eyes, he reached for her hand and stroked her hair. He wished he'd got here sooner. "I am sorry, Joy. I cannot believe he would do that to you. Are you hurt?"

She pulled away. "Only a few grazes and bruises. I'll live."

"You need to report him. He can't get away with this. I will go with you."

Joy shook her head. "No, let's forget this ever happened. He was drunk and not in his right mind."

Edward scoffed. "He knew enough about what he was doing. He cannot get away with this. He needs to take responsibility for his drinking before he hurts someone else, or worse, hurts you again." If only he had pushed him harder to get help. It was partly his fault that Joy got hurt. If only he had answered her call. If only he had dragged Ray to rehab and left him there. If only Edward had done something sooner, Joy might never have faced this.

"Let me sleep on it, Edward. I am so tired I cannot think straight."

He nodded. "Come here."

She hesitated then inched closer to him with only one arm around him. He embraced her tightly over the console, the wetness of her tears falling against the side of his neck. He patted the back of her head and breathed in her scent of flowers and soap. But she shifted away from his embrace and pulled away too soon. Did she not want to be touched by him? After what happened, she was obviously in shock and he understood that she might not want to be touched.

"Do you want me to come with you to your place?"

"No!" Joy said loudly. "No," she said again quietly. "I'll be fine."

"Then come back to my place. I can make sure you're taken care of and safe."

She shook her head and leaned away from him. "I'm fine Edward. I'm going to gather my composure and go home."

Edward nodded. "Okay but I'm checking in with you tomorrow, and you call me if you need anything."

How would he have lived with his brother if things had got worse? What if Joy hadn't hit him with the vase? He truly had no idea who his brother was. He was a stranger.

Chapter Twenty

CUTTING TIES

Edward followed George onto the worksite while Ray drilled holes into a plank of wood on a commercial building site. The site was filled with the roar of a chainsaw, the whirring of drills, and the shuffling of footsteps as tradesmen shouted instructions to each other. Edward stepped over gravel, flicking up stones and debris with each stride.

Ray stopped drilling and looked up at them. He spoke to a fellow workmate. "Can you finish this? Gotta see what these guys want." The man nodded.

"What's going on, George?" He avoided looking at Edward.

"We need to talk privately," said George.

He nodded. Ray led them to the portable building on site, climbing the stairs and dropping into a chair at a table. There was a sink with dirty dishes, linoleum flooring, a mini fridge, and four other chairs surrounding the table. "What's this about?"

Edward rested his arms on the table, waiting for George. Edward glared, fighting back his need to pound his fists into him. He had the audacity to show up here like nothing happened. Like he didn't attack one of their coworkers and jeopardize their contract. Like he didn't hurt Joy. "George has something to tell you."

George leaned forward. "I need to let you go, Ray. It's not working out."

Ray's face paled. "What the fuck? What do you mean?"

"We've given you warnings and you keep making the same mistakes: hammering the wrong pieces together, leaving a mess where your workmates have slipped, drinking on the job, coming to work drunk, and humiliating yourself in front of clients. It has to stop."

Ray stared at Edward, squinting, then turned to George again. "You can't be serious? I'm a good worker and I'm here today doing my damn job. Please don't do this. We have a few contracts to finish."

George frowned. "Sorry, Ray, but until you get your act together, you can't be here. Take your things and go home."

Ray pressed his lips together. "Edward, please. Don't let him do this. You know me. I've always been a great worker. I will stop the alcohol. I promise."

Edward averted his eyes. "It's done, Ray."

"No, I refuse to leave. You can't make me."

George shook his head. "Of course I can make you. I've got a security guard on speed dial if you don't get your arse off these premises in the next half-hour. You can go quietly or you can be forced off the site. Your choice."

Ray's hands fidgeted, then he bowed his head. "This is about Joy, isn't it?"

"What did you expect? After what you did to her, you don't deserve this job or anything else for that matter. I don't know you anymore, Ray."

"Go get your things and leave," said George.

Ray threw his hands in the air with a contorted expression on his face. He got up and walked outside, leaving them sitting on the table.

George turned to Edward. "Okay, I did what you asked. What the hell happened with Joy?"

"He attacked Joy last night because she doesn't want him. He asked her out but she shut him down. I can't forgive him, George. He would have raped her if she hadn't hit him with a vase."

George nodded. "Jesus, Eddie. I am sorry, man. Who would have thought he'd hurt Joy, particularly when he knows you like her? She's involved in one of your current projects. They could sue us, and his actions could destroy us. If you hadn't asked me to do this, I'd do it now that I know."

"I never told him in so many words but he knows. What he did is unforgivable, whether he was drunk or not. After the ambulance came to pick him up that night, I couldn't bring myself to visit him at the hospital or answer his call this morning when they let him out. I am surprised he showed up. I am done with him."

"I understand. You did the right thing here. He has to learn from his mistakes. I can't believe he did something like that." He sighed. "You up to telling me the whole story?" Edward explained what had happened. The state he found her in. He called this morning but she didn't answer. He hoped she was recovering. "My goodness, Eddie. No wonder you want him to suffer this way. I would've punched his damn lights out."

"I still want to hit him but what would it accomplish?" He squared his shoulders. "Let's check on Ray and ensure he's off the premises."

George patted him on the shoulder. "Sure, mate."

Edward sighed with relief at having saved the others from Ray's antics. It was safer to keep him at home until he got help for his drinking. He needed to make sure Ray actually went home.

After speaking with a client, two hours later, Edward stood at the front door of Ray's house and rang the doorbell. Edward needed to be clear about their boundaries. He needed to cut ties with him.

His chest constricted and he could barely breathe as he realised that he would no longer have a brother, but he couldn't recognise the person Ray had become.

When Ray opened the door, he already had alcohol on his breath. "Hi Eddie."

Edward pushed his way inside, noticing a few boxes with kitchen items stacked inside. A suitcase rested near the sofa. "Are you going somewhere?"

Ray nodded. "I thought I'd go back to England for a few weeks. At least while things die down around here."

Edward couldn't believe his brother was taking the easy way out. "Are you serious right now? You are running away. It's a cop out. What about making amends for what you did to Joy and getting help? How about realising the huge mistake you made?" He sneered. "I am disgusted by what you did, Ray. Explain it to me like I'm a five-year-old. I don't even know you anymore. Why did you do it?"

Ray remained tight-lipped. "You tried to rape Joy. Was it because she rejected you?"

Ray held his head down and shuffled his feet. "I'm sorry, man. I wasn't in my right mind and I had a bit too much to drink."

"Do you think?" Edward leaned in close to his brother's face, leering. "Stop calling me. You and me are done. Do you hear that? Done. I no longer have a brother." Ray's face paled and for the first time in a long while, Edward didn't care how his brother felt. He had no desire to help his brother anymore. It was time he stood on his own two feet. "I have bailed you out of fights, drunken states, police arrests, and I am tired of it. I cannot do this anymore. Hurting Joy was the last straw. It is time you grew up, Ray ."

"Please man. I promise to get help. I wasn't in my right mind. I never would have hurt Joy. Please, Eddie. You're all I've got. I know you told George to cut me off the contracts. I barely have other work as it is."

"It is what you deserve, and more. You need to pay for what you did to Joy."

Ray stared at his hands, nodding. "Fine, Eddie. I'll get help and show you I can change. I promise."

"I have heard that before countless times and I don't believe you." Edward stepped back. "From this day forward, I do not have a brother. Don't call me, don't visit me. I don't exist for you and you don't exist for me. I am ashamed of you. You're a rapist."

Ray stared at the floor and took deep breaths. "I am not a rapist."

Edward threaded his hands through his hair and paced the living room floor, bumping his foot into a box. "Damn."

Ray wrung his hands. "Don't do this, man. Please. Have a heart. We've been through a lot of shit together. You can't disown me like this. I have no-one. Literally no-one in my life."

Edward shook his head. "You should've thought about that before you hurt an innocent woman. You do need help but it will no longer be from me." His brother averted his eyes. "You are lucky she didn't report you to either the police or her boss." He scoffed. "I thought you were better than Mum and Dad, but you are exactly like them. No, worse. Only out for yourself and not caring about anyone else."

"Listen, man. I thought she might have grown to like me. I swear when I kissed her at the beach, it was like she was kissing me back. I was sure of it. But then she didn't want anything to do with me. I must have misunderstood. I thought there was a chance."

Edward lost his breath. What kiss? "You're lying."

"No, it's true. I kissed her because I cared for her. Still do, but she wasn't interested. I apologised for it too."

"How very generous of you. Please leave Joy and me alone." Edward stormed out of the house without turning back.

It was time to start a new chapter in his life, one not involving his brother. As far as he was concerned, he was an only child.

Chapter
Twenty-One

MORNING
AFTER

B ack at the housing project, Joy jotted down measurements in her notepad and scrutinised the imagined area between the bed and other furniture pieces. She envisioned the space and the positioning of each piece of furniture in the room, knowing that the bedroom suite would be delivered today.

She walked to the window with a slouched posture and stared outside, not focusing on anything in particular. She had cleaned herself up, ignored Edward's two calls, gone to bed, and then come here first thing in the morning. The work distracted her from reliving being attacked by Ray. If he wasn't Edward's brother, she would have reported him to the police and to Lian.

Through the large window, she spotted Thomas coming up the walk. She made her way to the entrance and opened the door. "Hi Thomas. What brings you by?" She ushered him inside and they walked over into the kitchen. Joy rested her hands against the recently delivered oblong table.

He lay a catalogue on the table. "The reason I'm here is that June and Richard wanted these marked furniture pieces for the other two bedrooms. They'd like your opinion as to whether these pieces would fit." It was a catalogue from an online store showcasing a Queen size designer hydraulic bed, matching bedside tables, an armoire, and a set of padded chairs for the dining area.

Joy nodded. "I think the bed is a great idea. Good for storage and decluttering. The armoire might suit their daughter's taste too. I can look into these, make enquiries, and get back to them." She picked it up and scanned through it.

Thomas stared at her. "Something is wrong. Are you all right?"

Joy's chest felt heavy. She couldn't rehash the incident. Why put the problem onto him? "I am fine. Just tired."

She forced a smile and changed the subject. "Has Richard been behaving?"

He took a step towards her, scanning the kitchen area. "Working with Richard has its challenges to say the least. I can't complain, Joy. He pays me well to manage his affairs and finances."

"Hmm. I know that's your way of saying he's a bad boss to work for, but you're too kind to admit it."

He laughed. "You could be right. But don't spread that around."

"At least once this house is done, you can work with your other clients. Do you have many?"

He nodded. "I have a few." He took a breath. "When we get this house done, I'll have more time on other projects." He rested his hands on the island counter. "I must say you know your design. The house isn't even finished and it looks great."

She wished she could ask him more about Richard instead of focusing on herself, but she kept tight-lipped. "Thanks. I couldn't imagine doing anything else other than my best."

He beamed, showing his bright, glossy white teeth. "It is important to do what you love. We all need meaning and purpose."

Joy nodded. "I couldn't agree you with more."

"Anyway, I had better get back to work. I'm meeting Richard for lunch. Did you want to go for a movie or dinner tonight? You could share what's bothering you in a more private place if you need someone to listen."

Not knowing how to reply to that, she ignored his question. "Richard has gone all out for his daughter, buying this amazing home for her."

Thomas smiled. "He has his quirks but Richard is an amazing businessman. He would do anything for his daughter."

"That's good."

He put up a hand. "About dinner?"

She shook her head. "Raincheck? I'm feeling a bit tired and not up to going out."

"Of course. I had better go." He turned towards the door.

Someone knocked. "Joy, are you there?"

She stood transfixed in her spot. "No," she whispered. Why was he here? "He isn't supposed to be here."

Edward had texted that Ray no longer worked with them and had been fired from his contracting jobs. He asked her to report Ray again but Joy just wanted to move on. If he tried to hurt her again, she wouldn't think twice about going to the police this time.

Thomas touched her tenderly on the shoulder. "You look pale. Are you all right? Should I get rid of him?" Joy nodded. Thomas opened the door slightly and walked out front, closing the door firmly behind him. She could see and hear everything through the window. "Hi Ray. Listen, Joy is not here. You can leave."

"Of course she is. Her car's here. I know she doesn't want to see me but I need to talk to her." Thomas blocked his way as he attempted to push past him. "Get out of my way, man." The front door swung open, and her heart raced as Ray made his way inside.

Thomas re-entered and blocked him again. "You're not supposed to be here," he echoed her words earlier.

Joy squared her shoulders and levelled her gaze at Ray, appearing as confident as she could even if she didn't feel it. "Please leave."

"I don't know what this is about, Ray, but Joy doesn't want to see you. She told you to leave," Thomas said.

Ray didn't budge, shaking his head. "No, this is not your business. You can leave if you like but I'm not going anywhere."

Thomas shook his head, his eyes dark. "Leave."

Ray put up his hand. "Please let me explain. Just give me five minutes, then I'll leave."

"It's fine, Thomas." Despite her words, Thomas didn't move. She glared at Ray, steeling herself. "What do you want?"

"I am here to apologise. I don't even remember anything, but you have to realise I was drunk. I wouldn't normally behave that way."

Thomas inched closer to Ray. "What the hell did you do?"

Ray snorted. "This is none of your damn business, Thomas. I don't care if you two are dating or friends or whatever. This is between Joy and me."

Thomas turned to Joy. "I will make him leave if you like. Say the word."

Ray waved him away, taking a step around Thomas and closer to Joy. She stepped back, putting distance between them again. "I am not going to hurt you. Please accept my apology. Please."

Thomas shoved him. "You hurt Joy?"

"It is none of your damn business, Thomas. Why don't you leave?" Ray snarled.

Joy exhaled. "You gave your apology so now leave." Her stomach churned at the idea that he would continue hassling her.

Thomas scoffed. "You need to leave, Ray. Respect Joy's wishes."

Joy stepped back on shaky legs. "Ray if you don't leave, I will report you to the police."

"You heard the lady," said Thomas.

Ray punched him in the shoulder. "Fuck you, man. You're not a part of this. Besides, I didn't intend to hurt her. I was missing my girlfriend."

Thomas moved between them again, his voice low and icy. "What did you do?"

Ray ignored Thomas. "Just tell me you forgive me, Joy."

She took a deep breath and lied. "Fine, I forgive you, but you need help with your drinking. Now, can you please go?"

Ray glanced at Thomas, shaking his head. Thomas's hands were balled into fists. The last thing they all needed was a fight on the job site. Finally, he walked to the door and disappeared down the path.

Her hands were shaking. With a warm caress, Thomas squeezed her shoulder. "It's okay. He's gone now."

She gave him a reassuring smile. "Thanks, Thomas. I appreciate you supporting me."

Thomas pulled her into an embrace. "If you need to talk about this, I am here."

Joy's heart warmed. "It's fine. I will get over it, but thanks."

Thomas pulled away. "I can reschedule my lunch with Richard. I am happy to stay and make sure he doesn't bother you again."

She shook her head. "No, you go. I will leave too and go back to the office in case he decides to come back. Thanks anyway."

Thomas nodded. "Are you sure you don't want to talk about what happened with Ray?" She shook her head. "Okay. No pressure but you take care of yourself. If you change your mind, please ring me."

"I will. Thanks again." Joy was thankful he'd been here when Ray barged in.

Back at the office, Joy sat in the staffroom talking to Lian. "I cannot believe he was suspected of murdering a prostitute. It's all over the news."

"I actually can believe it." Joy clutched her mug of steaming coffee. All she wanted to do was forget, but it seemed that the universe was conspiring to keep putting Ray in front of her. The staffroom had been crowded, filled with murmuring when she arrived as a news story reported that Ray had been arrested on Saturday and released due to lack of evidence forty-eight hours later.

Lian tilted her head and asked, "What do you mean?"

Joy hesitated. If she shared with Lian what had happened it could put Edward's job at risk. But Lian was also her friend. "He attacked me last night."

"What?" Lian stood up.

"Promise you won't let it affect our contract with Edward's company? Ray's already been fired this morning." Lian nodded so Joy told her a shortened overview of what happened.

Lian leaned forward and wrapped her arms around Joy. "Oh, honey, why didn't you tell me this morning? You should have taken the day off."

She swallowed and pulled away. "I am sorry, Lian. I should have told you but I didn't want to worry you or risk our contract with Edward. I just wanted to work and move on."

They sat on seats opposite each other. "How are you doing now?"

Joy shrugged. "I am still processing it but I feel bad for Edward. It's his brother, you know?" Joy sipped on a glass of water. "I feel as if it's surreal. I cannot imagine what it would be like if Jesse got arrested."

Lian tapped her fingers on the table. "Jesse would never hurt anyone, but Ray tried to rape you, Joy. All because you rejected him. He wanted to hurt you as much as you hurt him."

"I know, but something still doesn't feel right."

Lian picked at her nail. "Of course not. You were attacked. He obviously has violent tendencies that could escalate to the murder of a prostitute. Luckily, you escaped when you could."

"I know." She lifted her shoulders. "Who would have thought someone related to Edward could be so vile?"

Lian leaned forward. "I know you care for Edward, Joy, and I understand your need to have space but he might need your support. I know you two are close friends now and I'm not blind to the way he looks at you."

Joy nodded. "Maybe. We talked about it. He made it clear that he's not interested in a relationship and jeopardizing our contract."

Lian got up and refilled her glass of water. She sat back down to unwrap her sandwich. "Edward is very professional and that's good for work. Not great for you. Maybe after the project is done in a few weeks you can pursue something? After what is happening with Ray, it must be a shock for Edward too." She tilted her head.

"Yeah. I need to get back to work."

Lian nodded. "Me too, but if you want to leave early, please do."

Having worked through a full day, Joy was exhausted and wanted nothing more than to rest. The knock on the door delayed that plan. She went out and closed the door behind her, standing in front of the house. Her parents were inside and she wasn't in the headspace to introduce Edward to them or answer their million questions. "Hi Edward."

He frowned. "Hi. How are you feeling?"

She shrugged. "I'm fine but not really up to company today. Sorry."

Edward placed his hands in his pockets and looked past her for a moment, as if measuring his words. "I want you to know that Ray has left and he won't be bothering you again."

Joy jolted. "Left? But he came by the house this afternoon and wanted to apologise. I'm lucky Thomas was there to support me."

Edward's face drained of all colour. "I told him to leave you alone and he ignores me yet again. Why am I not surprised?"

"He must have come just after you spoke to him. Where did he go?"

"He said he plans to return to England. I have cut all ties with him, Joy." He gave her a reassuring smile. "I wish you had told me he kissed you at the beach. I know you turned him away."

She gasped. It wasn't her plan to tell him as she didn't want to cause conflict, but no doubt Ray must have told him. "I didn't want to cause problems between you two. Besides, I made it clear there would be nothing between us." He stared at the ground and Joy instantly felt guilty. "I'm sorry about his arrest. It was on the news in the breakroom."

"Thanks but like I said, we cut ties. I didn't think he was capable of something like that but now ..."

Edward shrugged and toed at the ground.

"I need to put this behind me, Edward. I'd like to offer you my support. You made it clear we need to keep our relationship professional. I can't do this today, relive everything. I just need to rest. Please. Do you mind leaving?"

His brow furrowed. "I am here for you Joy. I ... I care. Please don't shut me out. Let's talk about this." He reached for her and caressed her cheek but she moved back against the door.

She steeled herself against the softness of his touch and the sadness in his eyes. "I appreciate that but my head is spinning right now. I can't think straight. Ray's attack was just too much on top of everything. I can't talk about any of this if we're to be professional. I'm sorry."

He nodded, silent for a minute. "I am sorry too. For my brother."

"I have to go."

He walked back with a stooped posture. "I understand."

She turned around and rushed inside, leaning against the door and staring at the floor.

Her mother looked at her wide-eyed and rose from the couch. "Joy, what's wrong. Has something happened? Who were you talking to?"

"No-one," said Joy. She was about to walk to her room and had her head bowed when her father's voice alerted her.

"Don't you speak to your mother that way, Joy. What happened to you?"

She turned around and shook her head, anger rising at the judgement in his voice. "As if you two even care. Don't pretend to care now when you didn't care about me after Mia died. It's too late now."

Her mother inched closer towards her and reached out, but Joy stepped back. "What? We've always cared about you, Joy. Always."

"Get back here and talk to us. We don't appreciate your tone, young lady," said her father.

She laughed. "My tone? Wow. Here I am talking about my sister and you care about my tone. You blamed me for her death all these years, and you still both hate me."

Her mother's eyes dampened. "No, Joy. It's not true. Please hear our side."

She shook her head, rushed to her bedroom, ignoring the dark looks of her parents. Pushing her body back against the closed door of her room, she leaned hard against it, and cried.

The next day, Joy stepped into the police station feeling weighed down with an aching heart as she thought about Edward and how despondent he'd appeared. As much as she cared for him, she needed time and space to process what had happened.

Octavia had called her into the station but had been cryptic about the reason, mentioning only that it had something to do with Ray. What had he done now? Wasn't the man always in trouble? Besides, hadn't Edward mentioned that he was leaving the country?

She greeted the young policeman at the counter. "Hi, I am here to see Detective Senior Sergeant Marco Petrazini."

He nodded. "Sure. Please take a seat. He will be with you shortly."

Joy sat on her hands, glancing briefly at the people sitting in chairs and staring into space. She retrieved her phone again and scanned the display. A part of her was hoping for a message from Edward, but nothing. What did she expect when she kind of told him she needed space?

Marco approached ten minutes later. "Hey, Joy. Come on through." He walked down a narrow corridor through other cubicles and closed offices while staff mingled and worked at their desks.

She sat inside a bare room with four chairs around a square table in front of a small window letting in subtle light. "What is this about?"

Before he could respond, the door opened and in came Octavia, her wedged heels clacking against the floor. She smiled reassuringly, as if she'd had bad news. She took a seat beside Marco and inched the chair closer to the table. Her sharp, red manicured nails tapped briefly on the surface.

"Hi Joy. I appreciate you coming in." She faced Marco briefly then turned back to Joy. "We have questions about Ray."

Joy's head angled, her throat turning dry. "Why the sudden interest in Ray?" Did Edward go behind her back and report him?

Octavia stared at Marco as if they were communicating in code. She leaned forward and squeezed Joy's hand briefly. "We questioned Edward and he explained how Ray had attacked you in his home. Speaking as a friend, why didn't you tell us?"

Joy's hands sweated, a chill sliding down her back. "I couldn't. I ... I did it for Edward, not for him. I know Ray needs help and ..." She threaded her hands through her hair and bowed. "I didn't want this coming out. I just wanted to move on. Why did Edward tell you?"

Marco intervened. "Joy, I know you have heard about these local murders."

Joy nodded. "Sure, and I witnessed the aftermath of one of them, not to mention how two of these murders occurred to places I've been to. It's creepy."

Marco continued, shuffling through papers in a manila folder. "We believe there's a serial killer lurking out there, and we wanted you to be on your guard. Edward had no choice but to tell us." He took a breath. "Another thing

..." He faced Octavia then turned back to her. "The latest woman was found behind your office building."

Joy's hair lifted on the nape and her arms and hands became instantly clammy. "Jesus. It's at least the third time these women are being dumped in places I've been to. It can't be a coincidence."

Octavia's eyes softened. "We need to be honest about this case for your safety, but we also need to question you about Ray and the incident."

"What did Ray do?"

Octavia leaned back in her seat. "You may have heard on the news, Ray is a suspect in the murder of a prostitute."

Joy flinched. "Are you saying he's the serial killer?"

Marco curled a brow. "We are not saying that, but he we have some evidence against him for at least this murder. If you want to press charges, we'd support you, Joy."

Joy clasped her hands, facing Octavia. "Why are we always a target for these loonies, Octavia? Ray got violent with me while he was drunk but I didn't think he'd murder someone. Not that there's much of a gap between violence and murder, but no. Edward must be shocked."

Octavia's eyes darkened. "I know this is hard, but we need to ask you about the night of the incident. If this wasn't important, we wouldn't be asking, but we need details. I am sorry, Joy."

Joy nodded. "I understand." She closed her eyes and rested back in her chair, planting her feet firmly on the ground. If Ray was truly a murderer, she had to put her emotions aside and detach herself from the event.

Marco put aside the manila folder and pulled out a notebook from his jacket. "Take your time. I know this isn't easy but it is important. Not only so he doesn't hurt you again but for other women too."

"Okay," she said, exhaling. As she recounted the story of that night, Octavia moved her chair around to Joy's side and placed a gentle hand on her shoulder.

By the end of her story, Marco put away his notebook. "Thanks, Joy. I promise you he will not hurt you again. But this should have been reported."

"I am sorry but I was thinking of Edward and I just wanted it all to go away." Joy fought back tears. Octavia moved back to her position, opposite her. "Do you think he murdered these other women?"

Octavia pressed her lips together before replying. "We can't say at this stage."

Octavia stared at her hands. "We are looking into it further, but this serial killer appears to be someone who likes to exert control and manipulate women into submission. A narcissist who likes to break people down, bit by bit. Someone who gets excited by people's grief, pain, and suffering. A person who has no empathy, no humanity, and no remorse when he decides to murder and torture these women. He hopes not to get caught so he can continue to fulfil his warped fantasies."

Joy's body stilled as she wondered if Edward was even aware his brother might be a murderer.

Chapter Twenty-Two

GREAT MINDS

The next day, Joy sat inside a restaurant at the Docklands with her group of friends. Sitting near a large window with a view of the rippled water and Bolte bridge, she sipped a cafe latte attempting to relax and forget her troubles. Edward had been on her mind so she resorted to sending him a text message to check in with him about reporting Ray. At least he replied to one of them, telling her he was fine and had done what needed to be done. In spite of them not being in a relationship they were still friends.

Munching on a Caesar salad, Joy put aside her uneasiness and laughed at how Jamie glowed after talking about her upcoming engagement party. "I can't wait for your party. So exciting."

Jamie's eyes lit up. "I have found myself an amazing man. I fall in love with him more each day."

Liz squeezed her friend's shoulder. "Angelo is quite the catch. Have you got everything organised for the engagement party?"

She nodded. "It's all organised."

Gabriella leaned in. "Are you having a long engagement?"

Jamie's eyes lit up. "Definitely not. We haven't made a date yet but it could be within less than a year. It depends on the availability of reception centres."

Camilla rubbed her hands. "Oh, how beautiful, Jamie. I am envious."

Claudia winked at Jamie. "I am glad he turned me down when I first flirted with him. He was in love with you from the very beginning."

Jamie laughed. "I am sorry about that but I am sure your man is out there, Claudia."

Liz intervened. "Who would not want a beautiful, intelligent woman like you, girl? You hang in there."

Claudia put up her hands. "Hey, I never said I wanted a man. I am fine on my own, thank you very much."

Octavia gave her friend a reassuring smile. "I know we both have men out there waiting to be saved by us. But with my long shifts, I doubt I'd have time to go out with a man once, let alone have a relationship."

Claudia sighed. "You make the time, woman."

Bella stared at everyone around the room. "I have news, too." The group waited as she paused for effect. "I'm pregnant."

Joy burst from her seat and hugged her tightly. "Oh, congrats, Bella. That is great news." She pulled away when the others wished her well too. "How far along are you?"

"I'm two months but so far so good. Marco's ecstatic and cannot wait to be a father."

Camilla said, "It is a true joy to have a child, Bella. If you need any tips, I'm your woman. I can't wait for Mariana to have a play buddy too."

Bella's eyes lit up. "Thanks, Camilla. I'll hold you to that, but it's still a while to go."

"Was it planned?" Liz asked.

Bella nodded. "It was. We were both ready and we're not getting any younger. But with our careers, it will be a challenge. I only have Marco's mother to rely on. It's not like my mother was ever mother of the year." She became wistful.

Joy gave her a reassuring smile. "I'm sorry about your mother, Bella. But you have all of us as potential babysitters." The others agreed.

Bella forced her own smile back. "I don't want to be a downer but how are you doing with Edward and Ray?"

Joy shrugged, remaining silent.

Octavia clasped her wine glass. "I know it has been traumatising but if ever you want to talk, we're all here."

Joy leaned back in her chair. "Thanks, Octavia." She looked to Bella and the others. "I know you guys are there for me, and I appreciate it, but I am still trying to get my head around all of this. Plus, we got the last delivery today and by end of the day tomorrow, the project will be done. I feel guilty about being so relieved about that but I'm happy it's over. There are just too many complications and I need a break."

Claudia dug into her creamy steak and wiped off crumbs around her chin. "Understandable. Is there anything we can do for you?"

"No, thanks, Claudia. I'll be fine."

"When was the last time you saw Edward?" asked Liz.

She swallowed. "Yesterday. He stopped going to the housing project and is working virtually for now."

"What about Thomas?" Liz said.

"I broke up with him last week." She turned to Octavia. "I know you most likely can't say but I still need to ask. Do you guys have any leads on those other murders?"

Octavia leaned forward. "Not really, but if we did I couldn't tell you, Joy. We will find out who did this, don't worry. If this relates to you, we have your back."

Joy pursed her lips. "I know you do. But with these murders, don't you think it's strange that three of the murders occurred where I've been? Do you think it's a message?"

Octavia stared into her drink and took a quick sip of her wine. "I want you to look after yourself. After what happened with Ray and what you witnessed at the park, you need time to process. Focus on your self-care."

Jamie added, "Take it one step at a time. The police are still investigating. As Octavia mentioned, you need to take care of yourself and give your mind a break from all this. It is traumatising to say the least."

"You're right. Let's talk about something positive. I don't want to be morbid," said Joy.

The idea of facing her parents again stopped her from returning home. That afternoon, Joy rested her hands in her lap as she bowed her head, sitting on a hard bench at Williamstown Beach.

The cool wind cut against her cheeks as she watched the carefree passersby strolling alongside the shore, sunbathing, or huddling in groups loud with banter or laughter. Coming to the beach soothed her, and today she needed time and space to work through her situation with Edward. She really liked him. She yearned to wrap her arms around him and caress his cheeks and reassure him he'd be all right. But he made it clear he wanted nothing to do with her.

She spotted Ariana walk past. Joy rose and walked after her. "Ariana, wait."

Ariana turned with her brow raised. "Oh, hello, Joy. This is a surprise." She stood awkwardly with her arms hanging by her side and her posture drooping. Her eyes looked tired and dark.

"Come and sit with me."

Ariana hesitated but then broke into a smile. "Okay, but I can't stay long. I have to meet a friend." She sat on the bench beside Joy and texted on her phone. "Sorry. I need to text her, telling her I'll be a few minutes late."

Joy shifted, happy that Ariana appeared to be a bit more relaxed, but she still had bags under her eyes like she hadn't slept in a while. "That's great you're going out again. How are things?"

She shrugged. "Getting there slowly. I still ... aah ... work at the cafe. Nothing much is new. How about you?"

Joy didn't want to burden Ariana with everything so she decided to keep to the positive. "I'm loving my work. We've almost finished decorating a housing project and the clients love it so far."

"I admire your skill. I wish I had a skill like that but it's too late to learn. I should have gone to university a few years ago. It's too late now." Ariana stared at her fingernails, pressing against the cuticles.

Joy exhaled, wondering when being twenty-eight was considered too late for study. "It is never too late to learn. What are you passionate about?"

Ariana shrugged, gazing towards the sea and at passersby, gripping her bag strap as if she was ready to leave. "I only want to be happy, you know? Truly happy." She turned towards her. "I can't remember the last time ..."

"The last time what?" asked Joy.

Her lips pressed together. She toyed with the turtleneck of her long-sleeved black jumper. Ariana cleared her throat. "I was happy with Kathleen, you know, and now she's gone. I'll never have a sister again." Her eyes stared at a crow perching on the ground by the tree. Her eyes scanned the area, as if she was looking for someone.

"I am sorry. I hope you find the happiness you deserve. Will you be okay?"

Ariana bit her nails and crossed her legs, holding tightly on to her bag. "I am fine. I imagine you have more passions than just your work. Is there a special man in your life?"

Joy knit her brows, wondering if she had purposely tried to change the subject. "There kind of is someone special and I hope we find our way to each other."

"I am sorry to hear that but I'm sure you will work it out. I am still waiting for my Mr Right." A sound came from her bag. She rummaged into it and pulled out her phone. Her eyes changed to dark pools of terror as she read the text.

Who had sent her a message? Was it her friend? Something about Ariana didn't sit right with her. She wanted to get to know Ariana better and help bring her out of her shell. "Why don't you play volleyball with us?"

Ariana gave a nervous chuckle. "I don't think so, Joy. I'm not sporty."

"Neither was half of my team but it's a sport you can pick up easily. It is lots of fun. An old friend played with us a few times, but now he's left and we're looking for a new player."

"I will think about it, Joy. I might give you a call."

"Listen. Why don't you come out with my friends and I the next time we go out? It'll be good for you to go out. Kathleen would want you to be happy. I have a few psychologist friends. I am sure they'd be able to help you find your passion."

Ariana lifted up her loose sleeve and scratched her forearm, revealing a flash of a fresh purplish bruise. "It's fine. I have my own friends."

Joy wondered at Ariana's quick refusal. Kathleen had once mentioned how Ariana had lost her friends a few years ago and that she was a hermit. Maybe that had changed. "What happened to your arm?"

Ariana chuckled. "Oh, silly me. I fell on a slippery floor at work. Remind me not to rush around in a cafe. It's a hectic workplace." Her eyes misted and she forced a smile.

Joy got the sense she was lying but after she'd told the police to do a welfare check, there was nothing more she could do. Marco explained how there was no probable cause to invade her home or suspect foul play. All she could do was support her and check in on her at times. "Yes, I could never do what you do. Hospitality requires a lot of skill. Do you enjoy your work?"

"It pays the bills, I guess. Anyway, I had better meet my friend. She'll be worried."

"Of course, Ariana. It was great seeing you."

"Bye, Joy." She rushed off, making her way towards a kiosk.

Chapter Twenty-Three

JEALOUSY

Edward looked over at Joy as he shook hands with Richard and June. They all stood outside the front door of the new house late Thursday afternoon. He had maintained distance with Joy physically, but over the last two days had called her three times to ensure she was doing all right.

He missed talking to her, but a part of him continued to feel guilty for not having protected her from Ray. He should have known his brother was violent, and he had been stupid these past few years, helping him out when he'd failed to learn from his mistakes. He had encouraged the perpetuation of Ray's drinking. If he had been firmer in his decision to help, he could have prevented all this trauma for Joy. Now, he didn't feel worthy of her. She deserved better than him. She deserved someone who would protect her.

His brother had called a few times but Edward ignored his calls.

"It has been a pleasure to work with you, Mr and Mrs Stubble. If you have any questions, please do not hesitate to ask." The husband and wife smiled.

Richard leaned forward, holding a bunch of yellow flowers. "I will be giving you a high recommendation, Mr Astbury." He stared over at Joy who had her hands in her pockets. "And these are for you."

She took the flowers from him. "Thank you, Mr Stubble." She looked at them and peered at the card, a worried expression on her face.

"I must say you know your work, Ms Warrier. I will give you a high recommendation too. I am certain our daughter will be surprised." He shook Joy's hand firmly and scrutinised her from top to bottom in a way that set Edward's teeth on edge. As Joy tried to pull her hand away, he squeezed tighter. She looked at him with a wrinkled brow.

Edward broke the moment. "I am certain your daughter will appreciate the gift," he said. Richard released Joy's hand.

"Yes, I am sure too," said Joy. "Excuse me." She walked over to Thomas as he ended a phone call. Richard and June made their way to the car and Edward joined Joy and Thomas. Why had Richard scrutinised Joy as if she was his last meal? He was inclined to approach and ask him why he had been so disrespectful towards her. He wouldn't stand for it. But what would that accomplish? At least she wouldn't see the creep again.

Richard drove off with his wife.

Joy put aside the flowers and embraced Thomas. Jealousy threatened to bubble up in Edward. He had no right. Joy wasn't his. "I'll miss working with you, Thomas. I guess you'll have more time with other clients now?"

He nodded, a gleam in his eye. "I have a bucketload to get back to." He looked at Edward. "You do have a way with buildings, Edward."

Edward smiled tightly. "Thank you."

"What job are you working on next? Something as amazing as this house?" Thomas asked.

Edward shrugged. "I have a few projects on the go. It is always busy." The way Thomas looked at Joy brought a burning sensation in his chest.

Joy's shoulder brushed his, and he wanted to hold her in his arms and tell her that he couldn't breathe without her, but they were at work. Even if they weren't, he couldn't bring himself to say anything. It was clear there was still something between Thomas and Joy. But he couldn't blame her after the way he'd treated her. Always overthinking situations.

"Hmm," said Thomas. "I will be giving you both my recommendations."

"Thanks, Thomas," said Joy, gazing at Edward intermittently.

Edward nodded. "I appreciate the gesture." His stomach tensed. He couldn't bear to see Thomas placing an arm around her shoulders. "I had better go. Bye, Joy. Thomas," he said and walked the few feet to his vehicle parked in front of the house.

Joy knit her brows. "Bye Edward."

She looked downcast and he hated himself.

From the corner of his eye, Edward watched Thomas lean into Joy. "It's after five. How about dinner?"

Edward stopped in his tracks a few feet from his car, not daring to turn around, waiting for her response.

"Sure, Thomas."

"Great. Let's go. You can follow me."

They moved out of sight across the street. Edward scrubbed a hand over his face and a dull ache in his chest grew sharp. His legs felt heavy as he stepped inside his car and bowed over the steering wheel. Did he have a chance with Joy or was she in love with Thomas?

Turning on the TV on Friday night, Edward sat back against the couch, knowing that he wouldn't be able to sleep tonight. It was eleven o'clock but he wasn't tired and his mind flashed back to her sweet features. He wanted to reach out to Joy, but he didn't know whether she'd gotten back with Thomas after last night. If she had, it would be solve his problem for him, but if she hadn't, he'd be torn again.

Breaking news came on, reporting on a local, young woman who had been missing for a few days. The reporter appealed to anyone who may have seen this young, blonde woman with a concerned family. A photo of the missing woman came up on the screen, and he winced. This woman looked a lot like Joy. It was creepy. *Jesus*. Was this missing woman going to be another statistic or would they find her? Was she going to be a part of the series of female murders in the local area?

Switching the channel, he watched the start of an action movie and started dozing. His phone buzzed. He opened his eyes, stretched and reached for his phone on the coffee table. Checking the display, it came from an unknown number. "Hello?"

"Edward. It's Octavia here.

"What is it?"

"Joy doesn't know I called you but I thought you should be there for her. I believe she needs you. Physically, she's fine. But not emotionally. I'd rather explain it in person. Can you get to the police station right now?"

"Of course. I'll see you shortly." He ended the call, picked up his keys and rushed out the door.

Chapter Twenty-Four

A GIFT

T he day they'd closed the deal on the housing project she had hoped that Edward would reach out, but he hadn't. Nor did he reach out today. He'd been distant and avoidant with her and her heart broke in two. She knew she should move on, but it didn't stop her from yearning for the man.

Her friendly meal with Thomas was nice and ended at a respectable time, though she'd picked at her plate having lost her appetite. Since then, she couldn't eat or sleep. Edward was on her mind all day at work and all throughout the previous night, as well as in her dreams. He'd made a heavy footprint in her life and heart.

Honking slammed her back to the present and she hit the brake to avoid hitting the car in front of her. Before she could catch her breath, her phone went off a few times in a row with text messages. Focusing on the road, Joy ignored the messages and steered her car home. She couldn't afford any more distractions.

Parking in her driveway at home, she shifted her neck to remove all the aches and pains and gently massaged her shoulders. She had worked late finalising the Stubble's project paperwork and answering urgent requests for a new project. Lian had cancelled volleyball and rescheduled it to a beach game tomorrow instead. A Saturday afternoon under the warm sun with her toes in sand was just what she needed. Then she remembered that Edward might be there. She was equally torn between being excited and hopeful to see him again and being reluctant to go and face his stoicism. She yawned. That decision could wait for tomorrow.

Picking up her bag, she clicked her messages. A series of greetings and nonsense then *I left you a surprise in the boot.* An unknown number. The hair on her neck stood on end, her hands growing clammy. She hesitated and peered over her shoulder, eyes darting in all directions.

Joy took a cautious step outside, soft house lights casting a moonlit glow around her as she listened for sounds, voices, or cars. Nothing. It was dead-quiet. Her parents must have gone to sleep but had left the outside light on for her. Half of the street was dark. Nobody was walking the streets or hiding behind any trees as far as she could see. The rough wind brushed her cheeks and the coldness down her spine made her shiver. She had to get this over with. She was being silly. It was probably a wrong number. There was nothing in the boot.

For peace of mind, Joy walked to the back of the car. She gripped the unlocked boot and held onto it without lifting it. *Let's get this over with.*

Looking over her shoulder, the silent emptiness of the street taunted her. It was late and the few cars passing by made her hesitate. She had an uneasy feeling but shook it off. She steeled herself, knowing she had to open it. Her fingers remained on the boot for a few seconds and then she fully opened it. Flinching at the sight before her, a loud, terrifying scream woke up the quiet neighbourhood.

Joy sat frozen in her seat in the interview room, hunched over as if in a trance. The soothing touch of her brother, Jesse, gave her little comfort. She couldn't get the image out of her mind: the dead body of a young woman, dried blood caked all over her, deep gashes over her gaunt cheeks, terror in those open eyes, and her body lying at an awkward angle. Parts of her hair had been hacked off at the scalp. How would she ever sleep again?

"Detectives, this is ridiculous. Why can't you question Joy tomorrow? She is in shock," Jesse said.

Marco leaned forward and held her hand while Angelo looked on with concern. "I know this must be hard for you, Joy, but if we don't get the details from you while it's still fresh in your mind, you might lose it. I promise it will only take a few minutes."

She nodded, steeling herself. "I got a few text messages before I opened the boot. From ... someone." She handed over her phone.

Angelo took it from her. "We'll get forensics to check it over. See if they can track its source. He or she won't get away with this."

Joy looked up. "Who would do this? Why now, Angelo?"

Marco and Angelo gave each other a strange look. "We don't know yet," said Angelo. "But we have a few leads."

She knew these men well and loved their partners like sisters. "What more are you not telling me?"

Angelo played with the collar of his shirt. "Nothing. Listen we have a few more questions for you."

She sat cross-armed and faced Jesse who gave Angelo a quizzical look. "I am not answering any more questions until you tell me what's going on here. Who was that woman?"

Jesse intervened. "Is there anything you can tell us?"

Marco nodded. "We will eventually, but first things first. The woman needs to be examined by the coroner first."

This poor woman had been tortured before her death. "Please guys. Tell us what's going on. We won't go advertising anything."

Marco inched forward. "We got an anonymous tip. A woman claiming that she knows the killer and that he's been involved in all these murders, telling us Ray is innocent. She ended the call before we could ask more questions."

Ray was innocent?

"Why me?" she asked.

Marco shrugged. "We don't know why the perpetrator involved you, Joy, but we'll get to the bottom of this." He took a breath. "Do you know of anyone who might have a grudge against you besides Ray?"

She shook her head. "No, I don't have any enemies, Marco. I can only think of Ray being the one who hates me."

"Is this the missing woman I heard about on the news?" asked Jesse.

Angelo tilted his head. "We don't know anything right now. Octavia will be doing a press conference soon which will hopefully draw out the person who made that call. She might come forward. We have to appeal to the public, as someone would have seen him or know him. The public is our best source of information at this stage." The detectives asked Joy a few more questions before Marco got up.

Angelo rose too. "I'll organise a police officer outside your house. I know you live with your parents but it's best to be safe."

She nodded. "I understand." Joy shivered in the cool room, wondering why the killer had targeted her in this way.

As she made her way down the corridor with Jesse, who had his arm around her, she froze at seeing Edward stand up in the waiting area. What was he doing here?

"Hi Joy." He paced his steps slowly towards her. "I am sorry. I heard what happened a few minutes ago from Octavia. Are you all right?"

Joy swallowed, fighting back the images in her mind. She would definitely not sleep tonight. "I will be."

"Can I drive you home?"

"No, it's fine." She turned to Jesse. "I have my brother here. This is Jesse."

Jesse put out his hand. "I know it's not the best of circumstances but good to meet you, Edward." He faced Joy. "I don't mind Edward driving you home if you'd prefer."

Joy smiled at her brother. She couldn't deal with complications right now. "No, it's fine. Please take me home." She gazed at Edward. "I will call you and we'll talk." He nodded. She waved goodbye to Edward and followed Jesse outside the building in silence.

Chapter Twenty-Five

CLOSE AGAIN

On Saturday morning, the next day, Edward's breath hitched as he listened to more details of Joy's story.

They walked along the uneven ground with its worn, loose planks at the Williamstown pier. The glare of the sun blinded him without his sunglasses. The soft waves instilled a sense of calm that didn't fit with everything going on in their lives.

He kept his hands in his pockets, looking at the rocks jutting out of the water as he walked beside Joy "I am sorry you had to experience this."

She squared her shoulders and her eyes dampened. "I don't know why I'm being targeted and it scares me." She stared at the sea. "The detectives got a call from a woman telling them Ray is innocent. Have you heard from him lately?"

He shook his head. "Not lately."

"I only wish they find this serial killer before he kills anyone else."

"They will. Don't even think about it."

He didn't want her being alone when this madman might make her his next target. The policeman guarding her house would keep her safe. Marco and Angelo had given her strict instructions not to go anywhere alone and to take time off work. He would also make sure that she didn't go anywhere alone until they found this killer.

His heart broke at the way she trembled, her hands fumbled with nothing, and how her bottom lip quivered. He yearned to hold her tightly and keep her safe. If anything happened to her because of this killer he would never forgive himself for not saving her. If Ray was involved and wasn't truly innocent he would kill him. "Joy. I wish I could do more for you. I have ... I have missed you and want you to feel safe."

"I do feel safe with you and I missed you too." She sighed and inched closer to him.

It wasn't the right time to talk about them so soon after she'd experienced a traumatic event. Edward guided her aside so she could catch her breath. She leaned against the fence and he squeezed her shoulder. He twirled a strand of her hair around his finger. Their eyes locked and she fell into his arms as he held her tightly, stroking the small of her back and breathing in her jasmine-scented perfume. The smooth silk strands of her hair fit nicely over his hand, and he wished he could take her pain away. "Did they identify the woman in your boot?" They pulled away from each other.

Joy nodded. "Her name was Gina, and like all the women, she had blonde hair." She placed a hand over her mouth. "Oh, no. I just realised something." Edward gazed at her curiously. "This killer has been targeting blonde women of around my age or a bit older. Women who look like me."

It was crazy of her to believe that. "It's a coincidence, Joy." He rubbed her back again. She felt so good, so right under his hands. "Have the police mentioned anything like that to you?" She shook her head. "Well, there you go. It doesn't mean anything." Why did he sound unconvincing to himself? Surely it meant nothing.

Joy nodded, but her eyes looked at him as if in a daze. "I'm sorry for involving you in all this," she said as she clung to him, her tears causing his neck to become wet.

"I am here for you. I want you to know that," Edward replied. "Always." He didn't know what came over him as he couldn't bring himself to pull away, not wanting to take advantage of her vulnerability. If he asked her to stay in his spare room so he could keep her safe, would she stay, despite the policeman guarding her house? They could notify Marco that she was with him. That was ridiculous. The last place she'd want to be was with him.

Joy moved away from him. "Thanks for listening."

"Any time."

The moderate wind hissed through the trees around them and grazed his cheeks. He put a gentle arm around her. She drew closer. "I just want this to be over, Edward. I want the police to catch this crazy person."

He gave her a reassuring smile. "The police will find this man. Have faith." He yearned to tell her that he wanted her, but was the timing right when her life might be in danger? Did she even feel the same way? Her eyes were a mystery to him. "I care about you, Joy. I want ... I want you to make sure you're not on your own. Stay safe." He steered her back to his car.

"I know. I am lucky to have a lot of support. I guess we have to be patient a little while longer. Are you still coming to the game this afternoon?"

"I'll be there."

Edward shoved the ball as hard as he could over the volleyball net on the beach, the warm Autumn breeze adding to his sweat. Camilla hit the ball but it landed on the inside of their net. Turning to Joy, he slapped her hand, grinning. Yes. Another point for them.

Passersby, beach chairs, sandy towels, the gentle waves lapping across the horizon, all contributed to the feeling of a summer holiday. Seagulls flocked overhead and children played on their boogie boards while some people surfed and others lazed back, sunbathing. People savoured the warm weather while it still lasted as April started getting cooler.

Edward enjoyed Joy's presence beside him, shifting from one position to another, wearing tight jean shorts that displayed her tanned skin, matched with a white transparent shirt and sleeves rolled-up over a creme camisole.

The ball knocked him hard in the chest, jolting him out of his reverie. He gasped and turned to Joy. "Sorry."

Joy shook her head. "Come on, man. Wake up. Where were you just now?"

Lian yelled from the other side of the net, standing next to Camilla. "He's daydreaming, knowing he's going to lose this game."

Camilla laughed. "I second that, Lian. We can do this. My daughter's counting on me. Come on. Let's get on with it."

Edward looked over at Camilla who rubbed her hands together and grinned. He tossed the ball back and Lian returned it hard. It headed downward close to the ground across from Joy, who lunged low, scooped the ball up with both hands and threw it over the net. Camilla bumped it back over the net towards him, and he gave it all his strength, using the pads of his fingers to return it over the net. Camilla hit it back and it volleyed until his team gained on points, winning them the match.

"Yes," said Joy. "Great shot, Edward." They hi-fived, their faces within inches of one another's. She cleared her throat.

"How about lunch, guys?" said Joy, turning away and putting space between them again.

Camilla shook her head. "I have to take Mariana to a birthday party. Sorry, Joy. Raincheck?" She approached Joy and embraced her.

"No worries. What about you, Lian?"

Lian looked at Edward. "Sorry, no. I have ... ah ... something on. Catching up with a friend. But next time."

Joy looked to him. "Edward?"

"Of course. Why don't we go back to my place?"

"I have jalapenos, green peppers, mushrooms, salami, and olives. What's your preference for the Lebanese bread?" asked Edward.

"Everything but the jalapenos. I'd rather eat spiders than have that hot stuff. It'd give me a heart attack."

Edward laughed. "I hope you don't go eating spiders. Please don't."

She laughed. "Fine." Grabbing a chopping board from his kitchen counter, he handed her the ingredients and she started chopping the mushrooms for their pizza.

He invited her over to his place for lunch, wanting to keep her company until they got the news about the trial. It would be such a relief to put away this bastard. He would make sure he'd keep her safe even if it was over his dead corpse.

Edward hefted two trays with the pizzas and slid them inside the oven. "Do you care for a wine? I have sparkling strawberry or a drier white wine."

Joy sat on the kitchen chair. "Sparkling's great. Thanks."

Pouring her a glass, they engaged in small talk while he set the table. "What project are you working on now? Is it anything interesting?"

Joy licked her lips and he wondered what it would be like to taste those lips for the hundredth time. The way she flicked her hair twisted his insides. Her generous nature showed in the way she talked to others and the way she spoke volumes with her expressive eyes. She had a beautiful blend of strength and confidence with vulnerability and kindness. "An office building in the city. Would you believe it's an architectural firm?"

"It is not my employer. I know that much."

The ding of the oven's bell sounded, so he pulled the trays out and set them on the stove before serving them.

He put both plates on the table and sat opposite Joy, the wafting smells of sauce, herbs, and garlic increasing his hunger. "Enjoy."

Joy took a bite, her tongue wrapped around the crust, and the cheesy filling dripping down her chin. "Oh, gosh. This is delicious."

Edward's gaze lingered on Joy as she closed her eyes, savouring the food. She put her slice of pizza down on her plate, her face reddening. "I'm glad you like it." He cleared his throat. "Aah, I wanted us to talk." She glanced his way, frowning. "I wanted to mention how I have missed you these past weeks. The space between us killed me. I struggled to function without seeing you." He focused on his hands, not sure what he was attempting to say, but he had to be clear about his feelings. "I know we worked together, but it was hard to see you and not be with you." He wiped his mouth. "I know when you wanted us to get together, I declined, but it wasn't because of you. I had so much of my past come up and I was scared to trust in a relationship. I care about you. Now I feel bad about Ray. I should have known."

Joy leaned forward and patted his hand. "You have nothing to be sorry about, Edward. He is responsible for his own actions. You are not to blame."

He nodded. "Maybe, but still, I hated feeling the way I felt. I wanted to take your pain away and get you back to your old self. I only wanted to keep you safe and out of harm's way."

"I know, and I appreciate you worrying about me, but you are not to blame in any of this."

"Thanks for saying that, Joy. What about Thomas? Do you still care about him?"

Joy angled her head. "As I said before, I broke up with him. We had a casual sort of relationship, but nothing serious. He wanted more, but I couldn't give it to him."

"Why not?" She hesitated. "Joy, why didn't you go for Thomas if he wanted more?"

Joy picked up her glass and drank. "Because of you, Edward. I kept thinking about you every time Thomas and I were together."

Edward couldn't hold back. "I want you, Joy. I've cared for you and wanted you since the moment I saw you but was too stupid. I can't breathe without you. I can't sleep. I burn for you every day. I want you and only you. I like you so much it hurts, Joy, I might even love you."

Joy stilled. "You love me?"

"Yes. I love you so much, I don't ever want to share you with anyone. Not with Thomas, not with anyone."

She smiled. "You won't have to share me, Edward because I love you too. I think I might have loved you from the beginning but was too scared to be honest about my feelings."

Edward's heart soared and he wanted to shout his love from the highest mountain. "Will you take a chance on us, Joy? Can we be together?"

She nodded. "I would like that very much."

All time stopped for him as he took her hand in his.

Someone knocked on the door.

"Hold that thought." He rose and took two steps then turned around and smashed his lips into hers. She melted under him. Her lips were soft. He kissed her passionately, as if they wouldn't get another chance and she mirrored his desire.

Someone knocked again and he pulled away. "Sorry, I couldn't wait any longer."

Joy grinned and waved towards the door.

Edward opened the door and invited Marco and Octavia inside. "This is a surprise. What brings you two by?" He led them to the kitchen table.

Octavia looked around. "Oh good, Joy, you're here too so we can deliver the news to both of you."

"Have you caught the guy?" Joy asked.

She took a calming breath. "We've got him," said Octavia.

Edward was taken aback. Did he hear correctly? "What? Who is it?"

Octavia leaned forward. "The killer, and the man targeting you, is in custody as we speak and will not be able to hurt you anymore. He fits the profile and is connected to at least one of the victims. We'll keep digging until we find more evidence but have enough to charge him."

"Who is it? Can you tell us?" Edward asked again.

Octavia turned to Marco. "It's Richard Stubble who's been officially charged."

Joy gasped with a hand over her chest. "The client Edward and I were working with? Are you sure?"

"We have enough evidence to get him to trial," said Marco.

"What evidence?" asked Joy.

"For starters, we matched flowers he had in his home to ones at the dump site, among other things you don't need to concern yourself with," said Marco.

"Flowers? Didn't he give you yellow flowers with a card on Thursday, Joy?" said Edward. She nodded at him. "What did the card say?"

"Well, it was about how he thought my beauty matched my design work, particularly my glossy, blonde hair." Joy knit her brows. "Why would he do this to me? Why would he kill those women?"

Edward curled his hands into fists. If Stubble wasn't in jail at the moment, Edward would go deal with the creep right now.

Octavia pressed her lips together. She reached for Joy's hand and squeezed. "Richard is a narcissist and hates women. He thrives on the kill but mainly derives pleasure from the torture and screams of his victims. He likes to break down women's resilience and leave them totally helpless. All the women were tortured. He likes to humiliate and degrade them and most likely gets aroused by his kills."

"Are you sure it's him?" Joy said.

Marco nodded. "We have facts. His blood on the victim, no alibi, and video camera equipment stashed in storage with recordings of you driving home from Gabriella's house that night. As I said, he has no alibi and admitted to being attracted to you. He denies killing Gina or following you, but we have irrefutable proof. Richard's DNA, a strand of his hair and his blood, as well as prints on the body. As Octavia said, we can't link him to the other murders yet, but we will keep investigating those. We can send him to trial based on what we have so far," said Marco. "But we will need your testimony."

Joy nodded. "Of course, and that's great. If you believe you have the man, I'll be forever grateful." She paused. "You didn't give me many details about the woman in my boot. Can you tell me about her?"

Octavia took over. "It appears that Gina had been in your boot for a few hours before you discovered her, so judging from the time of death, forensic sweep, and your statement, we believe he carried her in a body bag and dumped her in your boot before you left work. Pretty gutsy, but then again, at night it is usually quiet so he would have picked the perfect time to do it.

"Jesus. That is depraved," said Joy. "Did she have a family? Children?"

Edward moved to her side. *Damn propriety*. He wrapped an arm around her and she leaned into him. Octavia smiled and shared a glance with Joy.

"Single, no siblings. Only parents. Devastated of course," said Marco.

"As soon as we know more about the court date, we'll be in touch," said Octavia. She got up and wrapped her arms around Joy. Edward stepped back to give them room. "I love you, Joy. I promise you this man will be punished to the full extent of the law."

She pulled away. "Thanks, Octavia. Marco."

Marco gave them a reassuring smile. "These other murders are our top priority, and until we link Richard to them, I want you to stay safe and not go anywhere alone."

"I will," said Joy.

Octavia and Marco said their goodbyes and saw themselves out. Edward turned to her. "Are you okay?"

Tears ran down her face. He pulled her to him, wrapping his arms around her. "I'm okay. I'm just relieved he's caught, and a little freaked out that we worked with him for so long."

Edward leaned back a little and wiped away her tears. "I get what you mean. To think he was so close to you makes me sick, Joy. I let him close under the guise of professionalism. I can't believe it."

She looked up at him and offered a smile. "Edward?"

"Mmm?" He replied as he wiped another escaped tear.

"Help me forget all this?"

His hand froze on her cheek and his eyes found hers again.

She smiled lovingly up at him. "I want you."

He couldn't find the words, so he leaned down and kissed her tenderly. She reciprocated with as much passion as the previous kiss and he couldn't hold back any longer. Kissing her deeply, he broke contact just long enough to lead her away from the kitchen towards his bedroom.

Fire in her eyes reflected the heat in his blood as she followed him. It was the way she leaned into him and parted her lips, suggesting she wanted more than a kiss. The way her breathing accelerated, as she craved his closeness and wanted an intimate connection. He would indulge her and himself, finally. With the man in custody, they were safe.

Opening the door to his bedroom, he guided her towards the bed and kissed her as they slowly undressed one another. He flicked off her t-shirt and camisole and unzipped her jeans with a gentle hand. Joy stepped out of them and threw them to one side when she drew closer.

He leaned in and his tongue tangled with hers in a smooth and tasteful dance.

Joy breathed heavily when he unclipped her bra. He dipped his head down and licked one nipple while his other hand slid lower to touch her slick heat beneath her panties. Gently pushing her on the bed, he pulled off his own jeans and his t-shirt then he slid down the final garment between them. His breath hitched and he dragged her thigh to one side. "I want you so much." Her body was trim and taut, inviting enough for him to want to taste her, but he held back.

Edward reached for his condom inside the back pocket of his jeans on the floor. The crinkle and rip of foil seemed to excite her. She let out a soft gasp as he slid the condom over his thick length.

She lifted her body upwards and moaned when he glided his palm over her mound, rubbing her tenderly as she closed her eyes and moved in a beautiful rhythm against his hand. She slid her tongue over her lips and reached for him. His manhood settled in her hand as she stroked the bottom to the tip. His heat level rose and his control waned. Those smooth, gentle hands gliding over him in waves brought him dangerously close, but he contained himself and put a little distance between them.

Their eyes locked as he leaned in and kissed her hungrily, his tongue dancing in her mouth and gliding in and out. He couldn't get enough of her. He needed her, wanted her, and craved the feel of her warmth, gentleness, and arousal.

Edward positioned himself over her body and thumbed her clit, watching as she closed her eyes and arched to savour his touch. She took his hand away and guided his penis to its home. He moved inside of her, working slowly. She pushed her hips up, demanding a faster pace. He answered in a rhythm which matched hers. Shivers rippled through his skin as she pressed her hands against his buttocks, their hungry tongues invested in each other's mouths. Writhing, he buried himself fully inside her until they climaxed in unison.

Joy lay back in bed naked while Edward grabbed a strand of her hair and moved it aside. "Hi there."

"How did you sleep?" he asked.

She chuckled. "Not much, considering you kept me up half the night." They had made love twice and she could not get enough of the man.

"Hmm. Ready for more?"

She nodded.

He leaned over her to cover his mouth with hers. His lips were firm as she met him eagerly with her own mouth, their tongues dancing in a way that made her heart pound and her body come alive. She tasted him with beautiful sweeps of his tongue, relishing the feel of his mouth hungering for hers.

He caressed her chin and continued to explore as she moaned and clutched the small of his back, wrapping her legs around him.

Edward massaged the centre of her chest and kissed the gaps in between her breasts while Joy tilted her head back, freeing up her neck for easy reach. He gripped her hips and slid warm hands over them, and over her waist.

His hands trailed up and down her breasts and abdomen, giving her gentle strokes while he kissed her delicate nipples. She leaned into him, savouring the feel of his stubble against her skin. His woody scent drove her wild and she spread her hands over his buttocks and squeezed. He bucked and she grinned. Her hands moved gently to the back of his head to inch him closer to her, feeling as if she couldn't get close enough.

He caressed the side of her face and lips before plunging his tongue deep inside her mouth again. Joy slid her own hands against the small of his back as he threaded his tender hands against the sides of her head. The feel of him made her moan and push herself against him. His lips moved down to her breasts again. With a gentle nip, he sucked her nipples while his hot fingers caressed the tender flesh between her legs. The way he was tasting her as if she was his last meal made her heart race.

Edward pulled away a moment and stared. "Joy, you make me crazy. I cannot get enough of you."

"I can't get close enough to you too," she said. Her hands brushed through his hair as he planted more hot kisses around her breast.

He moved down from her breast to the middle of her abdomen, tenderly stroking her skin as she wriggled and moaned. Sliding down further, he swept kisses around her hips and waist and looked up at her with desire. With a wicked grin, he teased her mound, inserting two fingers into her wet heat and massaging her pink pearl in a skilled, quick rhythm. "Come for me, Joy." Closing her eyes, he kept working his fingers inside and over her and she couldn't contain her excitement. He teased his manhood across her pelvis and kissed her hard.

Joy reached for him again, gliding a loose hand up and down his shaft while her heat got out of control and her climax came. She wriggled underneath him and inserted his manhood inside of her, locking her legs around him.

They fell into an easy rhythm while gazing into each other's eyes.

Joy was drinking water over the sink when Edward wrapped his arms around her. Tingles ran down her arms and his heated breath against her neck made her want him again. The way he knew all the right places to pleasure her, and how his expert touches showed he had wanted to please her.

Edward turned her around and kissed her hard again. "I can never get enough of you, Joy. Stay another night."

Joy wanted to say yes, but her parents weren't happy she was staying away from them after all these murders. She had mentioned Edward briefly, but there was a lot to work through before she was ready for him to meet them. "I might, but I need to let my parents know. They worry, you know."

He nodded. "Great. I would miss you otherwise." He grinned cheekily.

Joy chuckled. "You are hopelessly in love, aren't you?"

"Hopelessly. I'll take you right here if you say you are too."

"I am." As they dove into a deep, hungry kiss, her phone rang. She pulled away.

"Can't you answer it later? We were in the middle of something."

She wanted to stay in bed all day. Why did he know exactly what pleased her? Her ex-boyfriends had never measured up to Edward. He was thoughtful, kind, and loving, but had a passionate and sexy side too. "Hi Mum."

"Darling. We miss you. Are you coming home for dinner?"

She looked to Edward, wishing she could stay every night with the man. "I'll be home later tonight, Mum. I'm with Edward."

"When are we going to meet this man?"

"Soon, don't worry. I'll see you soon."

She ended the call and watched Edward's hungry eyes as he reached for her again and hoisted her onto the counter.

Chapter Twenty-Six

SURPRISE MESSAGE

On Monday night, Joy clipped her briefcase shut and retrieved her handbag, ready to go home earlier than usual and then out for dinner with Edward. She had dealt with her parents questions all through dinner the night before after leaving Edward's place. Then she spent the night tossing and turning, wishing Edward was there with her. Beside her. Inside of her.

Passing by Lian's office, she poked her head in. "See you, Lian. Have a good night?"

Lian frowned. "I am glad you're leaving work earlier than usual. You've been working extra hard lately."

She stepped inside. "I will research those lamps tomorrow. The client wants samples in a couple of days, so I still have time."

Lian nodded. "Okay, but now go and see Edward."

Her face warmed. "Now that they've caught Richard, hopefully things will get back to normal."

Lian tapped the pen over her notebook. "I hear you. What about Ray?"

"Edward's lost touch with him. He wants nothing to do with his brother after everything he did."

"I cannot blame the man. After what he did to you, it's unforgivable."

Joy shrugged. "He's the only family Edward has left, given that his parents hardly keep in contact. I kind of feel bad."

"That is tough. You have nothing to feel bad about. He's responsible for his own actions. You do realise that he might have killed the prostitute, despite the lack of evidence the police have? Until they find out who murdered her, Edward needs to keep away from his brother." Lian yawned. "I plan to leave too soon but you run off home. Have an amazing night, gorgeous."

"Speak for yourself, Lian." She waved. "Bye." Joy walked out of the building and towards the deserted underground park.

Clicking on the fob, she stepped inside her car and started the motor. Her phone rang. Staring at the display, she recognised Ariana's number. "Hi Ariana. This is a surprise."

"Hi Joy. I am sorry. Sorry for ringing you so late. Can we meet?"

Joy wondered if she'd heard correctly. "Of course, but I'm curious. What did you want to talk about?" Silence ensued. "Ariana. Are you still there?"

"Hmm. Sorry. Yes, I ... I wanted to talk about ... about possibly joining your volleyball team. I need more information. I realise after Kathleen ... Well, after she died, I know I need to change my life and go out more. I can't keep living this way."

Joy's heart warmed. "Of course. Where should we meet?"

"How about my house. I will text you the address now."

"Okay. I'll see you soon."

Joy tapped her fingers against the steering wheel, waiting. Luckily she would have time to meet Ariana and then meet with Edward afterwards. She didn't need to let him know unless she happened to be late for their dinner.

Five minutes passed by and nothing. Was she having second thoughts about meeting? Did she truly want to join the volleyball team? She could play as an emergency, seeing as Edward was back in the team. She smiled at the idea of how safe she felt being in his arms and wanted him with her every day.

She broke out of her reverie when the text message came through. Adding the address into her GPS, she put the car in drive and made her way to Ariana's house.

Joy parked her car after driving down the freeway for almost an hour. Her eyes darted around the isolated area with minimal street lighting. The curtains were drawn at a large mansion-like home with a fountain in front. An array of flowers decorated the garden. Rocks and pebbles surrounded the edge of the fountain. She hadn't known Ariana lived in such a large home, but she knew her parents were comfortable financially and must have bought this imposing house for her. But the upkeep would be astronomical.

A narrow concrete path led to the home, and wilting trees that lined the property had fallen leaves around them. A few dry, barren trees clumped together over the grass.

The street was dark as she took a breath and looked around the deserted space. As she stepped out of her car, she looked over her shoulders and in front of her, but no-one was in sight. No passing cars, no passersby, and no animals. She usually appreciated the aesthetics of nature and peace and quiet, away from the urban life. But tonight, an uneasiness settled over her without reason.

Gripping her bag, she pressed the fob to her car and wished she had arranged to meet Ariana in an open space, like a café or restaurant, but she must have felt safer in her home. She had shied away from crowds according to Kathleen, who never understood the reason that Ariana had changed these last few years.

Walking towards the house, she jumped at a noise behind her. Turning around, she saw a black cat scurrying down the footpath, possibly in search of its owner. She laughed at herself. Why was she nervous? It might be a quiet property but Ariana needed her. It must have taken courage for her to reach out like this.

She climbed two steps and approached the front door. A part of her wanted to get back inside her car and leave, but she wasn't the kind of person who would stand someone up. She was there for others.

Ringing the doorbell, she waited a few minutes and started to wonder if Ariana was home. The light was on so why wasn't she answering? Swallowing, she retrieved her phone and called her, but the voicemail came on. Strange. If she was home, she would think Ariana would answer her phone, particularly when she was waiting for her.

Joy felt a prickly sensation down her back. She should go and meet Ariana in the city where she didn't have to drive this distance tomorrow. But what if Ariana was in trouble? No, she wouldn't abandon poor Ariana now. Ringing the bell and knocking on the door, Joy decided she'd check the windows.

A shuffling sound from behind made her turn. In the corner of her eye, she saw the outline of a figure too tall to be Ariana. But before she could run, a strong, rough hand pushed a needle into her arm. Everything went black.

Joy opened her eyes and felt her way in the darkness, her fingers slipping through spaces in between bars. She tried to stand up but hit her head on steel. *Christ!* She was locked inside a small human-size cage. She was woozy and dropped back down to her side. The needle. She had been drugged.

The tangy smell of blood mixed with sweat and body odour made her cringe. Her body quivered and her throat felt parched. This couldn't be happening. She would never see her family and friends again. Never make love to

Edward again. Sadness hit her in the centre of her stomach and she couldn't breathe.

Her heart exploded in her chest and she took deep breaths. She clutched her arms around her belly, squeezing her eyes shut. Her chin and lips trembled. But they had caught him. The police must have the wrong person in custody, and now here she was.

Approaching footsteps made her cower. After a few seconds, the footsteps receded until they ceased.

Shaking her thoughts away, she clenched her hands and gazed through the gaps in the cage, the darkness and musty scent making her sick. Her back pushed up against the cold steel bars, her legs aching on vinyl flooring as her eyes roamed the bare, rough brick walls and a double bed. A light across the room flicked on. The spotlight in the ceiling illuminated a pair of ladies' shoes thrown willy-nilly to the left of the cage. Her spine chilled when she spotted a tray of implements near the door. A hammer, scalpel, knife, coiled rope, and drill rested on a dirty, white cloth. *No, No.* She had to get out of here. This had to be the real serial killer holding her in this cage. He planned to torture her in this room.

She didn't want to die. She had goals, and so much to live for. She refused to die without a fight and had to think of a plan. If she had to play along to buy herself time, she would play along.

Joy had to get back to her friends, back to Edward. Her love for him was undeniable and real. They deserved to have a life together. She was totally in love with the man and wanted the chance to tell him one last time.

A muffled voice in the distance made her jolt, but it got closer. Sounds of shattering glass, loud music, and crying made her wince. "Fuckin', I am King and I deserve to live like one. Call me master too. Now, bitch."

A sudden coldness at her core made her realise that he'd kidnapped another woman. Was it Ariana and was that why she'd never answered the door? Had she fallen prey to the demented killer too?

Chills ran up and down her spine as she bowed her head and cried. She had to get out of here before he killed her.

Chapter Twenty-Seven

A DISCOVERY

E dward approached the counter of the Chinese restaurant opposite the train station in Yarraville where he was meeting Joy for dinner.

A short, elderly woman led him to an outdoor area. She handed him menus. "A waiter will come by to take your order shortly."

"Thank you," said Edward. He scanned the menu and found a multitude of choices but would wait until Joy arrived.

Tables were scattered in a haphazard pattern, and guests either stared at their menus or ate from their plates. He gazed at a group of men passing by and a woman pushing a stroller, the warm wind grounding him in the present.

Twenty minutes later, Joy still hadn't arrived. She must be struggling to find parking as he did. He waited another five more minutes before reaching for his phone from his back pocket. He rang Joy but it went to voicemail. He rang twice more, leaving messages, but there was still no response.

Edward repeatedly rubbed his face as he shifted in his seat. He wondered if she had changed her mind about their relationship. But she had told him she loved him. She had to have a good reason for not showing up, surely.

He placed another call to Joy, but still no response. What if her car had broken down or she'd had an accident? No, he would not ponder the worst-case scenarios. There had to be a reasonable explanation for her lateness.

Edward left his seat and walked around the streets of Yarraville, hoping he would see her walking towards the restaurant. He stopped in front of an Italian restaurant, *Cose Belle*, which featured a pitched roof akin to a small federation style home, having distracted him for a minute. Then tapping on his phone, he tried her number again, but still no reply.

Walking back to the Chinese restaurant, his heart lifted at the idea that she might have arrived there now, but when he returned to his seat she was nowhere to be found. He gripped his phone, unsure of what to do next. Should he ring Lian, or the detective, or was he being paranoid? For all he knew she might have forgotten about their dinner date, but why wouldn't she answer her phone?

His phone rang and he sighed with relief. Checking the display, it wasn't Joy, but Detective Marco. His heart stopped, wondering if something was wrong like the last time she found the corpse in her car. "Hello, Marco. Is this about Joy?"

He heard an audible sigh. "What makes you believe that?"

Edward explained her absence on their date. "She is not answering her phone. Do you know something?"

"She might be in trouble. That's why I'm calling you. Her parents expected her home tonight before she was to meet you. Also, we discovered that Richard may have not murdered those other women. We don't know if Richard is working with someone else or if he is innocent. We've done a lot of digging, and new information has come up about a cold rape case a few years back. The DNA sample from that rape case had never been followed up on, but we are getting the sample processed now. It might show a match to these current murders."

Edward's legs shook and he held back a scream. "Jesus. What if he took her? Find her, Detective. Please."

"We will find her, don't worry. For now, I want you to go back home just in case you hear from her. I will ring her parents and go see them now."

"Stay home? Are you mad? I have to find her. She might be lying in a ditch somewhere." He had a sudden thought. "What makes you believe those cold rape cases might match the current serial killer?"

"We won't know for sure until the DNA is tested, but those women match these current murders by age, physicality, and temperament. In other words, they were blonde, around twenty-five to twenty-nine years of age, and had strong, independent personalities. We believe that rapist might have escalated in his crimes. But listen, Edward. Joy is strong. If he took her, she can take care of herself and will buy herself time. We will catch this guy. I have to go, but I'll be in touch." Marco ended the call.

Edward bent his head down low and rubbed his brow. His chest burned and he wanted to scream. He couldn't lose her.

Later that night, Edward sat in an interview room at one o'clock in the morning. "What is going on here? Why haven't you found Joy?"

Marco bowed over his notebook and Angelo played with the collar of his shirt, both looking gaunt and pale. Octavia's eyes were red, as if she'd been crying.

"Listen. The DNA sample should be ready in a couple more days. We have put a rush on this." He frowned. "We're dealing with an extremely intelligent man but we will find Joy," said Marco.

Octavia looked up at him, but her eyes appeared dazed. "We were convinced that Richard was the serial killer, Edward. He not only fit the profile but the murder he committed fit the pattern of those other women. I am sorry, but I promise you I have a plan. Someone knows this man and we can appeal to their sense of security and justice. The phone call we received from an unknown woman, telling us that Ray was innocent. She may know this man but is too frightened to come forward. This is the type of guy who will need a woman he can manipulate and control, and possibly someone who can do his bidding. This woman might be his partner, but an unwilling one who has a conscience. Potentially to lure in some of these women."

"Why would any woman put up with that?"

Octavia moved forward. "Self-preservation. Some women tend to get brainwashed. Survival would allow her to please the man. If she doesn't, he would most likely kill or punish her. I have no doubt he would have threatened to kill her or her family so she'd play along. I'm preparing a press conference for nine o'clock this morning."

Edward nodded. "I need to do something to help. What can I do?"

Octavia shook her head. "No. You will only get in our way and be putting yourself at risk too. What we didn't tell you before was that he carved Joy's name into the woman's skin. This man wants her, is obsessed with her, will most likely want to break her down because he knows she is feisty, strong, and independent. Joy will no doubt play along to not escalate the situation. She's smart. If you attempt to help, he will want to get you out of the way. Worse, he could kill Joy. Leave this to us."

He had an idea. "Use me as bait. Please. I can lure him in."

Angelo intervened. "We have enough to worry about with Joy. We are not going to be worrying about you too. Let's see how this press conference goes later today then we'll review."

Bile burned Edward's throat. He would willingly take her place so that she would not have to endure whatever the psychopath was doing to her. But he couldn't think like that. They would find her. They had to.

Edward sat in the audience with George while Marco, Angelo, and Octavia sat on a stage giving a televised press conference, their eyes forward, hands clasped, and seated opposite reporters standing with lanyards around their necks, holding recorders and cameras. They were about to start in the next few minutes.

Edward hadn't slept, counting the minutes until the conference and hoping that Joy would come home.

Octavia rubbed her hands, scanned her notes, and stared into the audience before turning to her companions and whispering to them.

George slapped Edward on the shoulder. "How are you holding up, Eddie? I know it must be hard for you."

Edward nodded, his legs feeling like lead. "I feel helpless. I wish I knew where she was, George. I wish I knew why the bastard targeted her."

George pursed his lips, putting a hand into his pocket. "From what you told me about her, she's tough, and the police will find her, man. Have faith."

"I hope you're right about the police but this man's smart. He's been able to fool them. What if he can still fool them? Somehow, he framed Ray and Richard. I'm sure of it."

George nodded. "I hear you, man, and now they'll put their focus on catching the real guy."

Edward knew in his mind that he was missing something, but what? "You're right. Have you spoken to Ray recently?"

George nodded. "Just yesterday. He mentioned struggling but he's determined. He asked about you."

Edward scoffed. "I truly do not care about Ray anymore."

George nodded. "The conference is about to start."

Edward's heart constricted and his mind was bombarded with thoughts. He wished it was him rather than Joy missing.

Edward glanced at Octavia who leaned in towards the microphone with a stern expression. Dark circles were etched under her eyes but her smile remained professional.

"We are appealing to the public or any witnesses to find the killer of Diane Jeens, Gina Armamdo, and several others to come forward. We are looking for a man between the ages of twenty-five to early thirties. He is likely be a born manipulator who exploits people and systems.

He is a man who likes to dominate his victims and is skilled with his hands but also highly intelligent. His latest murder victim was Gina Armamdo, and currently, a young woman by the name of Joy Warrier is missing. She has a loving family, amazing friends, a successful career, and the most generous of hearts. She has inspired her community by contributing in a skilful way with her interior design work and giving to others wholeheartedly without asking for rewards or renumerations. Joy has a kind heart and would do anything for her loved ones and her community. She deserves to have a future. Please; if you know anything about her whereabouts, come forward. We need to put a stop to these killings and we need to save Joy. We must fight for justice for these poor women."

Edward thought about Joy and what she was going through. He steeled himself. She was a fighter and strong and had to get out of this alive. She needed to.

Octavia continued. "We have detective Senior Sergeant Marco Petrazini who will provide you with more details of the case. Thank you."

Marco continued. "As Octavia stated, the man we are looking for is most likely in his mid-20s, early 30s, Caucasian, with a proficiency in technology, a high IQ, and is most likely skilled with his hands. We believe he resides in the local area. He may be working with a submissive partner. We believe he is a seasoned sexual criminal and may have escalated from rape to murder. The man thrives on humiliating and degrading women to compensate for his own sexual inadequacy." He took a breath. "Furthermore, his behaviour would have changed around the times of these murders. He would have been stressed and agitated more than usual and may have followed the news closely. The man would most likely have abused and dominated his partner more than usual around the time of the killings. He is likely to have no remorse and will only be anxious about getting caught."

Angelo took the reins by reciting the details again about further contact. "If you are watching, I want you to know that you will be caught. It's only a matter of when."

Edward's breathing accelerated as he pondered the profile of the man. Would he torture Joy or kill her? Would someone come forward? The person they were looking for was local, so it could be anyone in this room.

Chapter
Twenty-Eight

DISTURBED
MIND

Joy's heart thumped when the door swung open. Her blurred vision must have been from the effects of the medication. She looked up and could barely see a man swaggering inside. When he reached her cage and crouched, Joy's blood went cold.

"Well, hello Joy. We finally meet again."

Fingers touched her parted lips. "Thomas? What is going on here?"

He glared then kneeled opposite her. "If I can't have you willingly, Joy, then this is the only way I can keep you. My very own prized possession."

Bile rose in her throat, and her surroundings appeared surreal. Thomas's frame blurred in front of her and black spots appeared in her vision. This couldn't be happening. "Why are you doing this? What have I done to you?"

He scoffed. "What have you done?" He caressed his chin with his finger, staring into the distance. "Hmm. What have *you* done?" He banged hard against the cage, making Joy flinch. His perfect teeth gleamed in a sinister smile as he leaned in. "I loved you and you treated me like I was nothing. Deciding Edward was a better match for you than me. We could have had the perfect life. I thought you loved me too but you only used me because Edward was unavailable. I watched you the night he threw you out of his house, rejecting you, but you went back to him anyway. You wanted him from the start."

Joy winced. "I am sorry, Thomas. I do love you and I know you won't hurt me. Think about the great times we had. I care about you." She hid her fear by plastering her widest smile, hoping to appeal to his humanity.

He chuckled. "Oh, yes, you love me like a friend. But then you treated me as if you're better than me. You proved that you're a worthless bitch like all the rest of the female race. Not good for anything but flaunting your bodies and pretending to be in charge. Well, you're not in charge anymore, are you, Joy?"

Her chest tightened and she remembered how his mother had introduced herself to her family. She was a self-entitled woman who spoiled him. Her mind took her back to her old house.

"*I'm Janice and this is my son, Thomas. We wanted to say hello.*"

"*Would you like to come in?*" *asked Joy's mother, as she stood beside her.*

"*No, I only wanted you to meet my son, Thomas. Hopefully, we can all become friends.*" *She looked sternly at Joy.*

The boy pulled at his mother's cardigan. "*Mum, I think we should go. My TV show's on.*"

The woman nodded, touching her son's chin. "*Oh, darling. Of course. Anything for my king.*" *She turned back to Joy and her mother.* "*I will talk to you later.*"

As they were leaving, she overheard the mother saying, "*Oh, darling. Of course, I'll get you the laptop you need. Don't you need a few of those video games too that you like? Anything for my beautiful king.*"

"*Yes, mother. You're the best.*"

Joy focused back on the present, realising that over the next year before they had moved away that Thomas hated his mother. He didn't tell her outright but it showed in the sarcastic way he spoke to her. Even the times he lied to her about having a part-time job or not participating in sports. She had thought it was harmless, but now she realised it was a part of his temperament of manipulation and deception. He wanted control over his mother and had pretended to be someone else around her.

"Please let me go, Thomas. If our relationship meant anything to you, you wouldn't want to hurt me. You'd regret it, especially if you love me."

He scoffed and banged hard against the cage, making her cower. "You won't have a choice now but to cater to my sexual needs. We're going to have fun, aren't we? You proved you're not worthy of my love. I thought you were different, special, but you're like all the other bitches in the world. Now, I'll have you my way. I'll keep you for a while, but I call the damn shots." Joy stared into the dark recesses of his soul and managed a smile she didn't feel. She had to get on his side, but how long would it be before the police found her? She couldn't rely on them as they might never find her and had to find a way out of this. He grimaced. "I will be back later to enjoy the fruits of my labour."

Once he let her out of the cage, she could make a run for it or grab one of those tools resting on the tray. She wouldn't die without a damn hard fight.

Joy's eyes adjusted to the darkness. She reached out to the steel bars and banged against them, as if she could miraculously break through them. She was naked. How did she get naked? Thomas must have stripped her. Nausea set in at the humiliation she felt without clothes. The coldness of the cage made her cringe. Despite being woozy, she was jolted to attention when she heard the whimpering sounds of a woman.

A hint of light seeped from underneath the door. Against it, Joy made out the silhouette of a woman. She was shaking, head bowed. As the woman lifted up her head, her long, blonde hair fanned around her face, her squinting eyes looking past her. She appeared battered and bruised. *No, it couldn't be*. He had taken her too.

Joy realised that Ariana wasn't bound or tied up. "Ariana. Are you okay?" Silence, then more whimpering. "You have to go to the police. Now. He's going to kill us both." The woman didn't respond and kept crying. "Help me, please. Help."

The sudden push of the door knocked into Ariana's back making her flinch and whimper some more. Thomas turned on the light and Joy winced. He dragged Ariana roughly by the arms and pushed her outside. "I'll deal with you later, bitch."

Joy trembled, squeezing her eyes shut, hoping that this was a nightmare. She hyperventilated as Thomas's eyes scanned her from head to toe, licking his lips. Her jaw clenched and the pain in her chest made her feel as though she was about to have a heart attack. Black spots danced in her vision. Thomas bent down to her level and she scrambled back against the bars. She rocked back and forth. Joy had to push through her terror and make him believe she was his ally rather than his enemy.

His fingers reached inside the cage and trailed from the centre of her chest down to her navel, running his tongue over his bottom lip with heat in his eyes. She wanted to throw up but had to steel herself. She needed to survive at whatever cost to her dignity and self-worth. Roaming his fingers back up to her chest, he squeezed her breast. "You're a hard one to break down, aren't you?" Joy remained silent, not wanting to aggravate the monster. "I know you can learn to love me. I know I am a better lover than Edward. I can show you I am in control, always have been, and always will be. I am the Master of all women and I want you to call me King and Master. Now!"

Joy swallowed. "Please let me go. I can help you. Think about what we shared, Thomas. Why would you do this to me? If you truly love me, you'll let me go."

"Fuckin' call me King and Master or I will kill you slowly."

She swallowed. "King. Master," she said, fighting back her tears.

"That's right. What I say goes, and now we're going to have our own brand of fun."

"No, please. Don't do this."

"Or what? Do you think you can get me to change my mind about you? I have you and I call the shots. You see, I have all the women at my fingertips and what I say goes. No amount of reasoning can get you out of this. I deserve this and so much more."

She was crying on the inside and waiting for him to begin, but he swaggered out of the room and slammed the door behind him. How long would it be before he started torturing her?

Chapter
Twenty-Nine

A WITNESS

Thomas turned off the TV and faced Ariana. "They'll never catch me. They didn't even get the profile right. I don't work with my hands, now do I, bitch?" He glared.

"Please stop this. You can't keep doing this to me," Ariana said.

He hunched up his shoulders, swung out his right arm, and pounded into her face. She fell flat on the ground, blacking out. But he didn't stop there. He lifted her up by the collar and threw her against the couch. Then he yanked her by the arm and dragged her to the bedroom where Joy was.

He threw the woman to the ground, knocking her into the cage. "I think I'll give Joy a show of your demise. She's going to be your replacement, love. I've had enough of you."

"Please, don't, Thomas. You can't do this to Ariana. You would have loved her once?" Joy said.

He squinted, wondering why she looked so calm. "She was useful to me as my helper but now you're here. I don't need her anymore. You can be her replacement."

"Please don't hurt her. Use me instead. I will do whatever you want. Please."

Thomas laughed while kicking Ariana in the chest. The bitch squirmed against the wall, crying. He was sick of her weakness; she had to die. She might let something slip and he didn't want to worry about getting caught. But then again, she was too gutless and weak to go to the authorities, and she'd die just to please him. He could torture her slowly in front of Joy and break her down even more. "Hmm. Let me tell you something about sweet Ariana. She is not so sweet. The bitch let her own sister die. She brought her to me and watched me have sex with her. Some sister, ha?" The expression on Joy's face was priceless. She wasn't expecting that new piece of information.

He picked up a crumpled white sheet, lay it next to the cage, picked up coiled rope and pulled Ariana by the arm. "Stay still or I'll kill you quicker."

Ariana shook her head. "No, please. I'll do what you ask, Thomas. Please, no more. No more."

He glared. What he dreamed of. To be a master of all women. She had given him most of the women, so she had been useful, but like all women, they had an expiry date. Maybe he wouldn't kill her today and would only make her think he was going to. The terror in Ariana's eyes was a rush. He loved to scare her and then let her live with the idea that someday she might die. "I'll tell you what. Let me get my rush then I'll set you free. How's that?" The bitch nodded. He wondered if he'd use the wrench, hammer, or scalpel.

Having decided, he reached for the scalpel on the tray by the door and made the first cut.

Joy cried at the scene before her. Ariana lay on the ground in a crumpled heap. She wore an open shirt, had superficial cuts across her chest and abdomen, bruising and swelling around her eyes, and ripped shorts as evidence of him raping her at least twice. A rope by her side was a reminder of Thomas choking Ariana, making her believe he was going to kill her. Afterwards, he laughed, spat on her, and stormed out.

Not once, did he look at Joy while committing his atrocities towards the poor woman. She had screamed and pleaded for him to stop but he ignored her, acting as if she wasn't present in the room. Would she be next in line for his torturous fantasies? How could she have been stupid and not realised he was a psychopath, devoid of emotion and remorse? She might be able to appeal to any modicum of humanity that he might have left, but she doubted it after having tried to reach it earlier.

An hour had passed, and Ariana slowly roused from her unconscious state. Joy needed to get her attention as they needed to get out of here. She had no doubt that the creep would finish Ariana off the next time. If Joy was to be Ariana's replacement, her days were numbered.

Joy had to check on Ariana and see if she could help. "Ariana. Please. Help me. Help yourself. We need to get out of here, or he'll kill us both. Please."

Ariana shook her head. "I ... I can't. He ... he will kill me. No." Her eyes started closing again and her breathing appeared shallow.

Joy gripped the steel bars and pulled at them with force. There had to be a way out. "Please stay awake. He will kill you if you don't do anything. You have to act now before he comes back. Please help me out and I will save both of us. I have the energy to fight him but you don't. You need the hospital."

"I deserve ... deserve to die, Joy. Leave me alone."

Joy had to convince her. It was the only way to get out of here if the police didn't get to her first. She had to stay alive for Edward, her family, and her friends. She refused to give up without a fight. "Why do you deserve to die?" Silence. "Ariana. Please tell me why you deserve to die?"

Ariana's body shook as she wrapped her arms around herself, turning her head away. "Kathleen."

Joy winced at the idea that she had watched her own sister with this madman. "I know Thomas must have exaggerated about that. Can you tell me what actually happened with Kathleen?"

"I couldn't save her."

Joy couldn't give up and would stay on task until she got out of this damn cage. Hairs stood on the back of her neck as footsteps came closer. Her heart clenched tight in her chest and a dizzy sensation made it hard to keep talking, but she had to. "Please Ariana. Whatever happened to Kathleen, she would want you to save yourself. Save me. I can help." Joy shivered when the door suddenly opened.

He glared at Ariana and kicked her in the legs, carrying a bag of sandwiches. "You're dying tonight, bitch," he said.

Ariana squirmed, remaining silent.

He approached Joy and kneeled by the cage, a neutral expression on his face as he pushed the bag through the steel bars. She took it from him. "Here you go. You need to keep your energy up. Can't wait."

"Please, Thomas. Let me go and we can make it work. I'll leave Edward and go out with you again. We are friends and we can be lovers. Give me a chance to fall in love with you, but not like this. I need to be free to love you, Thomas."

His eyes softened for a few brief seconds but then hardened again. "What do you take me for, Joy? I haven't come this far out of stupidity. I can outsmart the police, even Edward. But you may get your wish soon."

He turned around, picked up Ariana, shoved her outside of the room, and slammed the door behind them. She had missed her last chance to convince Ariana to help. Now, she was doomed.

Pressing an unsteady finger across her temple, her eyes darted to something in the distance. Leaning forward, she noticed a glint on the ground. Was that a key?

Joy reached through the steel bars for the key but it was a little too far. *Damn!* She had to get the key. Ariana must have taken it from Thomas's back pocket when he was busy talking to her. It had to be for the cage.

If she didn't reach the key, she would be next. Who knew what he had planned for her? She couldn't imagine enduring what poor Ariana had gone through.

She wondered how long Ariana had been here. How long had Kathleen been here?

Joy took a deep breath, squeezed her hand through the bars again and stretched out her arm as far as it could go. Just a bit more. You can do it. She only had to reach another centimetre. Joy pushed hard against the bars, sweating with the exertion. Come on. Come on. She had to do this before Thomas returned.

Pushing herself even harder, her fingers touched the metal and she clawed it closer. Picking it up, she fumbled with the key as her heart raced.

Turning the key into the padlock, the clicking sound made her sigh with relief. Opening the cage, she relaxed her shoulders as she crept along the floor and reached the tray of equipment. A long white sheet lay underneath the tray, long enough to cover part of her naked body. She picked up a scalpel to defend herself. Why was there only a scalpel? Where were the other implements?

After wrapping the sheet around herself, she put her ear to the door and listened. It sounded quiet. She needed to find Ariana and save her. She couldn't leave without the woman after he'd told her he'd kill her tonight. She scanned the room. There were bars over the blacked-out windows.

Gently opening the door, Joy slowly walked down a narrow corridor, passed a bedroom and stepped inside while looking over her shoulder, gripping the scalpel. Sweat lined the back of her neck as she listened for any sounds around her. Cold chills ran down her legs. No-one was in the room. Passing by another bedroom, it was empty too. She tried opening the window but it also had bars.

She bit her bottom lip as she ran for the front door and opened it. A security door. Pulling down the handle, it was locked. *Oh, no.* Where was the key for this one? She wished she had something to break through the steel mesh, but it was hard and tough. She needed to look for a phone. She could ring the police before he found her.

Rushing forward, Joy headed into the kitchen, seeing the dirty dishes piled high in the sink, a bloody tea towel draped over the stove and two coiled ropes on the counter. Her back chilled and as she tightened the sheet around her body. Retrieving a knife and abandoning the scalpel, she wandered to more bedrooms down the hall, needing to find Ariana. How many bedrooms were there?

Creeping into one of the empty bedrooms, her heart seemed to explode and someone shoved her to the ground from behind. Her knife skidded across the floor, lost to her now.

"Where the fuck do you think you're going?" He dragged her away by her arm. Her muscles tensed as she gasped for air, knowing she had lost. If he restrained her again, she'd never find her way out again. The bastard would make sure of that. *Think, Joy. Think*.

She closed her eyes and went limp and Thomas relaxed a little as he kept dragging her down the narrow corridor. She had to make him think she'd given up, then she would pounce.

He dropped her inside the same bedroom with the cage in it, still with her eyes closed. In a split second, she lifted a leg and kicked him in the groin. "Oh, you bitch." He fell back, cowering in pain while she scrambled for the door. A hand fisted her hair and dragged her back, causing a gut-wrenching pain in her scalp."

"No, please Thomas. Let me go. Please."

Joy was no match for his strength. He pushed her back down on the ground and pounded into her until she was barely conscious. The last thing she remembered was Thomas pulling something out of his pocket. She was going to die.

Chapter Thirty

A STRONG LEAD

E dward rested his back against his couch trying to watch a documentary, but his mind wasn't following the program. He hadn't slept last night and his nightmares only showed Joy running in the distance. He attempted to catch her but she was too fast.

Closing his eyes, he bargained with God in hope that her life would be spared so they could be together forever. She had to survive this. She was a fighter and would work hard to get back to her life. He knew that in his heart, in his very soul. Now that he had found love, he couldn't lose it.

He jerked when his phone rang. Without checking the display, he answered. "Hello?"

"Hey, Eddie. It's me. I don't have long here."

He clenched a fist. "What do you want, Ray?"

"Please don't hang up, man. I heard about Joy, Eddie, and wanted to see how you're doing. I know you two care about each other."

He stared at the ground, considering ending the call. "I am fine. Is that why you're ringing?"

"Yes, I care about you and want you to know I didn't murder the prostitute. I was set up. You have to believe me."

"I don't know what to believe, Ray."

"Please, Eddie. I am telling you the truth. I did have sex with her but I swear on my life I didn't murder her."

"I need to go. Have a nice life." He felt nauseous even speaking to Ray, knowing he would never forgive him.

"I care about Joy. I know she'll be okay. The police will find her."

He rose and paced the carpet while holding his phone. "I doubt you care about Joy after what you pulled. How do I know you didn't organise this? Arrange to have someone kidnap her?" Silence. "Are you there?"

"I would never ... I'm not a kidnapper."

"Maybe not but you're a rapist." He ended the call and sat back on the couch, staring into the distance.

He couldn't sit by any longer. He had to see the police and discuss how he could help.

Edward stepped out of his car and entered the police station. He approached the front desk and asked for detectives Marco and Angelo.

The burly officer nodded and made a call. "Please take a seat. The detectives will be with you shortly."

Edward walked to the group of chairs and sat down, staring around the room as officers and detectives rushed down the walkway or to their own cubicles. Some responded to calls while others flicked through papers or stared at computers.

Marco walked towards him a few minutes later. "Hello, Edward. What can I do for you?"

"Can we sit down?"

"Of course. Follow me." He walked past multiple cubicles until he reached Marco's neat desk opposite another one that was cluttered, filled with dirty coffee cups, stained napkins, and high stacks of documents in the in-tray or scattered across it. "If you're wondering; that desk belongs to Angelo, and right now, he's following up on a lead with our forensics department on the DNA testing. He should be here in a few minutes."

"No judgement here," he said.

Marco frowned. "Oh, sure." He clasped his hands in front of him. "Anyway, what brings you by?"

"I wanted to discuss the status of your case and see if I can help in any way. It's been almost two days. Who knows what is happening to her?"

Marco angled his head. "We are doing everything we possibly can to find Joy. Trust in us and the system. If you get involved, you'll only be getting in our way."

He shook his head. "It is not my intention to do that, but I thought I could at least come with you once you find Joy. I need to be there when you free her." He took a breath. "What about tracking the mystery woman who called you? Did you find out who she was?"

He nodded. "That is classified, Edward. You know it is." He looked up when Angelo scurried to them.

"Hi, Edward." He faced Marco. "That information has panned out." He handed Marco a piece of paper."

"Let's go," said Marco.

"I am coming with you."

Marco stood with his arms across the waist. "No, this is official business, Edward. You'll only be getting in the way."

"Please, I promise I will stay in the car and not move a muscle. Please let me be there for Joy. I couldn't help Joy with Ray but I need to be there for her now."

Angelo sighed. "We really need to get going on this."

Marco motioned with his hand. "I don't have time to debate this with you. Come on, but do not get in our way or you will regret it."

Edward gave him a reassuring smile. "Thank you."

When they arrived at their destination, Edward saw a large mansion with a fountain, and rosebushes surrounding the front garden. Rocks and pebbles filled the edging of the fountain. The curtains were drawn. It appeared to be a normal neighbourhood, but this residence was nothing but normal if Joy was locked inside with a psychopath. Marco and Angelo still hadn't given away the identity of the killer.

A group of officers and the detectives had their bulletproof vests on as they snuck around the side and back of the house while others checked the front. Muffled voices and light, rapid footsteps sounded in the quiet street. With a long bar, a police officer pried open the front door. The group pointed their guns as they entered. The pain in his chest impacted his breathing and he bowed his head, praying that Joy would be all right.

What was he doing waiting here doing nothing? He had to find Joy. He refused to sit in the back seat of the car, knowing she was out there, suffering at the hands of a murderer and rapist. Quickly, he ran to the back of the mansion where the smallest team had gone.

Joy felt as if she was outside of herself and everything was in slow motion. Blood dripped down the side of her right arm, cut by a knife. The stinging pain made her clench her teeth, and her back ached as she lay like a rag doll back inside the bedroom, her back resting against the wall. Though she had no restraints, she couldn't escape this room again if she tried. Why hadn't he put her inside the cage? Did he have something else in mind for her?

She closed her eyes to preserve the little energy she had left, and realised that Thomas would not let her die today. He wanted to possess her and use her like a pet until he grew tired of her and threw her out like a piece of rubbish. Was this her fate? Would she die at the hands of a crazy person before she got the chance to marry, have children, and build her career to even greater heights?

Thomas came back into the room and slammed the door behind him. She shivered. He shoved her hard against the floor as she fought to get up, hoping to find a weapon. But the tray of equipment had disappeared. She had nothing. A slight bump underneath her distracted her. The floor was uneven.

He walked slowly towards her with a smirk across his face and kicked her hard in the legs. She cowered, shaking her head as he pushed her back inside the cage. Joy swung her left arm, and with her fingernails scraped his eye. He bowed in pain and the split second gave her time to run for the door. "You'll pay for that." She opened the door, but he pulled her by the hair and threw her to the floor again. "This time you can die. I've had enough of your shit. I can always find someone else. I always do."

Her rasping breaths sounded loud and her bottom lip quivered as she held herself tightly. She stared into his hard eyes when he reached for his back pocket and pulled out the same knife with its jagged edges. She retreated into the foetal position as he crept towards her. His hand gripped the knife and he swung it up high in the air and stabbed her deeply in the hand this time. She screamed at the pain.

Joy would not die this way, so she found reserves of energy she never knew she had and lifted herself up, attempting to shift her position. He swung the knife in the air and she took the opportunity to run behind the bed even though there was nowhere to go from there.

"You are a feisty one, aren't you? I love challenges. You want to play. We can play." He slowly made his way around the bed with a spring in his step. Her stomach twisted. He was enjoying himself.

Footsteps pounded down the hallway, followed by shouting. His eyes darted past her. Quickly, he rushed close to the cage and slid his hands across the floor. He pulled open a trapdoor and climbed down, shutting it over him.

The pain in her hand was unbearable and the room spun around her as her back pressed against the cold floor. Groups of feet surrounded her.

Marco approached and squeezed her shoulder. "My God, Joy. Are you all right?"

She ignored the stinging pain of her arm, hand, and whole body, the blood still dripping from her wounds. "I am fine. Thomas. He's in there. Get him." She pointed to the trapdoor.

"The paramedics are here," said Angelo, turning as two females carried a stretcher inside. They rushed to Joy and checked her vitals, tending to her wounds.

"Hang in there," said Angelo.

Both Angelo and Marco stepped inside the trapdoor and followed Thomas.

Edward made his way to the back part of the house and spotted a figure running from the side of it. It was Thomas. His stomach turned.

Thomas was the serial killer? It couldn't be. Why hadn't Marco prepared him for this?

His nostrils flared and he flexed his fingers and muscles. He couldn't let the bastard get away.

He bent down low behind a tree to avoid being seen and watched. Spotting a rock the size of his hand near the fountain, he picked it up and held it tight, spurred for action. Creeping out of hiding, he intercepted Thomas, hiding the rock behind his back. "Hello there."

Thomas lunged for him and together they wrestled on the rough ground. The rock fell from Edward's grip. Thomas pounded into Edward's face but Edward retaliated by punching him hard in the jaw. Thomas fell back. Where was that rock? He searched for it before Thomas got up, and when he found it, swung it hard into his forehead. Thomas lay unconscious on the ground, still breathing. He needed to suffer and rot in prison.

Bending down low, he pounded into him a few more times. "This is for Joy. Where is she?" The man grunted.

Edward stood over Thomas, waiting for the police to leave the house, and then saw Angelo and Marco coming towards him.

"What the hell?" said Angelo.

Marco shook his head. "You could have been killed, Edward."

"You are welcome, Marco. Where's Joy? Is she all right?"

Before he could answer, several police officers and the paramedics wheeled Joy outside. His heart soared, but as he got closer, it ached at the sight before him. She had a bandaged arm and hand, bruising around her eyes and a swollen cheek.

He hovered over her and held her hand. "Oh, Joy. Are you all right?" She nodded, but her eyes were closing. She was unconscious when he said, "I love you. So much."

Chapter Thirty-One

HOSPITAL VISIT

Joy roused from sleep and saw Edward holding his chin in his hands, slouching on the hospital chair by her bedside.

Edward had a hint of a smile on his face. "Hey, beautiful," he said. "Can I get you anything?"

Her throat was dry. "Water."

He rose from his chair, reached out for the jug of water, and poured it into a glass. Handing it to her, he said, "Here you are." Once she drank it down, he carried the glass back to the table. "How are you feeling?"

"As if I've been stabbed and beaten."

His eyes darkened. "I am so sorry, Joy."

She angled her head. "For what?"

"I felt helpless not being able to find you. I had this terror inside me, thinking that you might be dead. I should have known it was Thomas. Again, I couldn't protect you."

"No, Marco told me how you found Thomas outside. You stopped him from leaving. Thank you."

He beamed. "I am glad it's over and that I caught him by surprise. But he wouldn't have got far. The detectives weren't far behind."

She shifted on the hard bed. "You showed a lot of courage, fighting against a madman."

"I had to stop him. I don't know what I would have done if he killed you." He sighed and leaned forward, kissing her tenderly on the mouth. "I love you, Joy."

Joy's heart warmed "I love you too." He wrapped his arms around her and lay his head gently on her shoulder. She relished his warmth, feeling safe after all these months. Someone behind her cleared their throat. As she lifted herself up, she scanned the entryway and saw her friends there; Gabriella, Bella, Jamie, and Liz. "Hi guys."

Bella walked inside. "Oh, Joy. Thank God you're all right. Are you?" She nodded. "The others are waiting outside." She pulled Joy into a hug, then made room for their friends who came into the ward one by one.

Edward moved aside, grinning as her friends wrapped their arms around her. Joy found their overlapping voices created beautiful chaos after the quiet. When they stared at him, he nodded in their direction. "Hello, I'm Edward."

Joy intervened. "You know Camilla and Gabriella, but these are my other friends, Bella, Liz, and Jamie. They're like my sisters."

One by one, her friends greeted him.

Marco ambled inside. "Hey, gorgeous," he said to Bella. "I need a few minutes to update Joy and Edward. Sorry, Police business."

"Sure honey," said Bella who prodded the others outside the ward.

Edward moved to her side while Marco stood at the other side of the bed.

"What's going on?" asked Joy.

He leaned in. "I wanted to let you know that we have enough evidence against Thomas to put him away until his death. He will never get out."

Edward smiled. "Thank you."

Marco leaned forward. "We managed to get a lot out of him, given that he likes the notoriety. Anyway, we know he killed the prostitute and framed Ray. He admitted to killing those other women who went missing too. Richard's also innocent of the murder of Gina. Thomas is responsible for her murder, not to mention those prior rapes and deaths. He's been busy."

"Jesus. I cared about Thomas. I thought he was my friend. It was such a shock to know he had this whole evil side to him."

Marco knit his brow. "He is an expert manipulator. He admitted to loving you in his own warped way and wanted to replace Ariana with you. A new possession to lure his women."

"Why would he frame Richard?"

Marco sighed. "He didn't like the way the man was looking at you and decided to frame him too. The flowers were a nice touch to implicate him, for starters. I doubt Richard had any idea what the note said. Thomas had been the one to purchase them."

"Such a depraved mind," said Joy. "I wish I'd known. How could I be so stupid?"

Marco squeezed his hands, touching her shoulder gently and gave her a reassuring smile. "Don't beat yourself up about it. Psychopaths have two personalities. Like I said, expert manipulators. He's had lots of practice."

Edward gazed from Joy back to Marco. "What happened to Thomas's DNA all those years ago?"

Marco pressed his lips hard. "The system is broken when a DNA sample from Thomas all those years ago should have been processed back then but was left forgotten."

"What do you mean?" said Joy.

Marco brought a chair close to the bed and sat. "During those rape cases several years ago, Thomas agreed to giving a DNA sample. Rather than getting it processed, the forensics team got busy with priority cases and never suspected Thomas was culpable. As a solicitor, Thomas also had connections and managed to get it delayed to the point that other cases came up and his was forgotten. If it had been processed back then, he would've been in prison, but he was free to escalate to murder."

"Why was he tested in the first place?" asked Edward.

Marco briefly stared towards the window in deep thought. "His car was spotted in the area near the bus stop where that woman was taken."

"These serial murders could have been prevented, but Marco, as always, you and Angelo find the killers. Thank you," said Joy.

He reached over and squeezed her hand. "I'll be there when you testify, and no doubt the rest of the clan will be there too. We've got your back."

Octavia walked inside with a sombre expression. "Hi Edward, Joy, Marco. Sorry to interrupt but I wanted to give you news. Ariana's been arrested."

Joy's chest palpitated. "What?"

She took a breath. "She was Thomas's accomplice and lured those women to him. She watched her boyfriend murder and rape her own sister. In spite of her being brainwashed and traumatised, she will still need to serve time. What she did was wrong."

Edward's eyes darkened. "Are you are telling us that Ariana knew what she was doing? If she had come to us sooner, those girls would still be alive? How could a woman do that to her own sister? To those other women? She was as bad as Thomas."

Joy intervened. "Luckily, she saw sense at the end. If it wasn't for her, I might be dead. I think she might have helped me with the key to the cage. Surely it counts for something if she did try to help?"

Octavia nodded. "Ariana mentioned how she gave you the key. She wanted me to tell you that." She gave her a reassuring smile. "I'll be writing up a full psychological profile on Ariana and she'll get weeks of psychiatric evaluations. She will testify against Thomas, which will reduce her sentence, but she'll still have to account for her behaviour."

Joy clenched her hands, tears streaming down her cheek. "I struggle to understand how could she do that to Kathleen." She looked past Octavia. "I find it hard to believe."

Octavia nodded. "Thomas was a narcissist. He even threatened to tell her parents about her letting Kathleen have sex with him and taking drugs. Kathleen's overdose was an accident. Despite not intending to, he murdered her. In the end, he would have killed her eventually." She exhaled. "As for his treatment of Ariana, it eventually took its toll and she could no longer take the punishment, the torture, the humiliation. She had to help you, Joy."

Joy put her head down slowly and cried. Marco and Octavia gave her reassuring smiles while Edward reached for her hand. She couldn't imagine dealing with such a monster and was thankful he'd be in prison.

EPILOGUE (THREE MONTHS LATER)

Joy watched as Jamie put her engagement ring on her finger, then leaned in to kiss Angelo who had put on his ring earlier. She wore a long, flowing white satin dress and pearl accessories to match. Her hair was tied up in a chignon.

Angelo wore a black suit with Italian leather shoes, his eyes fixed on Jamie as he kissed her again. "I love you, Jamie. I can't wait to get married."

Jamie's eyes lit up. "I love you too, Angelo."

The guests applauded them, and Joy scanned the crowd around her. All her friends were present, as well as their families. Joy's parents had also been invited as her mother had recently become close friends with Jamie's mother.

The soft lighting in the room made it romantic and personal, with chairs backed up against the far wall and a buffet table set in the centre of it. Chandeliers hung from the ceiling and a fireplace warmed them on the cool night.

Edward touched the small of her back and whispered in her ear. "I cannot wait to make love to you, Joy. This party is giving me all the romantic vibes."

She whispered back as she glanced at Jamie and Angelo cutting their cake with joined hands. "I wonder if we can slip out early." They had moved in together a month ago and she couldn't be happier.

After eating by the buffet table and mingling with family and friends, Joy and Edward danced to a slow ballad. She pressed her body against his, knowing in her heart he was the man for her.

Joy's father approached. "May I cut in?"

Edward nodded. "Of course, Mr Warrier." He broke away from Joy and she smiled up at her father who had taken her in his arms. Over the past three months, she had had long talks with her parents about the past, and repairing their relationship was a work in progress.

"You are looking beautiful, Joy."

"Thanks, Dad."

"Listen, I hope you feel that you can talk to me now if anything I say or do bothers you. I am still learning, and you know ... How hard it is for me to ... Well, you know."

She laughed lightly. "I know, Dad, and it's okay. I understand you were going through your own issues with Mum and it was your way of coping at the time."

"Hmm. So true." He swung her around the dance floor as the music's beat gave them a spring in their step. "I want you to know I am proud of you. All you've accomplished at such a young age. Well, I am proud."

"I couldn't have done it without you pushing me, even if it was critical feedback."

His eyes darkened. "I only said those things because of my own issues. I believed you had potential. Please forgive me."

"I do, Dad."

In the distance, her mother stood close to Jamie's mother, Violet, and grinned in her direction.

When the song ended, she walked outside, away from the reception, and found Edward talking to Jesse.

"Hey, sis. I will leave you guys to it."

"See you later, Jesse. Thanks for keeping Edward company."

He saluted her. "No problem." He walked away and left them alone by a large tree.

Edward grabbed her hand and led her to a bench where it was quiet. "How are you doing after everything that's happened, especially with the trial coming up?"

"I am still processing what Thomas did to those poor women. How could I not know he was sick and evil like that?" She sighed. "I'm sorry that I hurt you by being in a relationship with him. I don't know what I was thinking, Edward, and I feel sick about it. How could I care about a psychopath? A monster?"

Edward caressed her hand as they sat side by side. "A monster has many faces and knows how to fool people. But they have a human side, and I believe in his own deranged way, he cared about you. When you rejected him, it triggered all his insecurities."

"Hmm," said Joy. "Poor Ariana too. I still can't get my head around the fact that she watched Kathleen with Thomas. What would possess someone to do such a thing?"

"She was so severely traumatised, Joy, that her fear of Thomas overrode her desire to save her sister. I cannot even imagine what it must have been like for her."

Joy nodded. "I can't imagine it either. Even to lure me to their house." She touched his cheek. "At least we know that Ray didn't kill the prostitute."

"It is a consolation, but I don't know if I'll ever be able to forgive him," said Edward.

Ray was currently in rehabilitation and hoped to change Edward's mind.

Joy heard voices. She glanced in the distance. Octavia stood near Claudia who was talking to someone on the phone, with her head down. Ending the call, she whispered in Octavia's ear and shook her head. She rushed inside. What was going on? Was she okay?

No doubt she'd get the news the next day, but for now, she would enjoy Jamie and Angelo's engagement party and share her life with the man she loved and who loved her back. All was well in her world.

Reviews are gold to authors and allow Lucy to keep writing. If you enjoyed this story, please consider rating and reviewing it here: https://books2read.com/u/3nBjy5

If you'd like to read Gabriella's story in Book 4, you can do so here: https://books2read.com/u/4jPKGX

ABOUT THE
AUTHOR

Lucy Appadoo is a prolific reader and author of the Friends In Crisis and Women Of Strength Series. After a childhood spent reading and imagining escapist worlds, Lucy has put her imagination into stories. Her work as a rehabilitation counsellor, and former work as a counsellor in private practice, have led to an interest in writing inspirational stories about authentic, driven women who manage adversity with strength and heart. She writes in the genres of romantic suspense/thrillers with significant life themes and contemporary romance.

Lucy's interests include researching crime stories and news to inspire her work, watching crime thrillers and suspenseful movies, travel, exercising, reading for entertainment or knowledge, meditation, and spending time with friends and family. She also appreciates her Italian background and culture, which has inspired her to write imaginative stories about her parents' childhoods, leading to The Italian Family Series novels.

Check out Lucy's website and sign up for a free suspenseful book:

https://www.lucyappadooauthor.com.au

ALSO BY LUCY APPADOO

<u>FICTION</u>

Women Of Strength Series – Romantic Suspense/Thriller

In Rio's Shadows (Book 1):

http://mybook.to/InRiosShadows

Shadows Of The Past (Book 2):

https://books2read.com/u/3JZe1X

Secrets In The Shadows (Book 3):

https://books2read.com/u/ml88kv

Friends In Crisis Series - Romantic Suspense/Thriller

Haunted By The Past (Book 1):

https://books2read.com/u/bw2ZeY

Twisted Obsession (Book 2):

https://books2read.com/u/4DW8pk

Web Of Lies (Book 3):

https://books2read.com/u/3JXazE

Love-Obsessed (Book 4):

https://books2read.com/u/4jPKGX

The Hearts Series - Romantic Suspense

Rising Hearts (Book 1):

https://books2read.com/u/mZwpoE

Forbidden Hearts (Book 2):

https://books2read.com/u/bQBKr7

Kindred Hearts (Book 3):

https://books2read.com/u/4AJKQK

Broken Hearts (prequel to Forbidden Hearts):

https://books2read.com/u/mgrnOD

Short Story Thrillers

Evening Interrupted:

https://books2read.com/u/3yZDjZ

The Dreamcatcher:

https://books2read.com/u/bzaLxn

Red Flags:

https://books2read.com/u/bWZ9W1

Collection of Short Story Thrillers:

https://books2read.com/u/bP5vwj

The Italian Family Series - Coming of Age Family Drama/Romance

A New Life:

https://books2read.com/u/mqqwZm

The Beauty of Tears:

https://books2read.com/u/bpqwk3

Dancing in the Rain:

https://books2read.com/u/bOr7LA

A Life By Design:

https://books2read.com/u/3J8ene

<u>NON-FICTION</u>

Grief & Loss

Moving Beyond Grief - How To Shift From Grief & Loss
to Joy & Peace:

https://books2read.com/u/mVNzDA

Stress Management & Anxiety

Holistic Spiritual and Mental Health - Building Resilience
and Creativity by Conquering Anxiety and Managing
Stress: https://books2read.com/u/47kG8A

Career Guidance

Your Holistic Career Path - Create Career
Change, Satisfaction, and Work/Life Balance:
https://books2read.com/u/bzYDz4